# FICTION
## – CAN BE –
# MURDER

*A Mystery Writer's Mystery*

## BECKY CLARK

MIDNIGHT INK
WOODBURY, MINNESOTA

MIDNIGHT
INK

FIRST EDITION
First Printing, 2018

Book format by Bob Gaul
Cover design by Kevin R. Brown
Cover illustration by Jeff Fitz-Maurice

Midnight Ink, an imprint of Llewellyn Worldwide Ltd.

**Library of Congress Cataloging-in-Publication Data**
Names: Clark, Becky, author.
Title: Fiction can be murder / Becky Clark.
Description: First edition. | Woodbury, Minnesota: Midnight Ink, [2018] |
    Series: A mystery writer's mystery; 1
Identifiers: LCCN 2017039535 (print) | LCCN 2017048439 (ebook) | ISBN
    9780738753706 | ISBN 9780738753324 (softcover)
Subjects: LCSH: Murder—Investigation—Fiction. | Women authors—Fiction. |
    GSAFD: Mystery fiction.
Classification: LCC PS3603.L3563 (ebook) | LCC PS3603.L3563 F53 2018 (print)
    | DDC 813/.6—dc23
LC record available at https://lccn.loc.gov/2017039535

Midnight Ink
Llewellyn Worldwide Ltd.
2143 Wooddale Drive
Woodbury, MN 55125-2989
www.midnightinkbooks.com

Printed in the United States of America

This is for …
Cynthia Kuhn for the cheerleading
Mary Birk and Leslie Budewitz for the nudge
Shannon Baker for the exuberant quarterbacking
Terri Bischoff for the trust
Jess Lourey for the introduction
Jill Marsal for the guidance
and Wes Cornwell for the unconditional support even
when he had no idea what I was blathering on about.

# Prologue

*M*elinda Walter settled her lean Pilates body—the maintaining of which took all her free time and could fund North Korea's military for a year—into the soft leather driver's seat of her sleek red 1959 classic Corvette.

It pleased her to know she lived in an area of Denver where she could keep a car like this unlocked overnight. Her husband begged her not to, but Melinda did whatever she pleased. Besides, she'd never had any trouble. Of course, it helped that she and her husband lived behind sturdy walls with a generously compensated twenty-four-hour guard patrolling the neighborhood. God bless America.

She dug her keys and Versace sunglasses from her Gucci purse and twisted in her seat to tuck the bag safely behind her briefcase. Her slick-soled Manolo Blahniks searched for purchase across the nubby floor mat. Melinda turned the key in the ignition and the engine roared to life, heater on full blast. Startled, she fumbled for the knob. She twisted and turned it, poked and punched it, but only succeeded in firing up the cigarette lighter and NPR. *Morning Edition* host Steve Inskeep was screaming at her about the historic amounts of snow in Boston.

"Shut up. I don't care." She managed to silence NPR, but the heater continued blasting icy air at her. Even though she didn't believe in regret, a moment snuck in where she wished she'd chosen one of the cars from the heated garage this chilly morning. "Dammit." She flipped through her mental Rolodex until she remembered the name of the mechanic who'd last touched her baby. "Joaquin. Good luck finding a new job after I get through with you."

The last person she'd fired had deserved it too. If a waiter wasn't absolutely certain the Boeuf Bourguignon was made with true French burgundy, why would he let her order it in the first place? What if she'd been allergic to domestic wine rather than simply appalled by it? So what if he'd returned to tell her it was made with a California varietal and ask if she'd like to order something different. He owed her five minutes of her life back, thanks to his inefficiency. That kind of shoddy customer service simply wouldn't fly with her. It was her duty to make management aware.

Melinda pulled forward on the circular driveway. The steel-gray overcast didn't require sunglasses, so she ripped off her Versaces with a grimace and glanced in the mirror. *I look better in the sunshine.* She checked both directions, then rumbled onto the street. Despite the frigid Colorado morning, before she'd passed the two other houses on her street the Corvette's blast furnace had warmed up the interior. A little too much. A flush crept up her neck and face. She tugged at her angora scarf. She began coughing, just a little at first, but then uncontrollably.

She gasped for breath. The car swerved. The steering wheel gyrated, spinning by itself. She blinked. Her neighborhood swam in her vision. She took her foot off the gas but hadn't the presence of mind to step on the brake. Her Manolos slid wildly out of control on the mat.

Breath barely came. She pictured someone pouring wet cement into her lungs and wondered what was happening. No air moved through her body. Breathing was a distant memory. *How can I be drowning in the driver's seat of my car two blocks from home?* She was sure she'd missed something important in the trajectory of this moment.

The Corvette jumped a curb, hit an ancient cottonwood tree, and came to a stop with two wheels in the wide planting strip between the street and sidewalk.

Melinda wanted to reach for the phone in her purse, but her arm wouldn't respond. Her mouth opened and closed silently like a trout on a riverbank. Her hands gripped the steering wheel and she couldn't pry them off, no matter how hard she willed it. Vomit exploded from her red-lipsticked mouth.

She sat paralyzed in her soft leather seat, Burberry coat stained with more than just the contents of her stomach.

With a violent shudder, her head dangled sideways and her eyes rolled back, her death grip on the steering wheel an apt cliché.

# *One*

detoured toward the intersection that had changed my life, my Kia, like the Lone Ranger's horse, knowing the way instinctively. The light was green, the Denver traffic heavy, and the strip mall parking lot already full. I sailed through on the green light, using my thumb and forefinger to flick the key hanging from my rearview mirror. My hand tremor was somewhat under control today and I hit it square, right where I intended. "Miss you, Dad."

I liked the days the light was red and I could stare at the parking lot for a moment, especially in the summer when the daylilies, salvia, and Russian sage bloomed, softening the edges of the asphalt with cheerful yellow, orange, and purple tones.

Today was not one of those days. The clouds hung low, blotting out the sun completely. I had absolute trust the stalwart Colorado sun would make an appearance soon. But for now, pedestrians in parkas hunched against the obnoxious March wind as I extricated myself from my self-imposed detour with a sharp right at the next intersection. In the passenger seat, the practically permanent *one of these days I'll get around to taking this stuff to Goodwill* lawn-and-leaf bag wedged itself against the door. My celery-colored, BPA-free plastic travel mug bounced precariously from side to side in the overly roomy cupholder.

I cranked the heater up a notch, wrinkling my nose at the musty odor.

A few miles later I careened down the street, nearing the long, circular driveway of Kell Mooney's McMansion, late once again for my writing group. My no-frills Kia made noises not typical for this kind of neighborhood. Kell's power-walking neighbors stared at me. "Lower your noses. You'll trip on something." I smiled and waved, glad my window was up. You'd think they'd be used to Kell's weekly writers meeting by now. They probably had their panic buttons curled in their palms and their rent-a-cop would come screeching up, humiliating me and irritating Kell. Didn't want that. I guess the neighbors were just watching out for each other. Was that what rich people did? My neighbors would stare, too, but only to see if my bangs were too long or if I was wearing knock-off designer anything. My neighborhood was wannabe. Kell's was the real deal.

I bumped into his driveway, took a deep breath, and hoped the right constructive words would come to me during our upcoming discussion today. Feelings got hurt no matter how carefully critiquers chose their words. We were writers, after all, covering the spectrum from quivering puddle of goo to granite confidence. Unfortunately, the spectrum changed from project to project, and with some writers, from minute to minute. A constantly moving target.

Kell's twenty-something valet was waiting, as he did every week, until all the members had assembled. He stood without an overcoat on this nippy morning. I felt a pang of guilt.

I pulled up, and he hurried to open the door of my blindingly blue Kia. I kept the bright color tamped down by a thick coat of dirt and grime. I considered it a public service.

"Hello, Charlemagne."

"I'm sorry I'm late. You don't have to wait out here for me every week. You must have something better to do. Inside. Where it's warm."

He bent at the waist until our eyes met. "There's nothing better than greeting one of Kell's loveliest friends."

"Surely you know by now that I don't tip. I do appreciate the flattery, though."

"I aim to please." He extended his hand to help me out. "I can wash it while you're here."

"My hand?"

He smiled indulgently. "Your car."

Every week I vowed not to be late and not to be embarrassed by my car and every week I failed. "You're sweet, but I can't let you do that. I'll make sure Kell knows you offered, though."

"I'm happy to do it."

"Which is why we love you." I threw my messenger bag over my head, the strap across my chest. I left what remained of my mediocre coffee in the cupholder. Delicious and hot coffee awaited me inside.

The valet helped me disentangle an enormous balloon bouquet filling the backseat. I took it upon myself to celebrate every publishing success the members of the group earned, no matter how big or small. Writing is difficult, solitary work, full of rejection and self-doubt. A cheering section—even a small one—goes a long way.

The valet ushered me into the grand foyer and handed back the balloons before driving my filthy car to Kell's pristine and perfectly sanitized seven-hundred-car garage. Lab-coated attendants with clipboards flitted about, dip-sticking and tire-gauging while making concerned clucking sounds over the vehicles.

At least that's how I pictured it. I never had to venture more than a few steps to retrieve my car after our meetings, as the valet had them waiting in a neat line. When we left it felt like a parade.

The idea of the valet listening in to know when we were winding down our meeting sometimes amused me, depending on the submissions we were discussing, but usually just made me uncomfortable. It was the same with Kell's household staff. The closest I came to having servants was watching *Downton Abbey*.

I waved off the housekeeper, preferring to wrangle my messenger bag and balloons by myself. As I neared Kell's enormous library, I heard AmyJo McFarland say, "Things aren't always as they appear. What makes you think I'm totally revising *The Zero Boy Summer*? Maybe I already sent it off to agents and am waiting to hear glorious songs of praise from them."

The idea made me smile. AmyJo hadn't submitted a manuscript to anyone but us in longer than I could remember. Unlike me—whose middle name might as well be Good Enough—AmyJo gets hung up on perfection, as if a manuscript could ever be perfect. That's a laugh. Somebody once said that manuscripts were never finished, only abandoned, which is a sentiment I heartily agree with. AmyJo does not, which is why she may never get her angsty young adult book published.

I leaned against the doorjamb, not wanting to interrupt the weekly drama. Half the critique group—Kell, AmyJo, Jenica Jahns, and Cordelia Hollister-Fiske—sat like King Arthur's knights around a huge mahogany table. AmyJo masterfully deflected every time someone asked her who she'd sent her manuscript to.

There's always something interesting going on with a group of writers. To an outsider, it probably seemed like we argued a lot. Because we did. But it was good-natured and we all thought we were helping, whether the issue was tricky plot development or trickier career planning. We mostly stayed out of each other's real lives, though, because none of us particularly wanted life critiques. Manuscript critiques were difficult enough.

I glanced at the side table laden with food and my stomach rumbled. Kell had his kitchen staff put out our favorites each week. As I decided to make my move toward a Key Lime Pie–flavored yogurt, Einstein Eichhorn pushed through the doorway, waving his arms at my balloon bouquet like he was dodging an angry swarm of hornets. I sighed, stepping aside to let him pass. His social skills were as miniscule as his intelligence was massive.

"Sorry. Had an emergency appointment," he said, a bit too loud. His shirt was buttoned wrong and his hair was wet. He didn't always remember to practice good hygiene, so at least this was something.

"Is everything okay?" I asked.

He executed a perfect sitcom double-take, completely unaware he'd just blown by me standing there. He set his backpack on the table. It was held together with safety pins and duct tape, and I wondered once again what his household furniture must look like.

He turned back to paw through the main pocket of his backpack. "I read a review."

All of us gasped and spoke at once, the gist being he really shouldn't do that but how lucky he was to have a therapist on call. He held up one hand. "In my defense, it was one-star and began, 'I don't know anything about astrophysics, but...'"

Ouch. Those hurt. Even I get those. Not about astrophysics, of course, but equally ridiculous. *I'm giving Ms. Russo's book one star because I ordered the wrong book.* Or, *this is a mystery and I hate reading mysteries,* even though the description clearly states it's a mystery. Or, my favorite, *I thought this was by Richard Russo, NOT Charlemagne Russo, whoever she is. I LOVE his books. Won't bother to read hers.*

It took volumes of emotional maturity to ignore those kinds of bogus reviews. I barely had it, but Einstein decidedly did not, as demonstrated by his weekly therapy appointment to wrangle his Emotional Quotient and Intelligence Quotient, constantly battling for space in his brain. His IQ won most of the time, I'm sure to the dismay of his therapist. He was a certified genius, the Mensa-card-carrying kind, writing serious, scholarly books about astrophysics.

"People should never read their reviews." I shifted the bouquet to one hand and used the other to grab a yogurt. "You might end up believing them." I placed the balloons in the middle of the big table, pleased that I'd remembered to ask for extra-long ribbons so we could still see each other through the table decoration. "These are for Heinrich." I peered through the ribbons. "I brought him cigars, too. Where is he?"

"Maybe he had to go back home and change, too." AmyJo grinned, knowing my penchant for spills.

"I'll have you know I didn't have to go home to change. I had an appointment with my agent." *Just a little white lie. Besides, it was none of their beeswax if I spilled coffee on my blouse and had to go back and change. Again.* "I thought I'd be the last one here. Sheelah's not here either?" I peeled off the foil lid of my yogurt and picked up the first of three spoons arranged in a perfectly straight row at my place setting. Not sure what the other two were for, but I felt fairly confident I could perform all my spoonly duties this morning with just the one.

"Sheelah had a dentist appointment. Not sure about Heinrich," Kell said. "I almost didn't make it either. God bless National Airlines for getting me on that red-eye before the storm hit Chicago." He raised his mug in salute. "I'm getting too old for all this travel."

"Nonsense. You're more active than all of us put together." Cordelia took a dainty sip of coffee. She probably wouldn't speak again for ten minutes.

I dropped my spoon while chasing a drip, making it clatter on the table. The housekeeper hurried to my side with a new spoon. I've been down this same road with her before so I graciously accepted the new spoon she held millimeters from the other two at my place setting. I used it to flick one of the balloons, making it bob and bounce. "I brought these to celebrate yet another of Heinrich's magazine bylines. He's on a hot streak. He's had so many short stories published I bet he's lost count."

"I know it's wrong, but I'm jealous of Heinrich." AmyJo nudged her cheesy scrambled eggs onto her fork with a crisp piece of bacon.

"You know he gets published because he puts himself out there and submits to editors." I knew I sounded like a naggy scold, but I couldn't help it. The guilt was strong with this one. "And since you still haven't answered, *did* you submit *The Zero Boy Summer* to an agent?"

Not only did she ignore me, she refused to meet my eye. Simply continued with her thought as if I hadn't spoken. "He's had such an interesting life and it gives him so much to write about. He's had a much more interesting life than I ever will. I'm sure by the time *he* was twenty-nine and three-quarters, he already had a bunch of stories. Real and fictional." AmyJo pointed the bacon at Jenica. "Even you have more stories than me and you're ten years younger."

Jenica shrugged, causing her spiked leather collar to poke the underside of her chin. "None of my picture books are getting published."

"Because you insist on submitting your manuscripts with illustrations." Kell dunked his donut in his coffee, transforming it to a sodden mess, making my gorge rise. "You know that's not how it's done in the industry, even if your boyfriend is an artist."

10

"Tattoo artist," AmyJo corrected. She turned to me. "Hey, get this. Jenica and her boyfriend won tickets to the Fillmore last night. Backstage passes, hanging all night with the band, the works. And here I thought I had a big night babysitting my nieces and getting them off to school this morning."

"Sounds fun … for both of you." I pointed ironically at Jenica's spiked collar and tight leather bustier. "Just getting home?" I teased.

"Ha ha. But yes." She flashed a grin.

Ah, to be twenty again. If someone had told me how ancient and matronly I'd feel at thirty, I never would have believed them.

I leaned forward apologetically. "I hate to say it, Jenica, but Kell's right about your boyfriend. I don't think he's the best illustrator for your picture books. Woodland creatures shouldn't have enormous boobs." My lips twitched. "Although it delights me to no end to picture story time with some unsuspecting librarian reading your sweet rhymes and showing those illustrations to a bunch of toddlers. The art he did for your *Bunnies to the Rescue* was downright pornographic."

Everyone laughed except Cordelia, who quietly tapped a delicate spoon around the shell of her soft-boiled egg. While the others joked about which picture book characters could star in adult films, I finished my yogurt and picked up the china cup and plate from my elaborate place setting.

As I chose some Danish and poured coffee, Kell called out, "So, Charlee, you had a breakfast meeting with your agent this morning?"

I kept my back to them, buying some time. *Did I say it was a breakfast meeting?* I held my hand on the coffee spigot even though my cup was full, trying to remember.

"I wish I had a hotshot literary agent like you," AmyJo said.

I turned and smiled, hoping I looked sincere instead of smug. AmyJo had known me for almost a dozen years. We'd met in a creative writing class in college and then later shared an apartment, so she knew all my expressions.

I tried not to advertise how glamorous my life was. Mainly, because it wasn't. I understood better than most the concept of grass being greener elsewhere. I'd learned it's because it's fertilized with bullshit. Lots of my writer friends—not just AmyJo—were envious of my publishing success. Nobody but me really likes the story of how I landed a high-powered literary agent on my first try who immediately got me a multi-book deal for my mysteries. It came with a sizable advance, the kind *Publishers Weekly* calls "a good deal." Better than a "nice" deal, not as lucrative as a "major" deal, but big enough that by being careful, I could quit my soul-sucking temp job to write full-time. Idyllic on paper. The reality, of course, was always different, more nuanced and veiled, and not green grass at all.

Like I said, fertilized with bullshit. Rather quickly, I'd realized I was just another cog in an overly complicated machine. My job was to churn out manuscripts fast, so my publisher could transform them into books, slow. My newest mystery, *Mercury Rising*, wouldn't be in bookstores for almost two years, at which time I'd be expected to drop everything and blather through six months of nonstop marketing and promotion by myself. I often found myself wishing for the good ol' days, which ended long before my time—those halcyon days when authors were held in high esteem and agents and publishers took care of all the business except for putting the right word on the page. But these days, I wouldn't be surprised if I were summoned to New York to scrub the corporate toilets.

Very few got to peek behind the publishing curtain, so I tried not to complain. At least not so much that my agent might hear about it.

"AmyJo, be careful what you wish for. Yes, I have a literary agent. But Melinda Walter is a raging bitch. She's downright sadistic to her assistant and absolutely delights in sending the snarkiest rejections to people." I shot her a worried look as I sat down. "Promise me you'll never submit a manuscript to Melinda."

"I'm from Iowa. I'm not a masochist."

"Why do you stay with your agent if she's so awful?" Jenica asked me.

Einstein added, "Surely with your track record you'd have no problem getting another agent."

"Plus, this thing with your royalties." Kell wagged a spoonful of cottage cheese. "Did you figure it out yet?"

I shook my head. "No. Still ongoing."

"I don't understand what's going on. I thought you had contracts with both your agent and the publishing company," AmyJo said.

"I do. But for some reason, my royalty checks are drastically smaller than they used to be and nobody can tell me why. I don't know if somebody is bullshitting me or if I'm just crazy." *Or if the reading public formed a committee to shun me.*

"Isn't there some sort of accounting involved?" AmyJo asked.

"Yeah, lots of it. And I've been prodding Melinda to get me a full accounting from the publisher, but she says they're dragging their heels getting it to her." I broke my Danish in half and buttery flakes crumbled to my plate. "For a tough, no-nonsense literary agent, she sure seems to be rolling over for them. I'm running out of patience with everyone, especially her."

"If you need attorneys or financial guys, I have a whole team on the payroll. Maybe it's bad accounting by your agent. I'd be happy to have them look into it for you," Kell said.

"That's really generous of you, but I think I'll give it a bit more time. My next royalty statement should be here in a couple of weeks. Maybe it'll be back to normal. But thanks." *Plus, if my royalties have dropped off because nobody buys my books anymore, I sure as hell don't want everyone to know. Some mortifications are best kept to oneself.*

Jenica frowned at me. "But you didn't answer my question. Why stay with Melinda?"

"I'm just a midlist author—not a bestseller, not a nobody. Melinda would still have rights to these books. Like a dope, I signed the contract she put under my nose. I was so thrilled and naïve I barely read it." I gave a rueful shake of my head. "Sure, I can fire her, but she'd still have all ten fingers in my books and in my wallet until one of us dies. Her contracts, I found out much too late, are notoriously iron-clad and in her favor." I stared, unfocused, at the far wall. "My relationship with her is like a marriage. Even if we get divorced, our lives are still tangled up. And my books are like our kids who never grow up, with custody issues that never go away." I looked around the table and realized I sounded like a whiny crybaby. "But don't worry about me. I'm this close to cracking the royalty mystery wide open." *If you define "close" as the distance between Earth and Jupiter.* "But the short answer is, Melinda loves my writing. That's why I stay with her. She's truly my biggest fan and there's no better advocate in the world than someone who's enthusiastic about your work and can get impossible things done in the publishing world."

"Probably because people are scared of her," Cordelia said.

"Probably," I said, laughing. "I know I am."

"Melinda Walter's got a good reputation in the industry. And in this world, all you have is your reputation."

AmyJo's words boomeranged me back to my living room when I was seventeen. I sat on the tufted hassock in front of my dad in the matching chair. He leaned forward, elbows on knees, all parental earnestness while he lectured me. "Charlee, all you have is your reputation."

If I'd have known those would be his last words to me, I would have flung myself into his arms and asked for all the knowledge he wanted to impart. Instead, I had rolled my eyes and minimized him and his words, as only a teenager could. I'd been sure he was chastising me for being late to my crappy fast food job, in my mind the only purpose of which was to make my hair reek of French fry grease.

*And what about your reputation, Dad? The blood stains in that strip mall parking lot are a good indication you probably didn't follow your own advice.*

"Charlee? Hello..."

I blinked, clearing out the past. "Reputation, right. Well, Melinda sure won't win Miss Congeniality, that's for sure. Last year somebody sent me a link to a huge anonymous website dedicated to people she has slayed verbally. They post all of her horrible rejections and then everyone comments. It's horrifying and hilarious at the same time."

"That doesn't mean people are scared of her," Jenica said. "That means people hate her."

My phone rang and I checked the caller ID. Queue Quaid, Melinda's assistant. Probably calling to tell me Melinda read my manuscript and had notes ready for me. Just once I'd like to submit a manuscript without anyone wanting changes. Brownies and beer will become diet food before that happens, though. I slid my phone past my plate, ignoring it.

A different ringtone sounded. Probably Q again, texting now. I continued to ignore it, getting up to refill my coffee cup instead.

"Must be important. You should answer." Kell stood. "Looks like everyone's done eating anyway. We'll meet you in the sunroom." Without him ringing a bell or yanking a velvet rope or clapping his hands, two women appeared and began clearing the breakfast items.

How did he do that? Did they just hover outside the door, peeking in at us? I've tried to figure out the system for years. It must be a combination of small workload and high salary.

I slipped my phone into my pocket, slung my bag across my chest, and carried my coffee to a couch on the other side of the library, out of their way. Everyone else gathered near the coffee urn to refill their cups before the meeting started.

AmyJo said, "Earlier? When we were talking about 'write what you know'? I still think it's really bad advice. I mean, how would we have any science fiction or fantasy if we could only write what we know?"

"I'm not sure that's what it means, AmyJo." Cordelia poured cream into her cup.

I glanced across the room, listening to their conversation.

"I think when people say 'write what you know,' they're talking about the emotion of writing," Cordelia went on. "Of course, you have policemen writing crime procedurals, and people remembering their time in junior high in order to write realistically for young people. But you don't need to have lost a child to write about how that would feel. Or have your house burn to ashes, or win the lottery."

*Or have carnal romps.* I thought about Cordelia's books. This buttoned-up, well-coiffed lady, wearing pearls and tailored outfits, had the most nimble imagination of us all and wrote the filthiest erotica I had ever read, which, granted, wasn't a lot. Only Heinrich could look Cordelia in the eye after we'd critiqued one of her submissions. Maybe his years of teaching high school English had steeled him against all things awkward. Or just made him dead inside.

Last week, Cordelia read a passage she'd written: *"The seemingly never-ending streams of ectoplasm emanating from his musket soon had me coated like a plasterer's radio. His plowing made me spray my vertical moisture all over his cream reaper."* Without a blush, vocal quiver, or minced word, Heinrich had told her, *"Seemingly* is weak. Lose it. And *musket* makes him seem old. Like Otto von Bismarck." He pronounced it with extra phlegm. *"Ja.* Make it a howitzer. And what's with the mixed metaphor? Is he a soldier or hanging drywall?"

Cordelia continued her explanation to AmyJo. "You already know how that would feel, even if it never happened to you. A little bit of research, a little bit of imagination, and a little bit of being observant about the world around you is all you need." She moved her cup under the spigot of the urn and watched as it filled with coffee.

It was conversations like these that made me love my writing group. I was incredibly blessed to have these people in my life, despite their idiosyncrasies. We bickered sometimes, but I didn't know how writers functioned without writing partners. All of us had different strengths we used to help the others, and our weaknesses didn't feel so insurmountable in a group.

"Well said, Cordelia." I raised my cup in salute and coffee splashed on the couch. One of the maids instantly loomed over me with a napkin. I accepted the napkin but waved away her assistance and blotted the spill myself. I'm sure she scurried away to assemble her arsenal of pine-scented this or morning-fresh that, ready to pounce on the spill the moment I stood.

AmyJo was the last to leave the room. She turned back with a smile aimed at me. "If we're writing what we know, I know what you could write about." She pantomimed pouring coffee on her own shirt.

"Very funny." I gave her a good-natured middle finger. I'd learned soon after my tremor developed that if I didn't make light of it and the problems it caused, then people would turn it—and maybe me—into a big pathetic deal. I'd rather they acknowledge my shake, even tease me about it, lessening the seriousness for everyone. Besides, my tremor was as much a part of me as my dark hair or the sound of my laugh, even though I had both of those before my dad's funeral.

Despite the maid's anticipated cleaning, I fished a stain remover stick from my bag and performed a little triage on the spill. I didn't know why I bothered, though. The sticks never worked. Most of my shirts and blouses had vague outlines of coffee, salsa, marinara, and/or soup. I chose my outfits using a complicated algorithm based on answers to questions like *Will my hair cover it, Who will I see today,* and *Does the stain match my shoes?*

I dug out my phone to return the call from Melinda's assistant and saw the low battery warning and a couple of additional messages. One text was from my mom and simply said *Hey, Bug,* so I knew she was just checking in. I replied with my favorite kissy-lips emoji and made a mental note to call later when I had time to chat.

I clicked on the other message and up popped Sheelah Doyle's ready-for-anything grin. *Sorry I didn't call last night. I know you wanted to see that movie today, but this &\*%^ tooth is killing me. Wish they woulda yanked it in the ER last night and been done with it. Rain check? And fill me in on crit grp. Ask if my chp was too long.*

Bummer. I'd been looking forward to hanging out with Sheelah after the meeting. I typed back. *Sure. No worries. Feel better!*

I returned the call from Melinda's assistant. "Hey, Q. What's up?" I heard her take a deep, calming breath, something she did often as Melinda's assistant. "What did she do now?" I asked, grimacing. "Are you quitting?"

"Charlee. Melinda's dead."

I gasped, almost dropping my phone. "What?" My mind raced. Had she been ill? "When? How?"

"A couple of hours ago. In her car."

"She was in an accident? I knew that car would get her into trouble."

"It wasn't an accident."

"Then what—was she carjacked? How awful."

"No, Charlee. I . . ."

"What? Tell me."

Q was silent for so long I thought we'd lost the connection.

"Charlee, it's bad. Melinda was murdered."

This time I did drop the phone. As I fumbled to pick it up, I heard Q's voice, along with a man's, in the background.

"Q, I'm at Kell's. I'll be there in twenty." I stood, collecting my messenger bag.

"No, Charlee. There's more. You need to stay there."

"I can't do anything here. I won't be able to concentrate."

"Melinda was killed exactly how you wrote it in *Mercury Rising*. Mercury poisoning in her car. Windows glued shut with Glu-Pocalypse. Heater glued on high."

I collapsed back onto the couch and sunk down. None of this seemed right. Dread caused my hands to tremble double-time. "Are they sure?"

AmyJo poked her head into the library. "We're ready to start. Are you coming?"

I nodded numbly, not really sure what she just asked. "Q? I gotta go."

"Charlee. Charlee! Stay there. Stay at Kell's. I told the police you were there."

The implications of this conversation began to come into focus. My chest felt like a vise. "Why would you do that?" Hysteria tightened my voice, raising its pitch. "You couldn't just give them my number?"

"Timing is important here, Charlee." Q paused. "I didn't think you'd have anything to hide—"

"I don't!"

"—and that you'd want to help."

"I do. Of course I do." I suddenly felt lightheaded, hearing how my protests sounded. Every word felt like a betrayal. I pulled my phone from my ear and stared at it, finally pushing the button to disconnect. Maybe it was a prank. Q was pranking me? About this? I'd heard Q make threats against Melinda's life, but they were jokes, right? Idle threats like we all make out of frustration. Not real.

Not a prank.

I forced my eyes from my phone to AmyJo, still standing in the doorway.

She frowned. "Are you okay?"

I shook my head. "Melinda was murdered this morning." The words felt oily and thick. They weren't my words. Wasn't my mouth.

AmyJo rushed forward and pulled me up from the couch. She wrapped me in a hug and I inhaled the calming scent of her coconut hair conditioner. My legs felt rubbery and I wasn't sure they would support me, even with AmyJo's help. She guided me to the sunroom where the others waited. As we walked in I must have looked like hell, because they all reacted, either by jumping up from their seats, or dropping their papers, or gasping.

"Charlee's agent was murdered. That's why her assistant was calling." AmyJo led me to an overstuffed chair and gently pushed me into it. Everyone was talking at once and coming toward me. I didn't hear what they were saying.

I raised my trembling hands and the room went silent. I glanced around but saw nothing. My eyes wouldn't focus. "They think I did it."

More voices, more soft focus. My mind worked backward to my manuscript. Mercury poisoning in her car. The perfect crime. But not too perfect—my detective had figured it out in the end and arrested the murderer. But perfect in my manuscript. And it worked. All that research. It worked. I'd been worried some reader would ask why my fictional victim didn't just crack a window or open the door to breathe fresh air. That's why I had to use so much mercury and glue the heater on high. Not "I." My bad guy.

My made-up scenario had worked in real life. I squinched my eyes tight, ashamed and sickened that even for a moment I was proud of my work. My research.

The voices became louder and I felt a hand on my arm. I opened my eyes to see Cordelia kneeling in front of me.

"Charlee, take a deep breath. Stay with us, here." Cordelia's voice was calm and her breath smelled like cream. I stared at the pearls around her neck. Counted them. Fourteen, before they dipped inside the collar of her sweater set. "Charlee." I felt her press the back of my head. "Head between your knees."

I took a deep breath. My vision cleared the rest of the way. I raised my head and saw the tableau of my friends in front of me—Cordelia kneeling, Kell and AmyJo standing behind her, Einstein in the chair next to me with Jenica perched on the arm.

"Melinda was killed in her car this morning. Exactly the way I wrote in *Mercury Rising*. I finished all my revisions and gave it to her last week." I searched each face for judgment, but only saw raised eyebrows of disbelief or frowns of confusion. In any other circumstance, I'd want to jot notes for future character studies. Clichéd reactions, but things become clichés because they're true.

Einstein checked his watch. "When did it happen, if you had breakfast with her this morning?"

I slid my fingers slowly up my forehead, spiking my bangs. "I didn't have breakfast with her. I lied. I was late because I spilled coffee on my shirt and had to go change before I picked up the balloons."

Jenica leaned toward me and nudged my long hair behind my shoulder. When she straightened, she pointed at a stain on my shirt that my hair had been covering.

I looked down. "That's ... an old one." When I raised my head, it seemed the atmosphere in the room had shifted. Just a bit, but I noticed. It felt like the judgment I had expected earlier.

Softly, Kell asked, "Does this have anything to do with you saying you're close to cracking the mystery of your royalty statements wide open?"

I stared at him. He looked like the same sweet Kell from my critique group, but this man just accused me of ... something. I searched the other faces staring back at me. Again, they looked like my writing group, but something in their expressions didn't match the people I thought I knew. AmyJo turned away. I wanted to talk, but words seemed impossible.

"Excuse me." Kell's housekeeper entered the room followed by two policemen. "These men need to speak with Charlee."

Kell waved them in.

They stopped about halfway between us and the doorway. One of them said, "Charlemagne Russo? Can you please come with us?"

# *Two*

For the eighty-seventh time, it seemed, I asked, "Am I under arrest?"

"Ms. Russo, you've asked that three times now, and three times we've told you no. You are not under arrest."

"I'm still wondering if I should have an attorney." I slid my hands under my thighs. Trembling hands looked guilty.

"You're not under arrest. You are certainly welcome to call an attorney, but that won't get you out of here any faster."

I sat in a small but tasteful room in the Cherry Hills Precinct of the Denver Police Department. Clearly it was an interrogation room, but the curvy teak table and three comfortable chairs seemed like they could have been swapped with furniture from a Silicon Valley CEO's office. The uniformed cops who'd escorted me here had delivered me into the hands of two plainclothes detectives who introduced themselves as "Ming-like-the-vase" and "Campbell-like-the-soup." Ming was a short Asian man with slicked-back hair. Campbell looked like he'd be right at home on the Broncos' defensive line. One Campbell easily equalled three Mings, but Ming seemed in charge. All that hair gel. I didn't trust him.

So far, they were playing Good Cop, Good Cop. I had coffee in an unadorned porcelain mug in front of me, as well as a bottle of water cold from the mini-refrigerator across the room. It sat next to the credenza that held the coffee service and a vase filled with a professional-level arrangement of yellow tulips and baby's breath. No expense had been spared in decorating this precinct, and they apparently wanted me well-hydrated for their musings about my whereabouts and level of guilt. I didn't drink either beverage, though, preferring to keep my hands on lockdown under my butt.

The shock of the last couple of hours had worn off and I was drifting into anger-and-frustration territory, despite what I suspected were aromatherapy candles strategically placed around the room. I was almost certain I smelled freshly peeled oranges, which I knew was supposed to be a calming scent. It didn't seem to be working.

"You understand I'm a fiction writer, paid to make stuff up?"

They nodded but continued asking questions, some more than once.

"Ms. Russo, tell us again who had access to your manuscript," Detective Ming said.

I sighed. "The seven members of my critique group—"

Campbell checked his notes by pointing with the tip of a pen, his meaty hand rendering it almost invisible. "AmyJo McFarland, Jenica Jahns, Sheelah Doyle, Kell Mooney, Cordelia Hollister-Fiske, Heinrich Gottlieb, and the one you call Einstein Eichhorn."

I nodded, pulling my hands out from under me and rubbing them to get rid of the prickly pins-and-needles sensation. I couldn't remember Einstein's real name, but they were detectives, they'd figure it out.

"Who else?"

"Melinda and her assistant."

"Not your brother?" Ming asked.

"Lance is a cop. He's not interested in fictional murder."

Detective Campbell looked at Ming. "I like Robert Crais and Jeffrey Deaver."

"I'm partial to the outdoorsy ones," Ming said. "CJ Box, Nevada Barr, Craig Johnson."

"Point taken. No, my brother didn't read my manuscript." I tilted my head toward Ming. "You know my brother?"

"Just by reputation—"

"I knew your dad," Campbell interrupted.

Ming cleared his throat, then changed course before I could respond. "Queue Quaid had access to your manuscript?" he asked.

"Yeah. Q was the one who told me about Melinda this morning." I used my thumb to brush condensation from the water bottle, happy to see that the stress only made my tremor a little bit worse. Maybe they wouldn't even notice. "My boyfriend, Ozzi Rabbinowitz, also read it, plus my regular beta readers." Ming opened his mouth but I answered the question I knew he was going to ask, again. "Like I told you before, they're the nonwriters who comment on my early drafts. Ozzi's sister, Bubbles. Suzanne Medina, my neighbor. And Dave and Veta Burr, friends of my parents from way back." I glanced up to see Detective Ming staring at my hands, so I wrapped them around my water bottle. The condensation felt unpleasant, so I wiped both palms on my jeans. But that looked guilty, like I was sweating, so I wrapped both hands around the porcelain mug instead. Then I tried to sit very, very still.

Ming twisted Campbell's notebook so he could read it. "Bubbles is ... Beulah Rabbinowitz Lukina?"

"Yes," I said.

Campbell-like-the-soup nodded too, making me feel like everything I said had to be verified. Which I guess it did, but it still made me fantasize about dumping a bowl of Cream of Mushroom on his head.

"Is your manuscript online anywhere?"

"No!"

"What about the experts you talked to in your research? Who are they?" Ming used his palm to smooth his hair, even though there wasn't a breath of air moving in the room to muss it. Was he as nervous as I was?

"They're not necessarily local. When I'm writing, I get as much information as I can from Google or the library, then I send out a call on Facebook. 'Who knows a dog groomer, or a ballet teacher, or a car mechanic, or a DEA agent, or whatever, who'd be willing to talk to me?' People respond and give me contact information for their sister or neighbor, or, in this case, their old high school chemistry teacher."

"We'll need her contact information," Ming said.

I pulled up the photos on my phone and scrolled until I found the screenshot I took of her message. I showed it to Ming, who read it and then passed the phone to Campbell, who copied the info into his notebook and handed my phone back.

"All I asked her was where someone could get a bunch of mercury and how long it would take for the vapor to kill an adult in an enclosed space."

"Did she ask why you wanted this information?"

"I was introduced as a mystery writer. I assumed she knew it was for a book." I collected my hair in a ponytail and fanned it against my neck. I thought about Ming's nervous hair gesture and stopped abruptly. "Now, I don't want to be rude or seem in any way unhelpful, but we're just going over the same territory. Can I go home now so you can look for the person who killed Melinda Walter?"

Ming smiled wanly. "Indulge me. Tell me again where you were last night until nine this morning."

I sighed loudly, like a teenager, and immediately wished I hadn't. "Late dinner with boyfriend. Asleep. Party store. Critique group."

Both detectives wrote in their notebooks.

When they finished I said, "I didn't kill Melinda, but based on the fact that whoever did kill her used details that seem to match what I wrote in my manuscript, I'm wondering if I'm in any danger. Or if my friends are. It seems pretty likely that the murderer is someone I—we—know."

Detective Ming paused, then shook his head. "Our investigation is clearly in the preliminary stages, but the facts of this case don't seem to rise to the level of a serial killer."

I glanced at Campbell in time to see the tail end of a look pass between the two men. But what was it? Concern? Impatience? Skepticism? Indifference? Were they annoyed by my perfectly reasonable worries?

"Will there be any protection for any of us?" I pressed.

Detective Campbell didn't even try to hide his condescending smile. "Charlee—may I call you Charlee?—there's no reason for you to worry. I know this is unfamiliar territory for you, but we've investigated many, many murders and you can trust me when I say, you and your friends are in no more danger than you were last week."

"We were in danger last week?" I felt my heartbeat quicken.

He waved his hand, dismissing my words. "You know how when people watch the news about terrorist bombings and such? Many of them begin to feel like it happens all the time and it's just a matter of time before they themselves will be targeted by a suicide bomber. But you know what? More Americans were shot and killed by toddlers in 2015 than were killed by Islamic terrorists. And you can check that with Snopes."

He smirked and settled back in his chair with an over-abundance of casualness. "There's no need for you to worry about a serial killer on the loose. Ming and I are on the job."

If he'd patted me on the head and handed me a lollipop, I couldn't have felt any more like a child who'd confessed her fear of a scary monster under her bed.

Ming smoothed his non-mussed hair again. "Just one more question, Ms. Russo. Did you like Melinda Walter?"

"Did I like her?" *No, not at all. She was a stone-cold bitch. Nobody liked her.* "Of course I liked her."

# Three

It was mid-afternoon by the time I left the detectives. I powered up my phone to call my brother. Lance would know what to do. I walked alone through the sunlit atrium of the police department and headed to one of the carved stone benches and sat, facing a faux jungle. Palm and ficus trees, ferns, oversized blooms, and a tangle of vines covered a two-story craggy cliff that rose above me. I'm no expert, but none of those plants seemed indigenous to Colorado. They sure looked real, but I knew that on the other side of the skylight, despite the cobalt blue sky that had finally made an appearance, was a cold March wind, not the tropics. Although with the way my world had been knocked upside down that morning, maybe the natural world was different, too.

I was the only one in the lobby. Even without Essence of Orange it was remarkably calming, especially with my back to the offices, detectives, and all the unpleasant questions and insinuations. Was that a waterfall I heard? I guess this was the kind of police station the property taxes in Melinda's neighborhood bought. I'd been to my brother's precinct. A walk through their fetid lobby made you long for a Silkwood shower afterward.

Before I dialed Lance, I got a text from Cordelia. It said, *Please don't mention that I read your manuscript.*

The ridiculousness made me read it again. And again. Still not understanding.

I replied, *Why not?*

She must have been staring at her phone waiting for me to respond because a new message immediately popped up. *It wouldn't be convenient.*

Convenient? I barked out a noise, then quickly covered my mouth with one hand. None of this was convenient. I typed, *Sorry. Already did. Why wouldn't it be*—I tried to type *convenient*, but my phone autocorrected it to *convincing*. I retyped *convenient*. This time it stuck. I waited for Cordelia to respond but she didn't. I considered calling her, but decided I needed to talk to my brother more.

It went to voicemail. I listened to Lance's outgoing message, then said, "Hey, I don't know if you heard anything through the grapevine or not, but I need to talk to you. I may or may not be in trouble. Call me as soon as you get this, but I'm calling your dispatch, too."

I clicked off and tried the other number.

"Denver Northfield Precinct."

I could barely hear the woman's voice over the background noise. I spoke louder to compensate, self-conscious in the quiet atrium. "I'm looking for Lance Russo. Is he working today?"

"Is this an emergency?"

"No. Maybe. No. I'm his sister and I need to talk to him." I glanced around the lobby, expecting stares or shushes, but there was still no one around, just the distant sound of muffled voices and ringing phones. "Can you tell him to call me?"

"I'll see what I can do." She hung up and I was alone once more in the jungle.

I made sure my ringer was on all the way, then dropped my phone in the front pocket of my bag. I stood and sighed, conflicted about ending my tropical vacation. Nobody had brought me a piña colada, but this peaceful interlude sandwiched between the nightmare-behind-me and the nightmare-sure-to-come was a welcome way to spend five minutes to collect myself. I would have liked a coconut-and-rum-laced concoction, though. And not to have been questioned by those detectives. And not to have been told Melinda was killed. And not to have written that horrible manuscript. Maybe I did need a few piña coladas.

I opened the door to a blast of cold wind and hurried to my car, politely driven here by one of the uniformed cops who'd picked me up. It then occurred to me that it wasn't polite at all, and I'd probably given permission for him to search it, too. Fine. I had nothing to hide. I waited for a couple of squad cars to pass me in the parking lot before I turned toward home, with none of them doing so much as glancing at me.

The detectives hadn't acted like they thought I killed Melinda, and I understood they had to question everyone. But I couldn't help but wonder how much trouble I was in. I gripped the steering wheel tighter than normal. It's not a crime to write a novel. It's not a crime to write a crime novel. It's not even a crime to write a criminally bad crime novel. But it doesn't matter if it was good or bad. Somebody used my imaginary crime to kill Melinda. To frame me? Because it was such compelling prose they simply couldn't help themselves?

Why this? Why now? Why her? Why me?

I slumped in my seat, powerless over my circumstances. Then I straightened a bit. The cops would figure this out. Cops solved heinous murders all the time. Despite their condescension earlier, they were treating this as a routine murder, if there was such a thing, and they said none of us were in danger.

I drove a couple more blocks. But what if they were wrong? What if I'd put my friends in some kind of danger simply by asking them to read my manuscript? I couldn't live with myself if anything happened to any of them. I had to figure it out.

I thought about my critique group that morning. Their faces when I told them. Kell's implication about my suspicions with Melinda and my royalties. I groaned. Why did I lie to them about meeting with her?

*Stop that. No use worrying about it. What's done is done.* I hadn't murdered Melinda. But somebody did. And it was probably someone I knew. And they probably knew where I lived.

A car honked. I gasped and jerked the Kia back into my own lane. My long-cold travel mug of coffee caromed around the cupholder.

Keeping my eyes on the road, I rooted around my bag until I felt my phone. I pulled it out and looked at it. No calls. What good did it do to have a cop for a brother if you couldn't find him when you needed him? I slipped it into my console with the pens and paperclips that seemed to find their way there no matter how often I cleaned it out.

I glanced at the phone every four seconds while I drove, willing it to light up.

If this real killer used one of my fictional scenarios, then what about all my other stories? Book number one was an arson cover-up. Book number two was a bomb in a package. Book number three was a maniac stalker in the lilac bushes.

I stopped at a red light and glanced nervously to my right. The guy in the Escalade looked like a murderer. Maybe the head of a drug cartel.

I locked my doors. And that lady in front of me with her cigarette out the window. Why couldn't she smoke inside her car? Did she just kill her lover and needed to calm down but didn't want her husband to get suspicious?

Across the street a woman pushed a double stroller. Really? Two babies? Not hiding an Uzi in there?

The light changed and I gave the Kia a bit too much gas, almost ramming the suspicious smoker. I slammed on my brakes, glancing in the rearview mirror at the same time. The guy behind me threw a middle finger salute and I raised my hand in contrition. Or at least I meant it to be contrition. What if he thought it was defiant and he pulled his handgun from his glove box, roared up next to me, shot me dead, then escaped to New Mexico? Another unsolved crime.

I saw a Facebook meme the other day that said the average person walked past a murderer thirty-six times in their life. I knew what it meant, but because of the poor sentence structure I made a joke that I'd just go the other direction on the thirty-seventh time. Now it didn't seem so funny. I'd seen at least thirty-six people today. Statistically, did that mean one of them was a murderer? Did Facebook know what it was talking about?

I shuddered. I turned my heater up a notch, but I didn't think it would help my chill.

Okay, let's set aside for a minute all the real murders seemingly going on around us all day, every day. Clearly, Melinda's murderer was either paying homage to my imaginative prose, had no imagination of their own, or was trying to frame me.

None of that seemed more comforting than real murderers all over the place, whether they were toddlers or terrorists.

But if it had something to do with *my* writing, *my* books, *my* imagination, then maybe I could figure it out and keep myself or one of my friends from being their next victim. But what if it didn't have anything to do with my books? What if this murderer was just too lazy to think up their own method? What about all those other genre tropes, all those rules and clichés we mystery lovers loved?

I was suddenly too hot and turned off the heater.

What about all those murders in movies and TV? Arsenic in elderberry wine. Dissolving bodies in chemicals. Firing squad. Axes. Well-placed kicks to the head. Gruesome stabbings. Feeding people to pigs. Burying them alive.

Geez, just avoiding the scenarios Adrian Monk dealt with would be a full-time job. And then there was Rockford, and Columbo, and Sherlock, and Castle, and Longmire, and those crazies on *Criminal Minds*. How could I be alert for all of them?

I pulled into the driveway at my apartment complex, where the security gate was wide open. I despaired that they considered this a secure complex. I flushed with shame at how many times I'd been happy when it had been left open for days at a time, probably broken. It was so much more convenient that way, instead of having to fumble with a key card. Plus, there was a pedestrian gate right next to it that didn't even lock; the only people that gate kept out would be those murdering toddlers who couldn't reach the latch. The other two pedestrian gates, on the north and south sides of the perimeter of the complex, weren't much better. I paid extra for security, so it shouldn't be a joke. I should feel safe. And I didn't anymore.

I parked in my space but stayed locked in the car while I scanned the area. I debated whether to move my car from my covered carport space to the empty guest space closer to my apartment. Snow was in the forecast, so I stayed put.

I took a deep breath, mustered my courage, and bolted from the car. Ten paces away I realized that in my rush, I'd left both my phone and my messenger bag in the Kia. I raced back and fumbled for my keys, eyes nervously darting around. I dropped my phone into the pocket of my bag, tucked it under my arm like a football, and re-locked my car. With my keys in my hand, I made my way up the sidewalk. As I neared my front door and began to breathe easier, a rabbit streaked out from under a juniper hedge and scared the bejesus out of me. I ran up to the door and shoved my key in the lock. I slammed the door behind me and leaned against it, fighting for control of my lungs.

The stillness of my apartment calmed me after a few moments. Everything was as I'd left it that morning. Dirty dishes still in the sink from last night's lasagne feast with Ozzi. Scarf I'd decided not to wear tossed over the back of the living room chair. Light on in the bath room down the hall. Wait. Did I leave the light on? I squinched my eyes, trying to remember.

Ozzi had tried to persuade me to shower with him before he left, but I knew from experience that it wouldn't have made either of us very clean. Quite the opposite. Plus, it was the middle of the night. He'd given up and used the hallway bathroom so I could get back to sleep. He must have left the light on. Probably. Why couldn't I remember? When did he leave? Was it before or after midnight? And why didn't he stay like he normally did?

I glanced again down the hallway. But the more pressing question right now was, why was my bathroom light on? Was someone here? Would a murderer need a light to kill me?

As I tried to decide whether to grab a knife from the kitchen and investigate or race out of my apartment, across several state lines, away from all of this trauma and danger to hole up in some off-the-grid cabin in a remote wilderness, my phone rang full blast with my brother's ringtone. For the second time in three minutes, I had no more bejesus. I scrambled for the phone and saw Lance's photo on the screen. My brother was two years younger than me but looked ten years older. It startled me to see how much he looked like Dad. Probably always would.

"Lance. Hey." I took a deep, calming breath and sidled along the hall toward the bathroom. My brother on the phone gave me courage. At least if I got murdered someone would know about it right away.

"You know anyone named Joaquin?" Lance often seemed to start a conversation halfway in when he called. Sometimes he made me wonder if I'd blacked out for three sentences of small talk and didn't remember we'd been chatting.

"I don't think so." I poked my head in the bathroom. Empty. "The reason I called earlier—"

"I know why you called." I heard the exasperation in his voice.

"You heard about Melinda?" Without waiting for an answer, I asked, "Didn't she live in a ritzy gated community? How could someone tamper with her car?" I tiptoed across the small bathroom, even though I recognized that with all the noise I was making, I couldn't possibly sneak up on anyone hiding in the bathtub. I yanked the curtain open. Empty.

"So?" Lance said. "Remember when we'd sneak into those neighborhoods and swim in their pools? It worked because we acted like we fit in. Hang on a minute."

"Don't be too long. My battery's dying." I sat on the edge of the tub and thought about who I knew who'd definitely fit in with Melinda's neighborhood. Kell, for sure. And Cordelia. Hell, maybe she did live there for all I knew about her. She was so inscrutable. She'd started out writing romance, but when she found out erotica paid better, she immediately switched genres. Very mercenary for someone who seemed so prim. Took us all by surprise. Like at our critique group Christmas party with the white elephant gift exchange. Instead of keeping the delicate bone china tea set she got, she swiped the *Led*

*Zeppelin Greatest Hits* box set right out from under Jenica's nose. What else didn't I know about her? Maybe I didn't want to know.

Lance came back on the line. "I've been talking to my buddies. Joaquin is the mechanic who worked on Melinda Walter's car recently. Is there any possibility he found a copy of your manuscript on her seat or something?"

"Yes, of course. That must be what happened." I blew out a huge breath and smiled, glad once again to have a cop in the family.

"Did you stop for coffee this morning?" he asked.

"And a blueberry muffin."

"Why didn't you tell the detectives that?"

"How do you know— -oh my gosh, I forgot to tell them. I do it almost every day. It completely slipped my mind. I'll call them about it."

"Go ahead or it looks bad. But they already know. And Charlee…"

"What?"

"I know you didn't kill your agent. Of course. But there's a process, protocol. Don't do anything… stupid. Just answer their questions and cooperate. It's going to take some time. Remember what Dad always said. Marathons start with one step."

"Dad said a lot of crazy things. Did he ever run one?"

"I don't—"

"And why are you telling me this? I thought you just said that mechanic, Joaquin, was the suspect."

"One of them. Gotta go. And you might want to lay low, hole up in your apartment for a while."

His photo disappeared along with my confidence. *One of them? Lay low?* Lance thought I was in danger? If I was in danger, then I'd put my friends in danger, too, even if the detectives refuse to acknowledge it. I couldn't lay low, couldn't do nothing.

How would I handle this in a novel?

# *Four*

I dug out a yellow legal pad from a stack on my desk. I glanced at the notes written on the first two pages, then tore them off, discarding them on a nearby stack of books. Research notes for my next book could wait. I had a real murder to solve.

At the kitchen table I hunched over the notepad and wrote across the top: *Motive, Means, Opportunity,* and *Alibi.*

I tapped my pen on the pad, contemplating each word. After a few minutes, I tore off the page. Everyone who read my manuscript had all the information they needed to kill someone using mercury.

Mercury was as easy to get as Glu-Pocalypse. The small beads were virtually invisible and odorless. Just by moving your feet you could turn a big blob into tinier, deadlier beads, disbursing vapor in a small car like Melinda's very easily. Especially with the heater stuck on full blast and the windows disabled. So *Means* was a useless category.

Same with *Opportunity*. The detectives wanted to know my whereabouts from Sunday evening through Monday morning. With such a huge window of time to tamper with Melinda's car, everyone also had opportunity.

Across the top of a clean page, I wrote the only two categories I cared about—*Motive* and *Alibi*—and drew a line between them straight down the page. Down the left margin I wrote the names of everyone I knew who'd had access to the *Mercury Rising* manuscript.

My critique group: Kell, Jenica, Cordelia, AmyJo, Sheelah, Einstein, Heinrich.

My beta readers: Suzanne, Dave, Veta, Bubbles.

Then everyone else: Melinda, Q, and Joaquin the mechanic. I forced myself to add Ozzi's name, even though the thought that my boyfriend was a murderer made me dizzy.

Actually, the thought of any of these people being a murderer made no sense, but I began to fill in any information I knew.

At the meeting this morning—geez, was it really just this morning?—Kell had said he'd been on a red-eye flight from Chicago. I wrote that and "National Airlines" in the space next to his name in the *Alibi* column.

In the space across from Sheelah's name, I jotted that she was in the ER last night and the dentist in the morning.

I scanned the page, freezing at Melinda's name. A wave of sadness washed over me and I thought about the people who loved her who'd she'd left behind. I remembered how my family had zombied through the aftermath of my dad's murder. Months passed before we didn't have to force ourselves to get out of bed every morning. That had been my first exposure to death, and it might be for Melinda's family as well. I knew she had a husband, Henry, but she'd never spoken to me of anyone else. Did she have parents? Nieces and nephews? Aunts and uncles? In-laws? One life touches so many, even if we don't realize it.

Sending flowers and a card seemed insufficient, but that was standard protocol, right? I mentally attempted several opening lines for the card I knew I'd be writing, but I rejected each. How do you comfort someone you've only met a few times, or never? What could I possibly say that would dent their smothering grief? Maybe by the time Melinda's funeral plans were made public I would have wordsmithed the perfect sentiment, but I doubted it.

This black cloud threatened to swallow me, so I tenderly arranged thoughts of Melinda and her family in my mental filing cabinet, to be pulled out when I felt I could properly manage my sorrow and perhaps even be useful to them. There was nothing I could do for Melinda's family right now, or maybe ever. But I'd try again in a few days.

I thought about calling Ozzi, even picked up the phone, but in the end decided that hearing your girlfriend is a suspect in a murder case should happen in person, and he'd be home in a couple of hours. The odds that the police had already contacted him were fairly slim.

My attention returned to my list. With a sigh, I X'd out the space for Melinda's alibi and almost crossed her off completely. But what if she'd done this to herself? Was she depressed? Suicidal? It seemed an overly cumbersome and melodramatic way to kill yourself. Did she stage it? Was she trying to frame someone? A rush of adrenaline surged through my body. That someone could only be me.

The only reason a person would use this method to kill someone would be to frame me, right? I balled my fists. No. Maybe they couldn't think of their own method so just used the handiest one, the one spelled out in my manuscript. But then they'd know it would implicate me, and none of my friends would—

Three deep breaths calmed me enough that I could focus again. I needed to remain analytical, not be thrown by emotions and hypotheticals. I wrote "suicide" and added a question mark under the *Motive* column next to Melinda's name.

Fifteen names, two alibis, and one motive. Not a very promising start. I forced myself to go back to the top of the list and carefully consider each name. I stopped at Cordelia's, remembering her cryptic text message. Opening my phone, I reread it. *Please don't mention that I read your manuscript ... It wouldn't be convenient.*

It seemed bizarre that she didn't want me to "inconvenience" her by telling the detectives she read my manuscript. But I certainly couldn't picture Cordelia in her kitten heels and expensive pearls murdering Melinda. Why inconvenient? And for what? What would her motive be?

The logical motives for murder—money, love, and revenge—flitted through my brain.

Could Cordelia be involved with Melinda's husband? Or Melinda involved with Cordelia's? Or Cordelia with Melinda? Or their husbands with each other?

Ridiculous. I shook my head to clear it, the human equivalent of an Etch A Sketch. Didn't work. *Was* it ridiculous? Cordelia wrote such over-the-top erotica. Was her imagination that nimble or did she have a life she kept secret?

I clutched the sides of my head, raking my fingers through my hair. The pressure felt good and seemed like it might quell the sensation that my brain might leak out my ears. Slowly walking my trembling fingers across the table, I rested my hand on my phone. With a long exhale, I pushed buttons until I was staring at Cordelia's contact page.

This was it. The moment I start accusing my friends of murdering my agent and trying to frame me for it.

"Ready, Charlee?" I stared at the phone in my hand. "Nope." But what choice did I have? Besides letting the police deal with it, that is. I set the phone down and gradually pushed it as far away as my arm would reach. The side of my face rested on the yellow legal pad for a length of time I couldn't determine. Long enough to drool a bit, not long enough for my problem to go away.

"This is ridiculous." I sat up, wiped the drool from the side of my mouth, and used my sleeve to blot the dribble on the yellow paper. Cordelia didn't murder Melinda and wasn't framing me for it. I grabbed my phone. None of my friends were capable of murder, and if I was going to get my life back, all I needed to do was clear them.

I pushed up my sleeves, sat up straight, and dialed Cordelia.

She answered before the first ring finished. "Charlee. Have you heard anything?"

After avoiding my text questions in the police station atrium, her bluntness caught me off guard. "Um … no."

"Oh."

"But I wanted to ask you why you didn't want me to tell the cops you read my manuscript."

"I don't … "

"Cordelia, a woman was murdered."

"I know, but … "

"The cops already know. You may as well tell me why it would be 'inconvenient' for them to know you read the manuscript." I used verbal air quotes to highlight my skepticism.

She heard them. "Perhaps 'inconvenient' was a poor word choice." She paused long enough for me to clench my lips together and vow not to speak first. "It's not what you think, Charlee."

I unclenched. "Let me be the judge of that." My words came out harsher than I wanted. I took a breath. "Cordelia," I said, more gently. "Just tell me."

In a quiet monotone she said, "My husband, Byron, was involved in an investment project that went bad."

"So? What does that have to do with—"

42

"It was with Melinda's husband, Henry."

My mind raced, trying to fit the pieces together. "I didn't know you knew Melinda."

"I don't. Didn't. But the men had dealings."

"Dealings? What was the investment?"

"I don't really know. It went very badly for my Byron but was quite lucrative for Henry. Byron has told more than one person he thinks he got cheated."

"How did he get cheated?"

"I don't know. Byron doesn't tell me many details." She added, "And I don't ask."

My brain was still grasping, and failing, to create the picture from these puzzle pieces. "What would that have to do with Melinda's murder?"

"Nothing," Cordelia said, much too quickly. "That's why I wanted to stay out of it and keep Byron out of it. It clearly has no bearing on her unfortunate murder and simply muddies the waters."

"Did the police ask about your husband?"

"No. They just asked if I knew her. I didn't lie." I heard her voice catch. "You won't mention it to them?"

"No." *Not unless I have to.* "Do you have an alibi for that night?"

"I was home." Cordelia paused. "All night ... with Byron."

That was some odd phrasing. Why not *I was home all night with Byron?*

"Charlee?"

"Yeah, I'm still here."

"You'll tell me if you hear anything else?"

"Yes, of course." *Unless what I hear is that you and/or your husband murdered Melinda.* "Talk to you later."

43

I added Byron's name to my suspect list. In both his and Cordelia's *Alibi* column I wrote, "At home with spouse." And in his *Motive* column I wrote, "Bad business deal with Henry?"

Then I added Henry Walter's name to the list. I knew next to nothing about him but always assumed he was some high-powered CEO, perhaps of his own company. With the information from Cordelia, that still seemed likely. I should have added him to my original list. The very first name. I thought back to all the mysteries I'd read and crime dramas I'd watched. The spouse was the murderer in a good sixty percent of them, and he would presumably have the most to gain from Melinda's death.

After a pause, in the *Motive* column for Cordelia, Byron, Melinda, and Henry, I added, "Affair?"

Just as I was beginning to believe he was the murderer, I remembered that Henry hadn't read my manuscript. It was a remote possibility, I supposed, that perhaps during a bout of insomnia he'd found it lying around, but Melinda had once told me her husband was too busy to be involved in her agency business. Plus, I couldn't picture Melinda leaving anything lying around. I'd never been to her house, but I assumed it was all white and chrome, sparsely furnished. Melinda was lean and sleek, so why wouldn't everything else in her life be the same?

She was also ruthless, and it made me wonder what kind of marriage they'd had. Had they always been rich? Was there any kind of prenuptial agreement between them? Melinda wasn't the kind to go in for chit-chat, so we'd never had any kind of heart-to-heart conversation, certainly not about her life. I'd done my share of worrying and whining to her, but only as it related to my writing career.

Suddenly curious about my relationship with her agency, now that she was dead, I went to the file cabinet and pulled out my contract with the Melinda Walter Literary Agency. I knew right where it was because I'd had it out recently to check on the language about auditing my royalties.

The three-page document didn't take long to scan. I breathed a sigh of relief when I read Clause 4: *After the initial term of this Agreement, either party may terminate this Agreement at any time upon thirty (30) days prior notice.*

In a little over a month, then, I could be free of any doubts about my royalties. I could take action on my own and figure out whether someone was playing fast and loose with my money or whether my sales had actually tanked, although I wasn't sure which I hoped for. I looked forward to dealing directly with my publisher without a middleman, only concerning myself with writing and promoting my books.

My relief was short-lived as I returned attention to my yellow notepad. I had two more suspects than when I started, and even more questions.

Gah. Fiction was so much easier than real life.

# Five

After staring at the notepad for twenty minutes, I took a break, trying to clear my head by visiting a few of my comfort reads until Ozzi got home. I sat in my favorite reading chair by the window but couldn't concentrate on my book. Not on any of them, in fact. Janet Evanovich, Carl Hiaasen, Gretchen Archer. Nope. Tried grittier with Wendy Corsi Staub. Hank Phillippi Ryan. Philip Donlay. Nope. Nope. Nope. Even pulled from my ever-growing stack of magazines. I simply couldn't keep pulling my eyes across the page.

I gave up and dropped my *Writer's Digest* to the carpet while staring at the brown winter landscape of my apartment complex, clumps of straw-colored ornamental grasses waving in the wind. Leafless beige trees. Dormant grass the color of sand. Banks of dirty snow plowed into the far corners of the parking lot. The sun began setting over the mountains, tinging my world with otherworldly light in shades of orange, pink, yellow, and blue. I watched the sky change colors behind the thin clouds, as if the artist couldn't decide on his palette.

I never got tired of watching the sun set from this window. Today it felt especially calming. Clear sky or cloudy, as long as it wasn't completely overcast, there was magic in a Rocky Mountain sunset. Most summer nights Ozzi and I sat side by side, holding hands in our matching anti-gravity chairs on my patio, keeping vigil, often with a margarita or one of our many favorite craft brews. In the winter, though, the sun went down before he got home from work, so we only had weekend sunsets. Only once, about three years ago, did we bundle up and try to watch from the patio in winter. We'd only been dating a few weeks and it seemed romantic at the time, but it was the stuff of erectile dysfunction commercials, all gauzy and ridiculous, and about a thousand degrees colder than was comfortable. We'd hustled inside, romance be damned, and ordered pizza.

I glanced at the clock. He'd be home soon. His third floor unit in another building in our sprawling complex faced east. We never saw sunsets over there, but we saw plenty of sunrises from his bed. Our friends kept asking why we didn't move in together. Both of us had big enough apartments and we got along great, but we liked this arrangement. We liked being together and apart, with some elbow room. He was in building JJ, I was in D. It was just enough distance for an easy, uncomplicated relationship. We had the occasional dust-up, but we agreed on just about everything important. Any arguments were usually because one or both of us were hangry, and finished and forgotten as soon as we shoved food in our mouths, proving my theory that anything could be solved with a grilled cheese sandwich. World leaders should try this.

The exterior lights of the complex kicked on. The ones on the three-story buildings glowed golden and cast long shadows on the walls, and the floodlights in the landscaping spotlighted the more dramatic plants and shrubs while illuminating the wide, curving sidewalks. The parking lot lights were already on, and more cars began snaking through the complex, headlights raking over the Monday night drive home.

One of the cars beeped its horn.

*He's home.*

Ozzi drove an absolutely silent Prius. He was in the habit of letting me know when he drove by, partly because I wouldn't hear him otherwise, but partly as proof to the judgmental greenies in the complex of his ongoing commitment to the environment. He might never recover from the sheer number and severity of stink-eyes he received from them whenever he'd idled his old Jeep in front of my building.

I had a brainstorm and closed the drapes before heading to the bedroom to change. In my haste, I bumped into the wall, jostling one of the oversized art postcards I'd hung there after one of my many forays to the Denver Art Museum. As I straightened Vincent van Gogh's *Starry Night Over the Rhone*, all blues and yellows highlighting the nuance of shadows of the night, a wave of melancholy washed over me. I'd chosen it in the gift shop because the stars over the water reminded me of standing at the edge of Grand Lake watching Independence Day fireworks as a kid, holding Dad's hand. I squared up the postcard. And my emotions.

It didn't take long to get ready. I needed this to take my mind off things. I'll tell him all about my craptastic day … afterward.

I pulled my hair over one shoulder and clasped a necklace behind my neck. I smoothed my bangs and fluffed my hair, leaving it long and loose, how he liked it. I stepped into an old pair of battered clogs, knowing my ankles would be cold, but only for the few minutes while I walked over.

With my long wool coat buttoned around me, I grabbed my keys and left, forgetting for a second my fear earlier that day. But only for a second. As I made my way down the curving sidewalk, I heard rustling nearby and snapped my head toward it. Nothing. A car door slammed and I snapped the opposite direction. My terror of maniac slashers in every bush roared back, pounding in my head. A voice erupted in laughter behind me and I stiffened. A teenager dashed across the sidewalk in front of me. I froze, then walked faster. A car slowed and pulled a U-turn ten feet ahead. I stopped again, legs paralyzed, fingers curling around the keys in my pocket. The car faced me, idling ominously at the curb. The interior was dark, windows tinted. Just as I was ready to turn and flee back to my apartment, a woman stepped out of the car, saying, "Thanks for the ride. See you tomorrow." She slammed the door and crossed in front of me, digging in her purse without even acknowledging me.

I flew the rest of the way to Ozzi's apartment, rocketing up three flights of stairs to his door. The fluorescent light buzzed and sputtered like punk wasps cruising for trouble. I took some deeps breaths while opening and closing my fists to calm myself in the cold night air before knocking.

Ozzi opened the door, and the ripe odor of his just-abandoned work loafers greeted me. He stood aside to let me in, but I knew something was wrong the minute I stepped out of my clogs. He still had his perfectly maintained scruffy beard and barely-there moustache that always made him look like he'd been camping for four days, but he didn't smile at me. Nor did he wrap me in a hug and greet me with the deep, hungry kiss I craved.

So I planted one on him. He responded appropriately, so whatever it was couldn't be too bad.

"Bad day at the hack factory?"

"I'm not a hacker," he said automatically.

"Websites, software, hacking. Whatever lets you sleep at night." I slipped him some tongue. Truth was, the boy had computer skills and if he ever wanted to put them to use and become an evil overlord, he'd be one of the best. He wasn't a bad kisser, either.

He cut short the make-out session, pulling back and looking at my face. "Not now, Charlee."

"Why'd you honk if you didn't want me to come over?" I put my arms around his neck, dragging my fingernails through his longish hair.

"Habit. I'm sorry. I should have called."

"You *must* have had a bad day." I nuzzled his neck and flicked my tongue in his ear, which usually fired up all his cylinders. His engine roared but stalled immediately, and he pulled away.

I had a surprise for him, though, and was glad I'd thought of it when it seemed we both needed a little pick-me-up. I unbuttoned my coat, slowly, deliberately, while he watched. I slipped out of the sleeves and let it drop to the floor. I stood in my most come-hither pose, naked but for the necklace.

He didn't come hither.

"Seriously? Nothing?" I struck a different pose.

"I'm sorry."

"I thought I was irresistible." I picked up my coat and shook it off. I left my pride there on the floor.

"It's me."

"You're irresistible?" I tried again, giving him a sexy pout. I began to feel foolish and guilty for thinking I could override the seriousness of today's events, even for a short time.

He frowned, either not understanding my joke or not listening.

"Last chance," I told him.

He shook his head, so I put on my coat, then opened it, flasher-style. Nothing. I sighed and wrapped it around me. When I took my hair out of the collar, I brushed my hand on the necklace. "Oh, look. I fixed it." I leaned toward him to show the jewelry. It was just a costume piece, but he'd noticed it matched my favorite sweater and wrapped it up last Christmas. I wore it a lot, but had dropped it, breaking one of the little ceramic flowers. "I love that Glu-Pocalypse."

"You used Glu-Pocalypse?"

"Yeah. It worked great." I shimmied and twerked like the cartoon tubes of glue in the commercial while singing the jingle, "accidentally" pushing my boobs together while letting the coat fall open. "If your force field comes unsealed, if your cup needs to be healed," I sang, hitting the rhyme hard, "if your kitchen faucet drips, or upholst'ry got some rips, Glu-Pocalypse! Glu-Pocalypse! Glu-Poc-A-Lypse!" I ended with a bump-and-grind of my own creation.

He ran a hand through his hair and didn't even smile or check out my lady bits. "Glu-Pocalypse. Like in your manuscript?" His eyes darted from my necklace to my face.

"You heard?" I swallowed the lump in my throat. This was a bad idea. "Lots of people use Glu-Pocalypse, Oz," I said quietly, stepping toward him.

He backed away.

I raised my palms. "You think I killed Melinda?"

He wouldn't look me in the eye. My mind skittered around, trying to find traction. How could he think this? Because I'd fixed my necklace with the same kind of glue I wrote about? The kind everybody in the world has stashed in their junk drawer? That's like accusing everyone who owns a knife of being Jack the Ripper.

"Why didn't you call me, Charlee? Why'd I hear this from my sister?"

"Your sister? It just happened! How did Bubbles hear about it?"

"The police called her."

"Oh. I didn't think they'd work that fast."

"They called me, too, but I didn't return their message."

"Why not?"

He shrugged. "Hoping to hear it from you."

"Why didn't you call me if you were so concerned?"

He shrugged again and we had a twenty-second stare-down.

Ozzi blinked first. "Why aren't you more upset? You show up for a booty call when all this is ... " He trailed off, shaking his head.

"How did you know it happened like my manuscript?"

"Bubbles said they were talking to everyone who read it and were asking questions about it. I made an assumption."

I continued to stare at him, knowing my mouth was set that ugly way it gets, but I didn't care. Let him see. He was being ugly too. "I can't believe I have to say this to you, of all people, but I did not kill my agent." I shoved my hands in my coat pockets. They'd still shake, but he wouldn't see.

"She was murdered exactly like—"

"Don't you think I know that?" I snapped. "Pretty sure that's why the cops hauled me in and questioned me half the day. And for the record, I told them the same thing. Because I didn't kill her."

"Then who did?" Ozzi's voice was quiet and calm, like he didn't want to make me mad. Too late.

"How should I know?" I yelled, and he flinched. Good. At least he was paying attention. "It was probably the mechanic who worked on Melinda's car. He found the manuscript in the backseat. That's what Lance told me." Kinda.

Ozzi took another step backward and leaned against the arm of the couch. "But what kind of motive would a mechanic have?"

His quiet voice made mine grow louder. "I don't know. You've met Melinda. You've seen her interact with the service industry. You said you wanted to strangle her that time she yelled at everybody at the Brown Palace. Remember?"

"That's just a turn of phrase."

"Is it? Are you sure you didn't strangle her?"

"Charlee, come on…"

"No, YOU come on."

He shook his head. "I don't have a motive."

"I don't either!"

He cocked his head. "You told me yourself that the only motives in murder are money, love, and revenge. I know you didn't love her, but you have been, let's say, concerned with your royalty statements. That she controls. That you think are wrong."

"I don't have to stand here and listen to this." I buttoned my coat. Halfway down, I stopped. "There's another motive. Jealousy." Jealousy, now that I thought about it, was more like a subset of love. But one doesn't quibble during an argument. One states opinions disguised as facts, the more emphatic, the better.

"Who was jealous of Melinda?"

"Not of her. Of me."

He looked confused, so I spelled it out. "Who do you know who is *always* talking about my success and how she wishes she had it?"

Ozzi raised his hands, palms up, in the classic *I don't know* gesture. Although combined with the look on his face, it was more like the *what the hell are you talking about now* gesture.

"Think, Oz. Who's an aspiring writer? Who begged you to talk me into letting her be one of my beta readers? Who's pushy and loud and always gets her way?" He still had the puzzled look on his face so I screamed, "Your sister, Oz!"

"Bubbles? Why would she?"

"I told you. Jealousy. Of me. Jealous of my success. Jealous that I'm an actual writer who writes actual books and has an actual literary agent managing my actual career. Jealous that I'm not middle-aged with the name of a performing monkey."

"Her real name is Beulah, named after—"

"Not the point." My fingernails dug into my palms. "She probably thought she'd be some sort of shoo-in to have Melinda represent her writing because of her *friendship*"—I dragged out the word and employed overly emphatic air quotes—"with me. Maybe Melinda rejected her as a client, so Bubbles got pissed and offed her."

Ozzi stared, open-mouthed, so I continued. "And if she did it, she's trying to frame me for it, too." My breath was fast and ragged.

"But why? She likes you. She told me a thousand times how happy she is I finally found someone."

"That just means she likes *you*."

"You're ridiculous. Not thinking straight." Ozzi's voice rose. "Let me get this straight. You think my sister read your manuscript and got jealous of the brilliance of your prose, leading her to bump off your agent, thus reducing the pool of people who might possibly get her published?"

"Why not? It makes as much sense as you thinking I did it."

"Just one problem, Charlee. She was with Mom. Besides, Bubbles isn't a writer. Never actually written anything."

I scoffed. "She just hasn't shown you any of her stuff. Lots of people keep their writing from their loved ones."

"Not my sister. She'd show me."

My jaw hurt and I unclenched it. "You know, you read the manuscript, too. You could have done it."

"Me? Why?"

"When I told you about my smaller royalty checks, you told me that she could have been embezzling from me and her other clients. Maybe you used your hacking skills on her computer and found proof, went to confront her, and she wouldn't confess, damaging your macho pride."

"That's the most—" He made a noise deep in his throat and stormed out of the room. I heard the refrigerator door open and the *pfft* of a bottle of beer being opened. I waited for him to return but he didn't.

I could have just called him to come over to my place after work, but no, I had to come over here and do the sexy thing that he didn't even appreciate. He could have just said he was tired or had to go somewhere. But then I wouldn't have seen this show. Wouldn't have seen his face. Wouldn't have watched him back away from me like I was some kind of murderer. When I walked through the door, he already thought I had something to do with the murder. The Glu-Pocalypse sealed it. Ha! I snorted wryly at my joke. Stupid Glu-Pocalypse.

I finished buttoning my coat, shoved my feet in my clogs, and left, slamming the door behind me. Screw him.

# Six

*I* slept late the next morning. My phone was off, the curtains drawn, and I was good with ignoring the world. But I knew I couldn't. I summoned the energy to contemplate a grilled cheese sandwich and grudgingly check my phone.

I groaned at the number of missed calls and texts. While I scrolled through them, the phone rang. Sheelah.

"Charlee! Finally. Are you okay?"

"I guess, but—"

"Where have you been?"

"I was—"

"Why was your phone off?"

"Because—"

"I heard what happened."

I kept quiet, waiting for her to take a breath. Frankly, the silence was fine with me.

"Charlee? You there?"

"Yes, I'm here."

"The police came to my house. They acted like you killed her."

I wanted to say "killed who?" but I figured that wouldn't be as sardonic and self-mocking as I wanted it to be.

"I got so flustered I couldn't even remember my dentist's name. I didn't know what to say."

"What did they ask you?"

"Where I was that morning, did I know Melinda, did I read your manuscript. And some questions about you. Stuff you've said about her, how you conduct your research, your relationship with the others in the group. I told them I'm kinda new so I don't really know much."

In critique group years, I guess a year was kinda new. But would the cops agree or think she was trying to cover for me with a lie? I groaned.

"What? Did I say something wrong?" I could hear the worry in her voice.

"No, you did what you had to, but ugh. I can't believe this is happening. I don't really know what to do."

"At least you have Ozzi for support."

"No, I don't. We had a huge fight last night. He all but accused me of the murder."

"I'm sure that's not true. It was just a misunderstanding. You probably overreacted because of all the stress you're under. I'm sure it'll blow over."

I curled my lip at the suggestion the fight was my fault, but I tucked away the idea to mull over later. "Maybe."

"Besides all that, how are you doing? Are you eating and sleeping? Or at least trying?"

"I guess."

"Charlee, I know you and Melinda weren't friends exactly, but it's still hard."

"Yeah. I'm confused and scared, and for a nonviolent person I'm having a lot of revenge fantasies. If I get my hands on whoever did this, it won't be pretty."

Sheelah made a noise I couldn't identify. "When I lost my kids I wanted revenge so bad I lashed out in every direction. Even at the cops. Especially at the cops. Speaking of which, be careful. They're not to be trusted."

I remembered Sheelah telling me about losing her family. I'd never asked, but the way she spoke made me think it was a car accident. "My brother's a cop. He's helping me."

"Is he? I'm sure he's one of the good ones."

"My dad was a cop, too."

"Again, one of the good ones."

Was he? "Up for debate. He died on the job. Big cloud hanging over it. Afterward, my mom ran away to New Mexico and my brother went to boarding school. I stayed with some friends, graduated early, and went to college." Weird and depressing how such a huge chunk of my pathetic history could be summed up so easily.

"That's terrible," Sheelah said. "You kinda lost your family, too." I didn't respond, couldn't respond, so she added, "I'm an idiot. I'm sure this isn't helping you at all. Want to get some lunch?"

"I'm making grilled cheese."

Talking to Sheelah was helpful, but the idea of going out into the world was beyond my capabilities at that moment. I didn't have a lot of close friends besides AmyJo, and she and I were so different it was often a chore to confide in her. AmyJo always wanted everything perfect, especially me. It was nice to have somebody like Sheelah. I wished she and AmyJo got along better, but they'd seemed like oil and water from the minute they met. If nothing else, AmyJo should have worshiped Sheelah for her ability to solve plot problems. She'd unraveled many knots in

AmyJo's stories. I wished she could do the same for my real-life problems.

"Ah, comfort food," Sheelah replied. "Want me to come over and keep you company?"

"Thanks, but no. I'm not fit for human interaction."

"Okay, but you call me if you need anything. I mean it, Charlee."

"I will. I hope your tooth feels better."

"Geez, that's so sweet of you. Everything that's going on and you're worried about me. I'm sure your problems will be cleared up before mine. Stupid dentist won't do anything until the infection is gone. Ten days on antibiotics. They better start working soon. The whole left side of my face hurts and it's all swollen up, too. I'm scaring babies and old people."

"Ooh. Send me a picture."

"You got it."

We disconnected and a text popped up with a selfie of Sheelah making a ridiculous face—cheeks puffed out, eyes bugging, mouth twisted. I laughed. Thanks to her, making a sandwich didn't seem so overwhelming for a minute.

The phone rang and I immediately picked it up, assuming it was Sheelah again.

"Nice picture," I said.

"What, dear? It's Veta."

"Oh, Veta, I'm sorry. I thought you were someone else. I'm also sorry I never returned your calls from yesterday and this morning. I've been ... busy."

"I understand. How are you?"

"I'm okay, but I'm trying to get my ducks in a row here."

"Charlee, the police questioned us." Veta sounded worried.

Dave and Veta had been so proud when I got my first book published, and they'd turned out to be excellent first readers for my manuscripts. Both of them were insightful and logical, always asking probing questions I'd never considered as I was writing. I'd given them an earlier draft of *Mercury Rising* than I gave everyone else because Dave was a retired biology professor, head of his department forever. I wanted him to check with his former professor comrades to help fine-tune the mercury poisoning facts for me. I had to ask him a couple of times, which was unusual, and Veta made excuses for him. Finally, I called and Veta must have made him come to the phone, but he brushed me off, saying, "I don't know anyone who'd know that." So I'd dropped it and checked with that chemistry teacher my Facebook friend had suggested instead.

"Don't worry about the police, Veta. They're talking to everyone who read my manuscript."

"I suppose. But it's still unsettling."

"I agree one thousand percent." I paused. "Do you remember what you and Dave were doing Sunday night into Monday morning?"

Veta was quiet a moment. "The police asked us that too. Do you think we killed that woman, Charlee?"

The hurt in her voice pained me. "No I don't, Veta. But I feel like I have to rule people out. At least for my own peace of mind."

"Of course you do." She paused. "Dave and I watched Netflix with some neighbors and then we went to bed. I can't prove to anyone that we were tucked in all night, but we were."

I sighed. How do you prove a negative?

"I'm sure you were, Veta. Have the police asked you anything more?"

"No. Haven't heard from them since that first call."

"Then I'm sure that means they don't think you killed Melinda. And I don't think you did either. Say hi to Dave for me."

"I will. And let's meet for lunch as soon as all this nastiness is cleared up."

I channeled my inner Columbo. "Hey Veta, one more thing. This has been bothering me for a while. How come Dave wouldn't help with my research for *Mercury Rising*?"

She was quiet for a moment. "Charlee, you can't tell him I told you this, but he's had to take a job at Walmart since he retired. He didn't want to talk with old colleagues and risk having them find out. He never even had time to read your manuscript."

"Taking a job isn't something to be ashamed of."

"I know, and he's actually starting to like it. The money helps and he's making new friends, but it isn't academia."

"His secret is safe with me."

After we hung up, I thought more about Dave and Veta. I loved when they came to our house to play cards with my parents. I'd sit in the living room, leaning on the wall just out of sight of my mother, and listen to them talk and laugh. I'd never heard adults argue like Dave and Veta. My folks agreed on most things, or maybe, because of Lance and me, they just didn't have the energy to form so many opinions. Dave and Veta were "childless by choice," as they announced constantly. That had seemed like an insult to me, being a child and all.

Dave proclaimed that his students were his children, but I knew that was a cop-out. I bet he never had to diaper one of them, or rush them to the emergency room during an asthma attack, or pay their college tuition.

But they seemed to like me. Whenever Veta saw me in the living room, hiding from my folks and listening to their banter, she'd make some excuse, then secretly bring me a plate of the fancy dessert they always brought. Typical desserts for us were store-brand ice cream, or brownies, or cake from a mix. Delicious, mind you, and always welcome on my immature palate, but Veta always brought something exotic. Baked Alaska, covered in meringue that melted on your tongue. English Trifle, with its layers of sponge cake, fresh fruit, and honest-to-god whipped cream. And fondue. Ohmygod, chocolate fondue. For that, she called Lance and me into the kitchen and gave us long skinny forks, waving her arm across a sea of confections to stab and dip. Pound cake, pineapple chunks not even from a can, whole strawberries, fancy cookies that didn't come in a family-sized box of value.

I remembered the wicked delight of accepting Veta's invitation to horn in on my parents' fun. Stabbing, dipping, and gorging on the sweet array laid out on the counter. "How'd you make the chocolate like this?" I'd asked, shoving the delicate fork in my not-so-delicate mouth.

Veta told me, "Science, Charlee. My kitchen is my laboratory."

The memory stopped me abruptly. Laboratory.

Dave and Veta Burr were excellent, critical readers for my first drafts. And, of course, they argued all the time. Could one of them have wanted to prove a point? And what would that even be? They seemed to know everyone in Denver but had never mentioned they knew Melinda. What would either one of them have had against her? Was Melinda just a victim of some intellectual discussion they were having?

I imagined them reading my manuscript and Dave wondering about the science involved in mercury poisoning. Veta would likely take the opposite point of view. Would one of them go so far as to try to prove the viability of my methods?

I sighed. I couldn't picture either one of them killing Melinda.

The memories of those desserts let my hunger pangs loose. I still craved a grilled cheese.

Despite the circumstances of its making, my sandwich turned out perfect enough to grace the cover of *Sandwich Monthly*. Not sure there was such a periodical, but there were magazines about most everything—

*Miniature Donkey Talk, Modern Drunkard, Cranes Today*. I know because I've had articles rejected by all of them.

While the grilled cheese was majestic in every way—butter-crisp, golden sourdough on the outside, the perfect ratio (3:1) of sharp cheddar and pepper jack melted on the inside, flowing from the diagonal knife cut—it didn't solve any problems. I shoved it in my mouth so fast I didn't even get to enjoy it. Worse, it didn't cure the dull throb in my head I suspected was caused by that bottle of wine I'd had for dinner. I considered brewing a pot of coffee, and even went so far as to pull the coffee from the pantry.

Then I went back to bed.

That's what professional writers did on a Tuesday morning if the situation warranted. And mine sure as hell did.

I woke up to a banging on my front door.

"Open up. I know you're in there. I see your car."

*Oh no, the police! They found me.* Wait. Was I hiding? That didn't seem right. I rolled over and looked at the clock on my nightstand. 1:48 … a.m. or p.m.? I blinked.

The pounding became more insistent. I used my palms to rub my eyes. Wouldn't my brother give me the heads-up if I was going to get arrested? Would he even know?

"Charlee, c'mon. What are you doing in there?"

I recognized that voice. My head began to clear. I propped myself on one elbow to hear better.

"I have a surprise for you."

My neighbor, Suzanne Medina. I flopped back down on my bed. Sooo not interested in any more surprises. I was awake now and grabbed my phone from the nightstand. A new parade of messages scrolled by. Nobody I wanted to talk to.

I glanced nervously toward the living room, but the banging at my door had stopped. I ventured out to make the pot of coffee I'd abandoned earlier. I still wasn't completely sure whether it was day or night—God bless you, Target blackout curtains model 43-529 with extra grommets—so I used one finger to draw them back, peeping out the sliding glass door near my reading chair overlooking the patio.

An eyeball stared back at me. I startled and fell backward into the chair.

"I knew you were in there. Are you avoiding me?"

"Hells bells, Suzanne. Yes. When people don't respond to someone at their door, they *are* trying to avoid you."

"Open the door."

That was the very last thing I wanted to do.

"I have a present for you." After a moment, the knocking on my front door started up again.

Maybe it was coffee. I cracked open the door. It wasn't coffee.

Suzanne stood there, stringy gray hair tucked behind her ears, which made them stick out more than normal.

"What's up?" I cracked the door a bit more and blocked the doorway with my body.

She picked up a big Amazon box that had been sitting at her feet. "I told you. I have something for you." She used the box to push me out of the way. Before I knew what was happening, she was in my living room.

"Geez, I was sleeping. Couldn't this wait?"

"Nobody sleeps until two in the afternoon except hookers and punk rockers. Now make some coffee and join the world."

I sighed and padded into the kitchen. Oh yeah. I'd had *two* bottles of wine for dinner. I moved them aside and measured water into the coffeemaker. I counted scoops of coffee into the filter but stopped with a jolt at three.

Suzanne was one of my beta readers. She could have killed Melinda. Should it mean something that she hadn't mentioned Melinda's death? No *I heard it on the news.* No *Isn't it terrible.* No *I'm sorry for your loss.*

Wait. Had it even been on the news yet? It had just happened the day before. Online, maybe, but unless you're scrolling around specifically looking for it, would you even see it? Melinda was a big deal in my little world, but I doubted she made a ripple in the Who's Who pond of the Denver populace.

I still held the coffee scoop in mid-air.

"Did you forget what you were doing?" Suzanne motioned toward the coffee.

"No. Yes. I'm just—"

"You're probably still in shock from what happened yesterday."

I wasn't sure if she was referring to Melinda's murder, or me being implicated in it, or me humiliating myself at Ozzi's. Gossip spreads through this complex like chlamydia on Colfax. "How'd you know about that?"

She shrugged. "I keep my finger on the pulse."

Still couldn't tell.

"On whose pulse?"

"Denver PD."

"What?"

She shrugged. "Everyone has a police scanner these days."

I didn't think that was true, but I held my tongue and finished making the coffee.

"Too bad about your agent. Weird way to die, too."

"What do you mean?" *How much did they talk about?*

"Jumped a curb and hit a tree in her own neighborhood? No skid marks? Seems fishy to me." Suzanne flashed her smile, and I'd never known how creepy it was until that minute. Her lips actually disappeared, making her look like a … what … shark. Yeah, a shark. I made a mental note to add that to my Character Traits file. It would be great for a killer. I gasped and turned my back on her.

I watched the coffee drip as I tried to collect my thoughts. There was no way my next door neighbor murdered my agent. Right? I mean, yeah, she read the first draft of my manuscript, and yeah, she was a weirdo with a Kindle devoted strictly to murder mysteries and thrillers. And, yes, she turned her second bedroom into a gruesome homage to murder, with floor-to-ceiling shelves filled with nonfiction books about serial killers, mass murders, and how-to references, but I always assumed she was yet another wannabe writer. Like Ozzi's sister. The world is lousy with wannabe writers. You can't swing a *Publishers Weekly* at a book signing without hitting a dozen wannabe writers.

I thought about how many times I'd borrowed those reference books from her, once even remarking that she would make a great serial killer. She'd replied, "Nah. Too obvious."

But was it? Or was it all simply preparation?

I felt a nudge on my back and shrieked.

"Wow. Maybe you don't need any coffee." Suzanne stood in the kitchen holding the Amazon box.

I stared at it, remembering the story I wrote with the bomb disguised as a gift. Absolutely cliché and trope-y, but my readers didn't mind. When the ribbon was undone, BAM.

She pushed it toward me. I backed away.

"It's on top," she kept saying as she jabbed it at me.

I knew I looked like an idiot by backing away with every jab. I bet my eyes had that crazy come-kill-me look that people must get when they're about to be murdered in their kitchen wearing their jammies and not even having had any coffee yet.

"Just take the one on top."

Suzanne reminded me of those elderly British ladies putting poison in one cup of tea. *This* one's for you, love. That's it, have a nice cuppa and a biscuit," one would offer sweetly. "No, not that one," the other would say, rotating the handle toward their victim. "This one's for you, innit?" It would look just like the other cup except for some barely noticeable sign you'd only see if you knew what to look for, like a sheen across the tea, or a few seemingly innocent sugar crystals on the rim.

"I don't need anything, Suzanne. And it's not anywhere near my birthday."

"Oh, for the love of—" She juggled the box and pulled open the flaps. It hadn't even been sealed, but that didn't matter. It could still be booby-trapped.

She shoved the box toward me and I saw three books sliding around. She shoved it again, right into my belly. I reacted by pulling out the stack of books. What can I say? Books of any kind are irresistible and almost never armed with a detonator.

I held the books in one hand, shuffling through them as I read the titles. "*How to Murder Your Darlings. The Handbook of Poisons, Potions, and Premeditation. Deadly Secrets of Deadly Women.*"

I glanced up at her. She was holding the empty box and grinning with those nonexistent lips. *How have I never noticed that creepy shark smile before?*

"This one's for you," she said, plucking *How to Murder Your Darlings* from my hands. "It's not about murder at all. It's about editing. Specifically, how to remove passages that don't fit your story, even if you love them. I thought you could use it."

I didn't know whether to be glad she wasn't here to murder me or upset that she felt so strongly I needed a book about editing. I decided to be glad I wasn't murdered.

But that didn't mean she wasn't a murderer.

I closed the door after Suzanne and felt sorry for myself for the next three and a half hours. Not in a row, of course. Some of the time was spent being angry at Ozzi and being scared and paranoid about whoever was trying to frame me. It all looked the same, though: me curled up on the couch watching a *Psych* marathon; empty chocolate chunk ice cream container on the coffee table; floor littered with tissues.

Geez. What a girl.

At a little after six, I heard Ozzi's familiar honk, like always, like nothing had happened. Ten minutes later, he used his special knock on my door. I ignored him.

"Charlee, open the door."

"No. Go away."

Silence. He went away? Just like that?

My phone chirped that I had a text message. Ozzi. I peeked out and saw him leaning on the railing looking at his phone.

*Are you okay? I'm here to apologize.*

I typed, *You said I was ridiculous.*

*I'M the ridiculous one. Let me take you to dinner. We can talk.*

My stomach rumbled but I typed, *No. Still angry.*

I heard a quiet thud. I used the peephole and saw he was leaning with his back on my apartment door.

*Please? I'm really good at apologizing.*

I leaned with my back to the door. We were six inches away but miles apart.

*I need some time. Lots going on.*

*I'm not giving up. Call me.*

I didn't reply, just kept leaning against the door, phone pressed to my heart. I jumped when it rang. I thought it would be Ozzi not giving up, but it was AmyJo. "Hey, Ames."

"How are you? I've been calling and calling."

"I know." I crossed to the couch and curled into the corner. "I'm pretending none of this happened."

"The cops questioned me."

I dug the remote from the couch cushion and muted the TV, feeling a stab of guilt for implicating her in this mess.

"What are you doing?" she asked.

"At this moment, I'm—"

"About Melinda."

"My plan is to lay low and stay home until they find Melinda's killer. That'll keep me safe if there's a lunatic after me, too."

"And the police might forget you're a suspect."

"Not sure that's how they work, but sure, *out of sight, out of mind* might be in their procedures manual."

"What if they never catch the murderer?" AmyJo said. "There are a lot of cold cases out there."

"Gee. Thanks for bringing that up."

"Like you never thought about it."

She was right. I'd been thinking about it constantly. "Yeah, but—"

"Oh, shoot, Charlee. I've got to go. But is there anything I can do for you? Do you need anything? More ice cream?"

My eyes drifted to the empty half-gallon container on the coffee table. "How did you know I ate all my ice cream?"

"Oh, please. I've never seen you go through a crisis without some chocolate chunk. I know you better than you know yourself. Call me if you need anything."

After AmyJo disconnected, I sat on the edge of the couch, hands clasped, elbows on knees. I knew I'd feel better if I wrote. I shut off the TV and padded down the hall to the extra bedroom that served as my office.

At my desk, the light from my MacBook pulsated gently, like an electronic finger beckoning. I lifted the lid and sat before it, waiting for my muse.

While I waited, I scrolled through the last few pages of the new mystery I'd started writing. Lots of writers take time off between completing one manuscript and beginning another, but I was firmly in the camp that believed in diving right into something new. After all, the best way to sell more books was to write more books. Which was also much more fun. Plus, I knew how to do it.

Geez, I hoped I knew how to do it. I reread the section I'd intended to submit to my writing group at the aborted meeting on Monday, but now, on Tuesday, a lifetime later, it wasn't speaking to me.

And my muse was off in the corner, filing her nails or something, completely oblivious to my need.

I didn't really believe in muses, but the imagery was so delicious. Some nebulous being who whispered in your ear, guiding your thoughts, helping create heavenly manuscripts. But they didn't always show up, even when invited. Instead, I believed in sitting in my chair every day. I believed in putting my hands on the keyboard and typing. My muse is BICHOK—butt in chair, hands on keyboard. No luck, no magic, just effort.

Of course, you have to know what you're doing. And at that moment I did not. Again, I read the pages I'd wanted my critique group to comment on. How could I write another murder mystery when the last one had ramifications far beyond entertaining someone for a few hours? How could I throw yet more violence into the world? How could I stomach what some sicko did with my words, my imagination?

I closed the document and stared at the folder on my screen. All my research. My entire outline. 13,462 words.

Click. The folder lit up. I dragged it toward the desktop trash can, finally dropping it in. I emptied the trash for good measure, the sucking *thwack* noise both terrifying and satisfying.

I opened a new document. No more mysteries. No more death and dying. I was branching out.

I thought about AmyJo. I read her angsty young adult stuff all the time. I could do that. My protagonist would be a high school girl with cancer—no, John Green already did that. Maybe a high school boy with cancer. No, a loser high school boy whose *younger sister* gets cancer and he must get his shit together in the three weeks before graduation to help his entire family cope with the situation. I started typing. But it turned out she didn't have cancer at all. Instead, she was being slowly poisoned by their parents who wanted to cash in her life insurance money and jet off to live on the beach in Belize and drink mai tais all day without the constant grind of raising kids. So he turned the tables on them, gave them the rest of the poison, and watched as they melted from the inside out, right there on the kitchen floor.

I dragged the pages to the trash and opened a new blank document.

A picture book, perhaps. Something in the style of Beatrix Potter. A sweet little bunny in a blue jacket. I had him frolicking in the farmer's field, nibbling carrots and making a nuisance of himself, always one step ahead of the frustrated farmer. Then BLAMMO. The farmer blasted him to smithereens, fricassee raining down on the heads of his brothers and his sweet, patient mother. "That's what you get for not controlling your child," shouted the farmer, not caring one whit about the blotches of bunny fur and entrails dripping from Mommy Bunny's little paisley bonnet.

*Delete.* I'd try my hand at writing romance. Maybe I could write myself over this fight with Ozzi.

I thought about the few romances I'd read. I knew the rules. Parallel stories of a star-crossed couple. They have a meet-cute, they're kept apart, they finally get together when one or both of them realizes they're meant to be happily ever after. Not something I necessarily subscribed to in real life, but, hey, anything goes in fiction, right?

I began writing about a darling fourth grade teacher and a hunky construction worker, both from central casting, at least until my first revision. He shows up for a parent-teacher conference, but she thinks he's there to fix the broken door in her classroom. Because she's darling, and he's good-natured with a mischievous grin—and did I mention hunky?—he fixes the door. Just when he finishes, the janitor walks in to do the repairs. The darling teacher with the single dimple realizes she was just cutely met, reaches into her purse for her concealed pearl-handled snubnose, aims it, and pierces the hunk cleanly between the eyes. He crumples to the floor, blood pooling around his head. She has a moment of remorse, because she *is* a darling elementary school teacher, after all. But she doesn't like to be made to look foolish. And now the janitor has so much more work to do.

I reread it. Shook my head.

Poetry. I'd try that.

*There once was a Reaper quite grim*
*Who stalked hatted men on a whim*
*When hit with a bat,*
*That head it went splat*
*And filled his beret to the brim.*

Nope.

*Shall I compare thee to a summer's day?*
*Dost thou hear the buzz of the bee, merrily alive,*
*Industrious?*
*Dost thou see the stinger, menacing closer,*
*Closer*
*Closer?*
*Piercing the sweet, delicate flesh of milady's*
*Red, rosebud lips*
*Pumping venom*
*Over and*
*Over and*
*Over again*
*Until nigh upon daybreak whence macabre Death takes her*
*Closer*
*Closer*
*Closer.*

I rubbed my eyes and turned on some lights. It was late, but I wasn't tired. Or maybe I was too tired. I shut the lid of my computer, remembering the *write what you know* conversation. Did I only know murder? Was that always where my brain scuttled? Were mysteries all I knew how to write?

If so, then I had to figure out who killed Melinda so I could get back to it. And maybe solving Melinda's murder would be a better tribute for her loved ones than simply sending flowers and a card.

# Seven

I stayed up the rest of the night studying my list of suspects and their possible motives.

Seventeen names. Fourteen of them people I knew. Spent time with. Shared secrets with. Slept with. My mind skittered and leaped, confused yet growing angrier by the minute. One of them must be a cold-blooded killer.

I still couldn't believe I might know a murderer, but why else would Melinda have been killed exactly as I detailed it? Mercury poisoning is pretty unique, if I do say so myself, reddening at my misplaced pride.

I doodled a fat blue question mark in the margin of the page, coloring it in with harsh, angry strokes. I pressed the heels of my palms to my eyelids and took a deep breath. I arched my back to work out a kink, then tapped my pen on every name, returning to the top of the list. Again. Again. Again.

By the time the sun came up I had a plan.

After a long, hot shower and an unsatisfying breakfast of Cheetos and a protein bar, I shoved my suspect list into my bag and drove to Dunphy's Auto Repair. I hoped it was the place Melinda used. If it wasn't, I had three more possibilities. An internet search showed that Dunphy's was about equidistant between her office and her home. And classic cars were listed as their specialty.

I parked on the street and walked up to the driveway of the business just as a man in dress slacks and a leather jacket swung open a chain-link gate and latched it on the right. He greeted me with a wave. "Car acting up?" He swung the left side open and latched it. Behind him, mechanics in blue-and-white-striped coveralls scurried around the lot and service bays.

"No," I said. "I was hoping to ask you some questions."

"About your car?" The man eyed my Kia at the curb. The rising sun highlighted the filth. "We only work on classic cars here, ma'am."

Ma'am. Ouch.

One of the mechanics revved an engine nearby, so I raised my voice. "Not about my car. But do you happen to know if you service Melinda Walter's car here?" The revving stopped halfway through the sentence so her name hung heavy over the parking lot.

The man turned his head toward the service bays. I saw one of the mechanics give an almost imperceptible nod and then scurry away. "Why do you ask?"

I pointed at the mechanic. "Is that Joaquin?"

"Are you a cop?" He started walking toward my car, but I didn't follow so he turned back. Now my back was to the service bays instead of his. I could see him glancing nervously behind me and I made a quarter turn.

"I'm not a cop, and I'm not with Immigration. I'm a friend of Melinda's. I might have left something on her backseat when she had her car serviced recently."

"Her car isn't here. I can't help you." Again, he walked toward my car. Again, I stayed put.

He returned and spoke quietly. "If you're a reporter, I'd like you to leave the premises now. I have nothing to say."

"Why do you think I'm a reporter?"

He gestured at my bag, where my yellow notebook was sticking out.

"I'm not a reporter. Like I said, I'm a friend of Melinda's."

He sized me up. "You may not be a reporter, but you must not know Melinda or you'd know she died recently."

"I'm aware. I'm also aware her car malfunctioned and your mechanic Joaquin was the last person to work on it."

We stared at each other. I was ready to scream and run if I needed to. But he looked the same way I felt. His face was taut and pinched without much color. Clearly, I was making him nervous.

"I don't know what you're insinuating, but if you think Joaquin or any of my mechanics did something to sabotage her car, well, I can assure you that would never happen. I run a professional business and we do quality work here. We've never had an incident like you're describing, and Joaquin—all my guys—are excellent mechanics and upstanding citizens."

"I'm sure they are. Look, I'm not here to make trouble. I just need some information. I'm not a cop. I'm not a reporter. I'm just a novelist trying to find my manuscript and maybe figure out some things about Melinda." The butterflies in my stomach multiplied and took flight. I balled my fists in my coat pockets while he stared at me.

Finally, he sighed. "Let's go inside. I need some coffee. Want some?"

Like I wanted oxygen. "Yes, please."

We crossed the parking lot into the office, furtively stared at by four or five mechanics pretending to be busy.

After he ushered me to a chair, closed the door, and handed me a steaming cup, he sat behind his desk. He sipped his coffee, staring at me over the rim. "So. You think we stole something from you out of Ms. Walter's car. What's your game? Blackmail? Phony insurance claim? With her gone, trying to make it a case of he said, she said?"

"What? No!" My coffee sloshed in my trembling hand and I placed the cup on his desk. I had to nudge aside a nameplate that read *Bob Dunphy.* "Let me start over, Mr. Dunphy. My understanding is that Joaquin worked on Melinda's car in the last few weeks." He nodded. "Melinda was my literary agent and she had one of my new manuscripts in her possession. I'm trying to determine if one of your mechanics—Joaquin, perhaps—might have pulled it out of the car. Maybe read it?"

All the tension left Dunphy's face and he smiled. "Well, first off, Joaquin is the only one who Ms. Walter allowed to touch her car, so there'd be no other mechanics involved."

"Are you sure nobody else would work on her car?"

He narrowed his eyes. "I thought you knew Ms. Walter. Do you really think one of my guys would do something against her wishes? They're not stupid. They wouldn't have wanted to take that risk. Ms. Walter was … demanding, as I'm sure you knew."

I nodded. "Yes, she was … demanding."

"I don't want to talk ill about the dead, but Joaquin actually drew the short straw. He seemed to have a way with her, though."

Like a snake charmer, perhaps. "That may be, but isn't it possible he could have read the manuscript?"

"Nope." Seeing my skepticism, he pushed a button on his intercom and spoke in Spanish.

I heard the tinny echo of his voice in the adjoining garage. It didn't take long before a muscular Hispanic man, maybe forty-ish, opened the office door. Dunphy waved him in and motioned me to speak to him.

"Joaquin, my name is Charlemagne Russo. I wanted to ask, the last time you worked on Melinda Walter's car, did you find a manuscript on the back seat?"

The mechanic rubbed the stubble on his chin. *"Cómo?"*

"It was a stack of papers about this big"—I spread my thumb and forefinger about two inches apart—"with a big black binder clip at the top."

Joaquin looked at me, then at Dunphy, who rummaged in his desk and pulled one out. Dunphy spoke in Spanish and I hoped he was translating what I said.

Joaquin shook his head.

"Joaquin, do you speak any English?" I asked.

He smiled and spread his thumb and forefinger about two inches apart, as I had. "Car stuff." When I didn't respond, he and Dunphy conversed in rapid-fire Spanish.

Dunphy said, "He wants you to know he's sorry about your friend, but he saw nothing like you describe."

*"Gracias."* My high school Spanish was rusty, since I took French, so I mimed reading a book. *"Inglés?"*

He smiled back, shaking his head.

"Joaquin is one of the brightest men I have working here. Fine family man, but he barely speaks English and doesn't read a lick of it." Dunphy sent Joaquin back to work, with apologies for the interruption.

Topping off our coffees, he asked me, "So what's the big deal about this manuscript? Surely you have another copy if you've lost it."

I stared at him, trying to decide how much to say. "You mentioned the police and reporters earlier, so I'm guessing you know Melinda's death was perhaps not accidental. So, I'm wondering…"

"What our alibis are?"

I blushed but kept eye contact with him.

Dunphy waved an arm vaguely toward the garage. "Ms. Russo, all the men who work back there are related to each other. Brothers, uncles, sons, cousins. We have a close-knit crew. We were all at Joaquin's daughter's *quinceañera* on Sunday. Everybody was there very late, including me and my wife, even though we open at six on Monday morning. Every single one of my mechanics was here with me to open." He pulled out his phone, pushed a couple of buttons, and handed it to me. "Pictures. A lovely girl and a fantastic party."

I swiped through the photos, seeing Joaquin with a beaming woman, probably his wife, posing with the girl and many others. There were photos of them in church, photos of Joaquin kneeling in front of his daughter and placing high heels on her feet, photos of groaning tables of food and gifts. There were selfies of Dunphy and there were photos of a packed dance floor. Even photos of people taking photos.

All time- and date-stamped from Sunday evening into the wee hours of Monday morning. The final one was a cockeyed selfie of two obviously drunk men, Bob Dunphy and Joaquin, at 2:56 Monday morning.

"That looked like some party." I handed the phone back. "But—"

"Ms. Russo, I don't want to be rude, but it seems to me you're implying that Joaquin might have had something to do with Ms. Walter's death. Like I said, he's a family man. Melinda lives not too far from here, right? Joaquin and his brothers all live way out past the airport, in Platteville. They pile into a van to drive over an hour to work every day, and Joaquin doesn't drive. Only one of the boys has a license. Do you really think Joaquin would leave his daughter's party, grab his nephew, and drive all the way down here to do harm to someone?"

It did seem far-fetched, especially seeing how happy Joaquin looked in those pictures. "Where was the party?" I asked.

"Platteville. Ceremony and reception at Sacred Heart Catholic Church, then after-party at Joaquin's house."

With the timestamps of the photos, it meant Joaquin couldn't have even left the party before three in the morning. Assuming he'd left right after that last photo was taken, he would have arrived at Melinda's around four, spent time tampering with her car, driven an hour back home, and still made it to work by six? The timeline didn't work.

We had a twenty second stare-down.

"I'm really trying to figure this out," Dunphy said. "He obviously didn't tamper with Ms. Walter's car. Wait. Are you accusing him of stealing your manuscript? What would his motive be? Put his name on it and pass it off as his own? Sell it on the black market?" He finished his coffee. "Ludicrous."

I had to agree. I finished my coffee and stood. "I guess you're right."

"But there is one thing. The last time Ms. Walter had her car in, it was picked up by her obnoxious assistant who insisted we keep a set of car keys here. It's not how we do business—we only keep keys while we're working on the cars—but she said it was what Ms. Walter wanted and threatened to send her down herself to explain things if I needed it." He shrugged. "The last thing I needed was her coming down here and tearing me a new one."

"So you kept a set of keys to Melinda's car here?" My ears perked up.

"Only for the past couple of weeks. Since the last time she had it serviced." He pulled a fully-loaded key chain from his pocket and unlocked his desk drawer. From the drawer he pulled out a pack of cigarettes. He slipped a finger into it and after some effort extracted a single silver key on a plain ring. Next he removed a small lockbox from a different locked drawer, which he proceeded to open with the silver key. "Can't be too careful." He handed me a set of keys, which was the only thing in the lockbox. "Since you're friends with Ms. Walter, can you please give these to her husband? He might want them, as a token, but I don't want to impose on him right now."

Neither did I, but I nodded.

# Eight

*I* sat in my car in front of the car repair shop and reconsidered my plan. I really, really wanted Joaquin to be more suspicious and/or have a flimsy alibi, and while his time could not be completely accounted for, it seemed highly implausible he randomly picked up my manuscript from Melinda's car because he saw it sitting there, had it translated into Spanish, read it, then used the information to stage Melinda's murder. Even if it was a lie that he didn't read English, it still seemed unlikely.

But I really, really wanted it to be him. He was the only stranger on my suspect list and now I had to cross him off.

I also had to take the keys to Henry. I wasn't sure he'd want keys to Melinda's totalled car, but who was I to judge? I still had the key to my dad's work locker hanging on my rear view mirror. I flicked it and started the car. While I was pulling my seat belt on, I got a text from Q.

*Your publisher sent papers you need to sign. I'll be in the office all day.*

I groaned. "That can't be good news." My publisher must have gotten word of Melinda's death. Since she was the sole proprietor of the agency, there were no other agents to handle my career. I was on my own. I just sent a simple thumbs-up emoji to Q in reply, planning to swing by after I went to Henry's.

When I got to the house Henry and Melinda used to share, I stood on the porch a long time before pressing the bell. I'm sure he knew I was there, since I'd had to stop at the gatehouse and let the guard know where I was going. Bless Henry for allowing me time to compose myself.

He opened the door and extended his hand. "Miss Russo, it's so nice of you to stop by."

"Hi, Mr. Walter. I hope I'm not disturbing you, but I wanted to give you my condolences. And these." I dangled Melinda's car keys between us. "Her mechanic wanted you to have them."

"Why were you talking to Melinda's mechanic?" He didn't take his eyes off the keys dangling from my index finger.

"That's a long story. But I understand if you don't want them." I started to put them in my jacket pocket, but he grabbed my wrist.

"No. I'll take them." He slid them into the pocket of his khakis. "Why did they have her keys?" He searched my face for an answer I didn't have.

He looked so tired and haggard, my heart broke for him. "Mr. Walter ... never mind. I won't bother you anymore."

"Not a bother. It's nice to have company for a bit. Will you come in? I just made coffee."

"Ohmygosh, I should have checked the time. It's so early. I didn't sleep last night, so I just assumed the whole world would be up."

"I haven't slept much either. It's hard to wrap your brain around the idea that you go to bed one night with your wife, then it's never going to happen again." He pointed a finger at me. "Don't take lovely normal weekends for granted, Miss Russo. Because then a Monday might come along and change your whole life." He twisted his wedding band, then abruptly stopped and rubbed a hand over his stubble. "I'm sorry. I don't want to be such a burden. Come in and have some coffee with me. Keep me company for a bit. And please call me Henry."

"Only if you call me Charlee."

"Deal."

He stepped aside to let me in, then led the way through the sprawling house to the kitchen. Melinda's home was not at all how I'd pictured it. Instead of sterile chrome and monochromatic decor, it was filled with warm leather furniture tucked with colorful pillows and throws, bright rugs on the wood floors. I was struck by two things in the kitchen—the gorgeous jade-colored countertop and the lack of any casseroles or flower arrangements on it. My hand slid over the surface before I could stop myself.

"Enameled lava from a volcano in France. Melinda searched for just the right thing for years. And this was it." He rapped it with his knuckles.

"France has volcanos?"

"I guess. It wasn't part of the discussion." Henry selected two dainty cups from a wrought-iron tree and filled them from a machine that looked like it cost more than my car. He handed one to me and waved me to a bistro table in an alcove. He sat across from me, sipping his coffee.

I sipped my coffee, too, relieved that his coffee tasted no different than the coffee I brewed in my El Cheapo brand coffee maker. I didn't need any more aspirational products in my life.

We sat in silence for a few moments before I spoke, almost inaudibly. "I wanted to find out about the funeral arrangements."

Henry cleared his throat. "There aren't any yet. There's going to be an autopsy, and the timing…"

I let the pause hang in the air for a moment. "I understand, but would you let me know as soon as—"

"Did Melinda seem depressed to you?" Henry asked abruptly. "I thought her antidepressants were working, but for her to deliberately crash into a tree ... "

It felt like he'd just forced me to swallow a rock. Melinda was on medication? He didn't know about the mercury? Was he trying to deliberately mislead me?

I thought my face remained impassive, but he said, "I'm sorry. I shouldn't be troubling you with this. Especially with all the financial turmoil you're in now."

Now I knew my face belied my emotions because I felt it flush. "Financial turmoil?"

"Oh, no. You don't know. I'm sorry, I shouldn't have mentioned it."

"Please, tell me." I gripped the edge of the table with both hands as I felt the flush traveling; only a matter of time before it hit my tremor and made it worse.

Henry took a deep breath and pursed his lips sympathetically. "The agency's assets were frozen as soon as Melinda's death was recorded by the coroner. Nobody can touch the funds. I asked our attorney if I can pay royalties to her authors, but he said I can't. It's a probate thing."

I made a mental accounting of my finances and it wasn't pretty. "For how long?"

"Nobody knows."

"What if I terminated the contract I have—had—with Melinda? Would they have to pay me as one of the creditors?"

"I don't think so. And your contract isn't with Melinda, it's with the agency."

I nodded absentmindedly. Melinda and the agency were interchangeable to me. "I should still terminate the contract."

"I understand." Henry rose from the table and shuffled through a stack of files on the corner of the counter. He handed me some pages from one. "Look at Clause 17, Dissolution or Death."

I raked my eyes over the front page and saw that it was a copy of my contract with Melinda. The agency.

Was two days the appropriate amount of time for spousal grief before the practicalities set in? I flashed back to when Dad died. Mom sent the insurance and police union guys away for weeks before she could face talking to them. Was it the difference between rich people and middle class? I glanced at Henry and then quickly looked away. Or was it the difference between people who loved their lost one and people who didn't?

"Clause 17. Third page." Henry waggled a finger at the papers in my hand.

I found the clause. *"All monies due Melinda B. Walter Agency, including commissions on royalties and on all secondary sales arising from literary material for which Melinda B. Walter Agency has sold primary rights, shall remain due and owing Melinda B. Walter Agency heirs upon the death or incapacitation of all principals of Melinda B. Walter Agency or the dissolution of Melinda B. Walter Agency."*

I had a million questions but couldn't form any.

Henry picked up our cups and refilled them. "I'm Melinda's only heir, so now I own the agency. As soon as everything goes through probate, I'll be your new agent." He handed me my coffee, then, standing over me, clinked it with his. "Congratulations, partner."

I set the cup down without drinking and flipped through the pages of my contract. My mind raced. My new agent? Did he even know the business? Did he have contacts with publishers? Editors? Anyone in the industry? I looked up at him. "How will you be able to just step into her business? Will you have a partner? Keep Q on as your assistant?"

Henry's face clouded. "Just between you and me, I don't trust that girl. It's crossed my mind that she could have cut Melinda's brakes or something. She had all of Melinda's keys, knew her schedule, hell, knew everything about her. And you of all people should know Mel wasn't the easiest to get along with."

He was blaming Q for Melinda's death? He barely knew me. He shouldn't have been talking like this. I studied the contract.

His voice lost its edge and he sounded downright perky. "How hard can agenting be? It's just a game of numbers, profit and loss, right? It'll be fine, Charlee. You'll see. I just wish I could send you your royalties as soon as they come."

"Henry, I don't mean to be rude, but I do want to terminate my contract with the agency, like it says in Clause 4." I pointed to it while I read. *"After the initial term of this Agreement, either party may terminate this Agreement at any time upon thirty (30) days prior notice."* I raised my eyes. "Consider this my thirty days notice."

He nodded, still smiling. "And in four years or so, I'll be happy to discuss it."

"Four years?"

"Read Clause 2. You're not through your initial term yet."

I closed my eyes and took a deep breath. This was exactly what I'd been telling my critique group the other day. I'd signed a horrible contract. But that wasn't why I was there. I had to set the contract aside for now because I was supposed to be investigating my list of suspects.

And Henry was fast rising to the top. All this, plus what Cordelia had told me about the business dealings gone bad with her husband, and my musings about romantic affair scenarios between the two couples didn't seem so over-the-top now.

"Do you know Byron Hollister-Fiske?" I asked. "He's the husband of my friend Cordelia."

"Byron? Cordelia? What do they have to do with anything?" Henry narrowed his eyes at me. "What have they been saying?" He walked across the kitchen, then turned. "Why are you really here?" He yanked the contract from my hands. "I think you should go."

# Nine

*I* was more than happy to leave Henry's house and hurried to my
car parked in the driveway. I'd hoped to get a feel for his alibi
while I returned those keys, but a "lovely normal weekend" wasn't
much to go on. I hadn't bargained on any bombshells about my career
or financial straits, either.

My hands trembled as I pulled forward in the circular drive. As I
passed the house, I saw Henry watching me from a window. He didn't
even pretend that he wasn't. Just stared as I rolled past.

Stopping at the street to check for oncoming traffic, it occurred to
me that this might be exactly what Melinda did Monday morning. I
shuddered.

I pulled out and drove slowly down the street. After several houses I
saw an area where the grassy planting strip had been churned up. Dark
soil with tufts of dry, dormant grass; a fifty-year-old cottonwood tree with
a gouge, about bumper high—none of which I'd seen earlier when
searching for Melinda's address. I pulled to the curb and stared at the tree.

"I'll figure this out. I promise."

As I drove away, I remembered what Henry said about Melinda being depressed and on meds. Suicide had been one of my theories as well, except I seemed to know something Henry did not—mercury poisoning was an excessively brutal and complicated way to kill yourself.

I had to stop at the gated community's guardhouse again on the way out. The guard wore a brown quasi-military uniform with an *Elite Protection* patch on the pocket. No weapon that I saw, but a walkie-talkie clipped at his shoulder. Tufts of gray hair poked from his cap. He came to my window, smiling as I rolled it down. "Have a nice visit, Ms. Russo? I think poor ol' Henry needed it. Just between you and me, this isn't the kind of neighborhood where women bring casseroles. And I don't think I've seen him leave since he got the news. Maybe I'll stop by after my relief guy gets here."

The sun was brighter now and I squinted up at him. "Are you here every day?"

"Most of 'em."

"What about at night?"

"Never work nights. They want the young bucks for that. Daytime all's we do is let pretty girls in and out." He winked at me.

I put my elbow on the window frame. "Who worked Sunday night?"

He placed his hands on my roof and leaned in. I leaned away. "I know what you're getting at, but you're barking up the wrong tree, Missy. Nobody but residents went in or out that night. Ms. Walter's accident was just that—an accident. The police made similar insinuations and I don't 'preciate it." He banged his hands on the roof and stepped back before tipping his cap. "You have a nice day now." He opened the gate and waved as I drove through.

So Elite Protection didn't know about the mercury either.

All the way to Melinda's office, I thought about those expensive enameled lava countertops completely devoid of signs of condolence. The contrast with our kitchen after Dad died was stark. But our house was small. Maybe flower arrangements were overflowing in Henry's formal living room. Maybe, despite what the guard said, casseroles were all tucked away in hidden freezers.

As I pulled into a parking place at the agency's tony office building in Cherry Creek, I thought about the uncomplimentary things Bob Dunphy and Henry had said about Q. I turned off the car and pulled the yellow pad from my bag. Across from Henry's name, in the *Alibi* space, I wrote, "'Lovely normal weekend,' but how to prove?"

I looked at the notes I'd made for Q. Last night, under *Motive*, I'd written, "So much bullying/resentment." And with Henry's mistrust of Q, and her insistence that the garage keep a set of Melinda's car keys, my head was spinning.

I stared through the windshield toward the office building but my eyes were unfocused. Of everyone on my suspect list, Queue Quaid had the only tangible motive, what with being verbally abused by Melinda for ten hours a day for several years. Anybody would snap. Opportunity? Definitely. She had keys to Melinda's house, cars, and office, and she kept her schedule, so she always knew where she was. The mercury could have been put in her car any time after Melinda parked it.

I thought about all the other people in the world who'd been verbally abused by Melinda posting on the *Dear Horrible Writer* website. Twenty years as an agent. I opened the calculator app on my phone and punched some numbers. Roughly 250 working days per year. Twenty rejections per day? Fifty? I had no idea. I calculated somewhere between 5,000 and 12,500 rejections times twenty years. Anywhere from 100,000 to 250,000 sarcastic, demeaning rejections.

Melinda told me once, quite gleefully, that one of the best parts of her day was sending rejections to the inappropriate queries she received from writers. Most agents, or their assistants, simply deleted the queries that had misspellings or pitched a story not in a genre they represented or were poorly written.

Melinda wasn't most agents, however. Her letters always began, "Dear Horrible Writer ... please don't ever send me anything again ... "

But I knew many people who submitted queries to her over and over. Out loud I always questioned why they would subject themselves to that, but deep down I knew. Every writer, me included, thought their books were, if not remarkable, at least publishable. And Melinda anointed enough bestsellers every year to make the gamble of humiliation and heartbreak worth it.

Writers could choose to keep their pain private, or diffuse it by kvetching about it publicly. Perhaps on an anonymous website.

I wished I'd logged on to the *Dear Horrible Writer* forum last night. Maybe I would have gotten lucky and somebody would've been on there bragging about killing Melinda. I'd solve the case and be a hero to the police. Ozzi and my critique group would apologize to me in a generous and overwrought manner—maybe with a lavish all-expense paid trip to Fiji—but I would remain gracious, blushing, waving it off with a sublime twist of my wrist and a modest "Pshaw."

Could happen.

The one time I was on there, I scrolled through the postings, mostly images of letters and emails from Melinda but cropped in such a way as to keep the recipient anonymous. And to illustrate that a picture is indeed worth a thousand words, I still remembered one under a steaming pile of poo. Pages and pages, each more horrifying than the last. They all began and ended the same way: "Dear Horrible

Writer ... Very truly yours, Melinda B. Walter. PS—Seriously, quit writing. You're bad at it."

Occasionally, one of the commenters copped to being the recipient, but most often there was a stream of comments "deleted by the webmaster." The nondeleted comments fell into two categories: maudlin or wildly funny and over-the-top, often in the form of imagined responses to Melinda. The deleted comments I assumed were of a more threatening and graphic nature.

I sat up straight. Suddenly I had a zillion more suspects. *Someone with a vendetta killed her and is trying to frame me. Someone on that forum.*

I hurried into the building and took the elevator to Melinda's office on the third floor. I'd been there so many times, but I wondered how many more I would come in the future, especially after it became the Henry Walter Agency. I pulled open the door to find Q, with her hands on her hips, staring at the copy machine behind the reception desk.

She turned when I walked in. "Know anything about copiers?"

"Can't say that I do." I dropped my bag on her desk and stood next to her. The doors to every compartment on the copier hung open. "What have you done?"

"Nothing. I pressed the button to print and it didn't. So I started to ask it why."

"Did it answer?"

"Not yet."

"Maybe it's a computer problem and not the printer. Did they have a fight?"

"It would've been in the last half hour because it printed that stuff for you." Q gestured toward a packet of stapled papers.

I saw the cover letter from Penn & Powell Publishing. "Is it bad news?"

"Only if it won't start working again."

"Not the copier. The papers." I waved them at her.

"Oh. Yeah. We're not getting paid anytime soon. You're not getting royalties and the agency isn't giving me my paycheck. That bitch is hassling me from the grave. All the assets are frozen."

Just like Henry said. "So why are you here?"

"Why not? What else do I have to do?"

"Um ... anything?"

She shrugged and continued staring at the copier as if she could repair it with a scorching scowl.

I shoved the papers in my bag to be dealt with later. It wasn't ten o'clock yet and I was already out of energy. Certainly didn't have enough to tell Q that Henry was taking over the agency.

"You know that *Dear Horrible Writer* website?"

"Yeah."

"Do you think my manuscript could have been leaked on there?"

"Nope."

"Why?"

Q slammed one of the doors on the copier and it bounced open again. "Because." She got down on her hands and knees and peered into the inner workings of the machine.

This interrogation wasn't working out quite like I wanted. I tried a different tack, hoping for more than a monosyllabic answer. "Hey, I picked up Melinda's car keys from the mechanic and gave them to Henry."

She didn't take her eyes from the copier, just said, "Oh." No surprise or question in her voice.

"Yeah. Joaquin and his boss said you threatened them to keep the keys there." I leaned against her desk, trying to look casual.

She did a slo-mo turn toward me and sat back on her feet. "What are you trying to say?"

"Nothing. But it seems weird. Why were you so adamant that someone else had a set of Melinda's car keys?"

"Are you accusing me of something?"

Now that I had her attention, I wasn't sure I wanted it. But I stared, vowing not to blink first.

She blinked first. "I made them keep the keys because the last time Melinda had to remove hers from her key ring, she broke a nail and I heard about it for a month, like it was my fault. It's so stupid. But Melinda makes people do stupid things."

I kept staring. "Do you have an alibi for her murder? Like from Sunday night until the accident Monday morning?" My palms began sweating and I wondered how those detectives keep their cool.

"I'm not sure it's any of your business."

It dawned on me that after knowing Q all these years, I could be talking to a bona fide cold-blooded murderer. Up until now, it had all seemed like more of an academic exercise, like plotting my novels. Pretend, safe, a bit surreal. But it was too late now.

"Q, nobody would really blame you if you ... and I'm sure there were extenuating circumstances, but—"

"You really think I killed Melinda?"

*Did I? Did I really think that?* "Well, you had motive, means, and opportunity, which everyone knows is—"

"I also have an alibi."

She paused long enough that I said, "Which is ... ?"

"I run the *Dear Horrible Writer* website. I'm the moderator of the forum."

"You? But—"

"I've always felt bad for those writers. I thought I could show them it's not because they're horrible writers, it's because Melinda is—was—a horrible person." She paused, then added, "Please don't tell. It'll make it really hard for me to work at another agency if word gets out."

"The cops will find that website. They probably already have. They'll trace it back to you and it won't look good. Get in front of it. Tell them it was you. Ask them to keep it quiet and they might. It won't help their investigation to make the website public knowledge. But if you make them go down some dead end, they won't be happy."

She looked at me like I was twenty pounds of stupid in a ten-pound sack. "They already know about it. They questioned me. For a long time. Of course I told them my alibi. I was on the site most of Sunday night, posting, chatting, and deleting things. Thank God it was all timestamped."

"What about early Monday?"

"Since when did you become a cop?" Q dropped back to her hands and knees to peer into the guts of the copier again.

"Q, it might just be that Melinda's killer is lurking on your forum. Even if you didn't knowingly leak the manuscript, maybe something happened."

She didn't turn around. "I didn't leak anything, Charlee."

"Why didn't you delete the site? Shut the whole thing down after she was murdered?"

"Why would I?"

I didn't answer.

"That's what a guilty person would do," she said.

Or someone who wants people to believe she's innocent. "I don't know what to think, Q."

After a long pause, she said, "I will delete it. There's no reason for it now, but the cops asked me to leave it up."

"Why?"

"I don't know. But you won't say anything about me running the website? To anybody?"

What good would it serve to vilify Q if she wanted to stay in the agenting business? "No, I won't tell anyone you're behind that website." *Unless I have to.*

"Thanks, Charlee."

I gathered my bag and left. Waiting for the elevator gave me a chance to absorb what she said. Very noble of Q to worry about the delicate feelings of rejected writers, but why couldn't she have just reworded the rejections? Even if Melinda sent all the rejections herself, which I couldn't believe based on the sheer number of submissions she got, Q could have followed up with a softer email of her own. "Dear Not-Horrible Writer ... I read your submission and it wasn't quite as bad as Ms. Walter intimated, blah, blah, blah."

Maybe there was more to it. Was it possible to fake those timestamps on her postings? How long would that have taken? Would it be a big deal, or could you do it with the push of a button? I had no idea. If Q was the administrator, it must mean she could access the code, but did she have the skill to do something like that?

A reluctant copier had flummoxed her.

# Ten

When I got home, the first thing I did was pull out my notepad. In the *Alibi* column beside Q's name, I wrote "website admin—timestamps."

The second thing I did was log on to the *Dear Horrible Writer* site and scroll, hoping to find some kind of confirmation of what Q had told me. Five minutes later, after pages and pages of comments, my breath caught and my muscles went taut.

I skimmed one particular comment again, the one with the reference to *The Zero Boy Summer*. AmyJo's working title. I read the last paragraph four times. "I've seen things that would kill Melinda if she knew. Luckily, I'm a good person ... or am I?" The comment was signed "AJ."

AmyJo? It couldn't be. That title wasn't particularly original for a young adult novel. But also signed AJ? It had to be her. I checked the date. Two days before the murder.

I stared at it and finally took a screenshot. The idea that I was preserving evidence made my stomach roll. AmyJo? I continued to stare at the comment, creating scenarios where it made sense that AmyJo murdered Melinda. None made sense. It simply wasn't possible. Was it? I picked up my phone to call her but changed my mind. I grabbed my car keys and jacket twice to go to her apartment, both times flinging them and myself on the couch instead.

"Okay, this is ridiculous," I finally said to my empty apartment. "There's got to be a logical explanation for this." I just couldn't figure it out due to extreme lack of sleep and nutrition. I heaved myself from the couch and returned to my computer. I jiggled the mouse and the sleeping screen awakened, showing once again the confusing comment.

I dialed the phone.

"Hi, Cha—"

"AmyJo, did you post a comment on the *Dear Horrible Writer* forum?"

Pause. Then a defiant "Yes, I did." Quieter, she added, "She's really mean."

"You submitted *The Zero Boy Summer* to Melinda?"

"Yes. And she rejected it. Of course. I told you guys it wasn't ready, but you all said I should start sending it out."

"Not to Melinda! There are so many other agents who aren't evil. I would have helped you make a list."

"I'm not a child, Charlee."

"No, but you are from Iowa and your glasses are perpetually rose-colored. You should have—wait." I paused. AmyJo wasn't stupid. Nor was she a masochist. "You just wanted to prove to us your manuscript wasn't perfect, and a rejection from Melinda allowed you an easy I-told-you-so. But why didn't you mention it?"

AmyJo grunted. "Seemed impolite with her being murdered and all."

"Impolite? How 'bout suspicious?" I leaned into my computer screen. "What does this mean? 'I've seen things that would kill Melinda if she knew.'"

"Have you ever been to her house? Dirty clothes all over her bedroom, sink full of dirty dishes, hair clogs. So many hair clogs." AmyJo paused. "I don't know why, but I took pictures. I'd never post them. I wouldn't be able to look my minister in the eye again, so I deleted them."

My brain turned into a Tilt-A-Whirl. "You were in her bedroom?"

"Yeah. I've been cleaning her house for a few months."

"You've been ..."

"Cleaning her house for a few months. Yes."

"For a few ..."

"Yes! Months." I heard the impatience in her voice. "I'm back working for my sister."

"What about your library job?"

"I still have it. I work for DebbieJo on my days off."

"Why didn't you tell me?"

"I don't know. Embarrassed, I guess. Don't get me wrong, I love the job. There's something very satisfying about turning a huge mess into something beautiful and shiny. But I'm almost thirty and I can't quite support myself." She paused. "I didn't think you'd understand."

"Oh, AmyJo. Of course I understand. Why wouldn't I?" But did I? Really? I got the whole need to make more money, but cleaning Melinda's house? That just seemed weirdly coincidental.

"Because you're successful at what you do and I'm ... not." When I didn't respond, she added, "I will say, though, I haven't lost my touch as a house cleaner. Zip, zip, zip. In and out in under three hours."

I didn't know what to think, so I said rather lamely, "Well, I'm glad your sister had an opening. Hey, Ames, I gotta go, but I'm glad we cleared that up."

"Charlee, I didn't kill Melinda."

"Of course you didn't. Talk to you later." I disconnected with trembling fingers, then pulled up the browser on my computer. I couldn't remember the name of DebbieJo's cleaning service, even though AmyJo and I had both worked for her after college. AmyJo moved back to Denver with me from Des Moines because she wanted a taste of big city life, and it didn't hurt to have her sister and a crappy job here as a safety net, either. AmyJo didn't think cleaning houses was the world's worst possible way to earn minimum wage like I did, however. I'd blocked it out. Like PTSD.

I typed "housecleaning Denver." 9,350,000 results. Seriously? There were only five million people in all of Colorado. Apparently everyone gets two housecleaning services. We're messy here, I guess.

Squinching my eyes tight to better access my memory, I had a vague recollection that the name was overkill. A rubber ducky hovered on the periphery of my brain. Yellow. Rubber. Squeaky. My eyes flew open and I typed "Squeaky Clean as a Whistle" in the browser. A map, address, phone number, and reviews popped up. I clicked on the first one and had my phone dialed as soon as I read, "I can't say enough about DebbieJo's team."

"We'll make your home squeaky clean as a whistle. DebbieJo speaking."

"Hi, Deb, it's Charlee Russo."

"Charlee! Hi. What's going on? I hope you're not looking for a job." DebbieJo chuckled, and I pictured the dimple that matched AmyJo's when they smiled.

"Perish the thought. I couldn't please you back then and I certainly couldn't now. I was just talking to AmyJo, and she said she'd been doing some cleaning for you, and—"

"Yep, she was chomping at the bit to clean this huge house we have on the schedule, like it was—oh, golly, I'm sorry, Charlee. I forgot you knew Melinda Walter. That was really awful, wasn't it?"

"Yeah." We held a respectful silence. "Why was AmyJo chomping at the bit?"

"You know how she is. Sees something she can make perfect and rolls up her sleeves."

"But why that house in particular?"

DebbieJo paused. "The Walters tip pretty well and it's a fairly easy clean, with just the two of them living there."

That made sense, I guess, despite what AmyJo had said about the biblical proportions of hair clogs.

DebbieJo continued. "There's a lot of square footage, but no dogs or kids to clean up after."

"Speaking of which, how are your girls? Must be pretty big now." My segue sounded disingenuous, even to me. But DebbieJo didn't seem to sense any insincerity. Must be a maternal thing, thinking everyone wanted to know every detail about your kids.

"They're great. A handful, but great. Good to get away from them and regain our sanity every so often."

"Got a trip planned?" I asked, proud of my sly way of verifying AmyJo's babysitting alibi. Even if it was weird that she'd been cleaning Melinda's house, if she had an alibi, then that was all it was—weird. Not criminal. Not nefarious. Just weird. And I could live with weird.

"We took one last weekend at the Broadmoor. Heavenly. Thank goodness AmyJo likes to stay with the kids. She even took them to school Monday morning."

I grinned. Alibi confirmed.

After some more chitchat and an estimate for cleaning an apartment my size, we said goodbye. Still unclear about one thing, I called AmyJo.

"Hey, why did you want to clean Melinda's house so bad?"

After a few beats she said, "Because I wanted to find something to give me an edge, maybe a boost of confidence when I submitted my manuscript to her. It was stupid, but I wanted her to have a house decorated in pink lace with puppies and kittens frolicking. Something to prove she wasn't as horrible as everyone said."

I thought about Q saying Melinda made people do stupid things. "Sometimes, AmyJo, things are exactly as they appear." Tears surprised me by welling behind my eyelids. I suddenly felt a sense of relief I hadn't felt in days. "The good news is, DebbieJo verified your alibi."

"You called my sister? To verify my alibi?"

Uh oh. "I'm checking everyone. You're the second one I've crossed off. You can't imagine how this feels. Don't be mad."

"I'm not mad. It's just weird, having my best friend think I killed somebody."

"Not any more weird than thinking all your friends might have killed somebody."

"I guess," she said. "Who'd you cross off first?"

"The mechanic who serviced Melinda's car. I didn't get any kind of creepy vibe from him or his boss. The guy was sweet and barely speaks English. I doubt he reads it either. And even if he did, any motive would be a stretch. Plus, a murder this involved is clearly personal and it would have been random for him to find my manuscript and then go to all this trouble."

"So, you're investigating this?"

"I guess I am. I realized if I wanted to get my life back to normal I needed to take some action. I couldn't just hide under my covers. Plus, it was my manuscript. I feel more than a little responsible."

"Charlee, you're not—"

"I know. But I *feeeel* responsible. Like it wouldn't have happened except for me."

"Well, I've been working on a theory. Wanna hear it?"

"Desperately."

"You know how we always joke about Einstein's IQ being higher than his EQ? I think Mr. Thaddeus Eichhorn II has finally fallen off the deep end, lashed out, gone kookoobananas."

Two words in that sentence caught my attention—"kookoobananas," because it was the perfect AmyJo-ism, and "Thaddeus," because I always forgot that was Einstein's real name.

The first time I saw Einstein's real name written out was on one of his book covers. He told me he fought with his publisher about it, but he lost. When I asked him why he didn't want it revealed, he said the world was better off without another Thaddeus Eichhorn. When I asked where his father was, he simply said, "Dead," with a grimace like there was a bad taste in his mouth.

Maybe AmyJo was right.

"I don't trust him anymore, Charlee. And remember when I asked him to help me get that job at the University? He told them I was milquetoast and that I liked little kids."

"I still don't even understand why you asked him for that reference. And you know he meant *milk toast* because it's homey and comforting. Remember that story he told about his mom making it for him when he was sick?" I knew AmyJo was rolling her eyes because I'd seen her do it every single time we talked about this.

"But—"

"And he wasn't saying you were a pedophile. He was trying to tell them you wrote for kids."

"Well, what they heard was that I was a wishy-washy pervert unfit to work there."

I bit my tongue, because it was more likely she was unqualified to be an assistant professor.

"I let it go at the time—"

"No you didn't."

"—but now it all sounds shady. He probably didn't want me knowing so much about him. I'm thinking he pretends to be emotionally stunted so he has plausible deniability."

I doubt their paths would have crossed much with AmyJo in the English Department and Einstein in Physics, but I told her I'd mull it over.

"And speaking of plausible deniability, Sheelah and Heinrich both missed the critique group meeting Monday. You should investigate them, too."

"And there's also the love triangle theory," I said.

"Which is … "

"I thought about it after I talked with Cordelia. She said some things that were kind of weird and it just made me wonder if there was some romantic angle between her, her husband, Melinda, and Melinda's husband."

"Shut the front door!" AmyJo uttered her most objectionable oath.

I nodded even though she couldn't see me. "And Henry was weird when I mentioned Cordelia and Byron."

"You talked to Melinda's husband, too? You've been a busy little beaver." AmyJo was quiet for a moment. "Did he have an alibi? You know, the husband is always the prime suspect."

"I don't know about his alibi. I didn't ask outright, but he said something vague—wait, I have it right here—" I grabbed my notepad. "He said they were having a 'lovely normal weekend.'"

"That's not much of an alibi."

"I know, but I wasn't going to come right out and ask."

"Did you ask that mechanic you ruled out?"

"Yes. He was at his daughter's *quinceañera*. His boss was there too. Seemed legit."

We were both quiet for a moment until AmyJo asked, "Have the police talked to you again?"

"No."

"That's probably a good sign. They must know you didn't kill Melinda. What was it like when they interrogated you? Was it like on TV?"

"Didn't they talk to you?"

"Yeah, but they came to the library and we talked on the mermaid bench in the Storytime Room. Didn't seem much like an interrogation. We even had cookies. For a little guy, that Detective Ming can put away the Thin Mints."

"No cookies for me, but they were very polite. Played Good Cop, Good Cop." I remembered Sheelah saying my dad must have been one of the good ones and felt my chest tighten. "I've been thinking about my dad."

"Oh, Charlee, I'm so sorry."

"I feel like I'm back in that time of my life. Up seems down, black seems white. Nothing makes sense. It's like when that asshole told me the whole department was required to attend Dad's funeral. Required. Like they wouldn't have gone otherwise."

"Between us and the cops, we'll figure out who killed Melinda," AmyJo said in a soothing voice.

"Will we? You said yourself that murders go unsolved all the time. What makes you so certain?"

"Because you and I are on the case. It'll be perfect."

A slow smile formed on my lips. Everyone needed a friend like AmyJo, positive, perky and persistent.

"But who'll be Good Cop and who'll be Bad Cop?" she quipped.

"You're from Iowa. Guarantees you'll always be Good Cop."

I officially crossed AmyJo's name off my suspect list.

# Eleven

Yesterday's grilled cheese wasn't as satisfying as I'd hoped, so I used up the last of the bread and cheese in another attempt. Today's was equally photogenic and melty, but again, it wasn't rewarding. I could only conclude it was me, not it. Not ready to break up though.

I was leaning against the kitchen sink when a knock on my door interrupted my last discouraging bite. I tensed, then relaxed when a voice called out "Flowers!" and then tensed again when I suspected a ploy. Oldest trick in the book. I tiptoed to the peephole. Eighty-something Barb Singer from upstairs held a vase filled with Crazy Daisies in one hand and a plate of cookies in the other.

I opened the door. Looking past Barb's nest of gray-blue curls, I spotted Detectives Campbell and Ming knocking at Suzanne's door.

I hastily ushered Barb inside and slammed the door, but not before Detective Ming scorched me with his gaze while calmly smoothing his slick-backed hair.

"Hi, Barb. Are you okay? Those guys out there startled me."

"Hello, dear. Yes, of course, I'm fine. I'm not made out of Waterford crystal, you know." She handed me the flowers. "These came upstairs by mistake."

"Thanks for bringing them down."

"And you have a couple of newspapers out there but my hands were full."

"I'll get them later."

"And I made too many cookies again. Chocolate oatmeal." She carried them to the kitchen table.

"Yum. Thanks, Barb." I chuckled, immensely happy to have a retiree living right above me who loved to bake. "You should adjust your recipes. You always seem to make way more than you need."

"You know what they say about an old dog and new tricks."

"If you were old, I might agree with you." I placed the flowers on the coffee table and pulled out the card, recognizing Ozzi's handwriting immediately. *Cops asked me about you. I told them you were perfect.*

"From your beau?"

I nodded. "Ozzi." I loved that he was trying to apologize, but I still wasn't ready. I fluffed the flowers, filling the empty spaces with the wild, unnaturally-colored daisies. I wondered what the detectives asked Oz and what he answered, but I was too proud—and scared—to ask.

I motioned to the couch. "Sit down and I'll get us some coffee."

"Aren't you going to call him?" Barb asked, shrugging out of her coat.

I didn't know exactly what face I made, but she said, "Ah, apology flowers. You get that coffee and we'll have a nice little chat."

In the kitchen I texted a simple *Thanks for the flowers. They're pretty.* And got a simple, *You're welcome. I'm still sorry. Call me* in reply.

I carried two mugs into the living room and sat next to Barb on the couch.

"You shouldn't let a little tiff with your beau make you lose your head." She sipped her coffee, then licked her lips and tipped her head ever-so-slightly toward the platter of cookies.

I jumped up, removed the plastic wrap, and held the platter out to her. She took one and balanced it on her knee. "Thank you, dear. Don't mind if I do."

"Let me get you a plate for that."

"Don't be daft. Why dirty up extra dishes?"

I loved her.

I set the platter on the coffee table in front of her and reached for one but saw walnuts jutting out so I withdrew my hand, trying to act nonchalant. I'd told Barb a couple of times, years ago, that walnuts made my throat itch so I avoided them. She didn't always remember, but I never reminded her. It wasn't her job to remember my allergies, and I refused to hurt her feelings.

She made a *tsk-tsk* sound. "You girls and your diets."

I didn't want her to regret her efforts, so I said, "No, it's not that. I just ate. I'll have these later."

She tilted her head and stared at me while chewing a bite of cookie, clearly assessing my truthfulness. Apparently I failed her test because she said, "You can't let an argument with your beau put you in a tizzy, Charlemagne."

"Do you and Don ever fight?"

An enormous gale of laughter erupted out of her tiny body, which led to an alarming fit of coughing. She took a sip of coffee to quell it. "Oh my. Of course we have arguments. But after sixty-three years of marriage, there's not much we haven't already resolved. Now we just bicker over what to watch on TV. I love those cooking shows but he loves the History Channel." She sipped again. "He's lived through most everything they broadcast. It's hardly history to him. And he complains that I watch all those recipes being made but all I ever make are the same old things." She chewed a bite of cookie, then leaned toward me. "Everything but chicken soup gives him gas. Why would I want to branch out?"

I laughed. "Why, indeed." I sipped my coffee while she finished her cookie and reached for another. "Sixty-three years. That's amazing."

"You reach a point where even though the romance is gone—have I mentioned the gas?—there's such a deep tapestry of your life together that the threads simply can't be pulled apart. Even if you wanted to." She nibbled her cookie.

"A tapestry. What a lovely image. I'll have to steal that."

"Even though you and your beau haven't been together as long as we have, you already have a tapestry."

Nodding slowly, I said, "I suppose we do." I thought about my parents and my fight with Ozzi about the murder. "But some threads get ripped."

"Rips can be mended, dear. If you want them to be."

Are all old people so wise and comforting? "I'm sure glad you live right upstairs, Barb. You're like my surrogate grandmother."

"Where are your grandparents, dear? Do they live nearby?"

"My mom's parents died before I was born, and my dad's parents quit coming around after he died. Whether from too much grief or not enough love I don't know. Doesn't matter. The effect was the same."

"Oh, Charlee. I didn't realize your father died. How awful."

Barb's face was so full of concern it made me feel bad. I felt like a little black storm cloud, raining on everyone I came in contact with lately. I smiled and said brightly, "It was a long time ago. Water under the bridge." I finished my coffee and stood.

I could tell she didn't believe me, but she took my hint and stood too.

"I've bothered you enough today, dear. Now I must get back up-stairs." I helped her with her coat and she said over her shoulder, "Now go call that handsome beau of yours."

"I already texted him."

"Texted. *Pfft*. That's no way to get lucky."

"Barb!" I felt a tingle creep across my face and my ears got impossibly hot.

She let out another full-bodied guffaw and let herself out of the apartment.

I was still blushing as I used a fingernail to jimmy the walnuts from an otherwise perfect cookie. A hopeless task with such small pieces. Damn those cooking shows teaching her mad knife skills. I slid the platter across the kitchen counter and tried to ignore its mockery.

As I carried our cups to the sink, I heard a familiar rustling from the juniper bushes under my kitchen window. Barb must have let their dog, Peter, out when she got upstairs. I quickly shoved my feet in snow boots, grabbed a jacket, and headed outside, stepping past the orange plastic bags filled with two editions of the *Denver Post* I'd neglected to bring inside.

The sidewalk had been cleared of snow so I followed it to the edge of my building, where there was a grassy area between my building and the next. There were several shrubs, but Peter's favorites were the two juniper bushes under my kitchen window. I watched them thrash back and forth.

"Peter, come here," I called, squatting down.

The rustling stopped and the junipers became still.

Don Singer called out from his balcony above my patio. "Everything okay down there?"

I looked up and nodded at him before turning back to the bushes. "Peter. Now." I used my alpha dog voice, hoping he knew I meant business. And that I might be alpha dog.

The wrinkled, shoved-in face of an irresistibly perky pug poked out from the junipers. When he saw me, he raced toward me, slowing only to wiggle through his favorite gap in the filigree of the wrought-iron fencing by the sidewalk. The bunny he'd cornered shot out the opposite direction.

Peter O'Drool was the full name of Don and Barb Singer's dog. He was as charming as he was odd. Like a snapshot of your grandma in the Louvre.

As was his habit, he'd come down to potty, but instead of trotting back upstairs when he was done, today he'd become sidetracked by a rabbit. Also as kind of a habit, I'd started retrieving him for Don and Barb because at their age it was increasingly difficult for them to step over the knee-high decorative fencing to get close to the junipers to coerce him to come home, especially in bad weather. Plus, their alpha dog voices oozed with unconditional love. I hoped Peter sensed my love was completely conditional. It wasn't, of course, but he didn't need to know that.

With the snow on the ground, I was glad I didn't have to step over the fence either. With my luck, I'd slip and have to deal with cold, wet snow on my butt as well as cold, wet nose on my face.

When Peter squirted through the fencing, I braced myself before he could bowl me over with his frantic, quivering love. "Dude. Relax." His tail curled over his hind end and he wagged them both so hard I thought they might fly off. When he calmed the teensiest bit, I scooped him up.

"Should I bring him up? Did he do his business?" I lifted him toward Don, who was waiting on his balcony.

"Yep. Prodigious amounts, too. Makes me jealous."

I laughed and carried Peter up the outdoor stairway, to be met at their door by Barb holding a loaf of something wrapped in plastic.

"Banana bread," she said, handing it to me. "I forgot to bring it down before. But I didn't forget to add lots of walnuts, just how you like it."

"You don't have to give me so many treats, Barb. I'm always happy to see Peter." I set him down and he orbited me three times before racing into the apartment.

"Oh, dear. I'm so sorry." Barb pointed at my fleece jacket covered in snow, dog hair, and drool.

"No worries," I said. I stuck my head around her and called, "Bye, Don. Bye, Peter."

Using cold hands, I picked up the newspapers at my door. Back in my warm apartment, I studied the loaf of banana bread. Yep, full of walnuts. I set it next to the cookies on the countertop and sighed.

I knew better, but I zapped leftover coffee in the microwave. I wasn't going to be able to sleep that night anyway, if the last couple of days were any indication. I tasted it, grimaced, and rinsed my cup.

The newspaper crosswords beckoned me as a welcome diversion from my ineffective sleuthing. I'd added as many suspects as I'd crossed off and had even more questions than when I started. One step forward, fourteen steps back.

Maybe if I ignored my investigation, it would be like when you try to remember the name of some song that ear-wormed into your subconscious. No matter what you do, you can't conjure up anything but two lines of the chorus. And those might not even be right. So you forget about the stupid song and start washing dishes, mindlessly scrubbing a pan you should have soaked, when all of a sudden the title, singer, and all three verses pop right into your brain and off your lips like a miraculous karaoke visitation.

Could happen.

I dumped the newspapers out of their plastic tubes and onto the table. I junked the ads and sports sections—since football season was over—and made a neat pile for recycling. I set aside the sections I wanted. I decided to make a new pot of coffee and try to enjoy what used to be my ritual. But it seemed a ritual from some other life.

I stared into the coffee container. Barely enough grounds for half a pot. It's a bush-league sort of coffee fanatic who runs out of coffee. Lame. While the tiny pot brewed, I organized the sections into the order I wanted to read them—first Tuesday's, then today's.

I loved everything about the newspaper. The comics, the often poorly edited articles, the unintentionally funny headlines, the crazy letters to the editor. But mostly I loved the ritual. I'd been reading newspapers since before I could read. My parents subscribed and, like clockwork, the daily landed on our driveway and I'd race out so I could be first to read the comics. I never failed to find one that amused me, and before I was twelve, I probably cut out a hundred of my favorite full-color ones from the Sunday editions.

It was a true love affair I had with newsprint, and I didn't understand why so many people eschewed it for bits and bytes. Sure, online editions have news that's actually up-to-the-minute, and sure, you could seek out more detailed coverage of the events you were interested in, and sure, your news wasn't curated by some lonely editor in the middle of the night.

But only a newspaper smelled and felt like a newspaper. Every whiff and crinkle sent me straight back to sitting on Dad's lap. He held the broadsheet in front of us, encircling us like a shield. I felt safe in our paper fort, despite some of the photographs and words he tried to hide from view.

When I was very little, he'd read the comics to me. After I could pick out certain words, I'd point and "read" to him. As I got older, we'd discuss the actual news of the day, analyzing quoted sources and content rather than, like I saw so much today, the distillation of complicated content into pithy, not-quite-accurate Facebook memes. Every Monday in fifth grade we had to bring in articles clipped from the paper for Current Events. I wondered how kids did that today, when so many people didn't subscribe to any newspaper. Surely fifth graders still discussed current events.

The coffee finished brewing and I poured myself a cup. Much tastier than the zapped version. I glanced longingly at the banana bread and the cookies that would go so well right now. I squinched my eyes and tried to remove the walnuts from the treats using only the mighty power of my desire. I opened my eyes to learn that my powers were nonexistent. At least as far as deleting walnuts was concerned. I presumed my crossword skills remained intact.

I decided to skim through the news, then get busy on those crossword puzzles, my true love.

The first section combined world, national, and Colorado news. Ferry disaster in India. Women and girls kidnapped in Africa. Politicians misbehaving. Mountain snowpack totals. LoDo shootings. Roundup of new craft breweries.

Quickly turning the pages, I stopped short at page five. Melinda's photo stared back at me. The headline read, *Death of Denver Literary Agent*.

I read the short article, tears stinging my eyes as I learned of her early career and current philanthropic work, which I'd never known about. She was on the Board of Directors for many local charities and nonprofits, but the one that jumped out at me was the Children's Hospital. As far as I knew, Melinda didn't like kids. Never expressed any interest in them, nor had any in her life. But maybe I didn't know. Maybe she had a niece or nephew with a medical issue. My hand fluttered to my chest. Maybe she'd had a child who had died. I contemplated that for a moment, racking my brain for any mention she'd made of a child. Nothing came to mind. Then why the Children's Hospital? I hated to think the worst of her, but how could volunteering to serve on a hospital board help her in any way? A literary agent wouldn't be trying to drum up business there; that Venn diagram didn't seem to intersect at all. Could it have anything to do with her murder?

I read the article from the beginning, slower, with this in mind, but nothing clicked for me. I took a deep breath at the end of the article. "The investigation continues."

The accompanying sidebar article showed a photo of Melinda's crumpled car. It looked like it was taken at an impound lot, even though they reported that the accident had happened in her neighborhood. *Mystery Deepens in Agent's Murder.* The reporter used vague language like "it's been reported" and "unconfirmed sources" but told a compelling story about Melinda's accident. It ended with, "Anonymous police sources confirm their investigation continues but admit they've never seen an accident quite like this."

Holding my breath, I rummaged through the stack for today's paper and stared at page two.

In all of literary history, there have been only four acceptable types of author photos. One, informal, while staring at a computer keyboard or perhaps reading a book. Two, the author gazing steadily at the camera, either smiling or serious depending on their genre. Three, with some sort of hobby or pet, also informal.

And mine, plastered all over my website and social media, and on the back of every one of my book covers. Arms crossed, looking bemused while leaning against a photogenic brick wall.

The one I stared at now, taking up three column-inches on page two of today's *Denver Post.*

*Local Author Questioned in Agent's Death.*

My beloved newspaper had betrayed me.

# Twelve

*Local Author Questioned in Agent's Death*
*By Jonathan Crier, The Denver Post*

*Sources confirm local mystery author Charlemagne Russo has been questioned by Denver Police in conjunction with Melinda Walter's death on Monday. Walter, found dead in her car under mysterious circumstances, had been Russo's literary agent for nearly seven years, securing publishing contracts for such books as Ashes to Ashes, Fragments of Fear, and Pursued to Death.*

*It has been reported there was an ongoing disagreement instigated by Russo over possible questionable accounting practices on the part of Walter or of Penn & Powell Publishing, or both, resulting in a serious decrease of royalties to Russo. Unnamed sources claim Russo was reportedly furious over a substantial drop in income and the purported cover-up of financial information.*

*Penn & Powell state through a spokesman they are shocked and*
*saddened by these events and allegations and will cooperate fully*
*with the authorities in their investigation.*
*Russo refused to comment when contacted.*

Refused to comment? Nobody ever called. I thought back to the missed calls I'd deleted. Wouldn't—I looked at the byline—Jonathan Crier have left a message if he was so desperate to speak with me?

Jonathan Crier. Seriously? Writing for the newspaper with a name like that? I couldn't decide if it was destiny or irony.

Should I call him? To yell? To set the record straight? I hadn't refused to comment. And how did he know about the royalties? I pressed my palms to my eyes. He'd made me look so suspicious.

I called my brother. "Lance, did you read the paper today?"

"No."

I filled him in. "What should I do? Do you know this guy? Should I call him? Didn't he make me sound guilty?"

"No."

"Oh, good." I let out a whoosh of air. "I was hoping it was just my imagination. Wait. No, what?"

Lance paused. "No, you shouldn't call him." Another pause. "Reporters are tricky."

"In general, or do you know this guy?"

"I'm at work. I gotta go." He was gone.

Even for Lance, that was an odd conversation. What wasn't he telling me? Was he one of the unnamed sources? It was easy enough to find out I was one of Melinda's clients, but who else knew about the royalties? I groaned. My entire critique group.

Once again, the only way to set the record straight was to find Melinda's killer. No tiny print retraction buried where nobody ever noticed would do. Online, this bogus story would live forever uncorrected in the cyberspace archives, like the ridiculous story about vaccinations causing autism that kept circling the planet years after it was debunked by scientists. Or that one alleging that brown recluse spider eggs used to fill Beanie Babies in the 1990s were starting to hatch. Or the regular rumor around Denver that our beloved theme restaurant, Bonita Fajita, was closing. Personally, I thought that seemed like the perfect marketing ploy. Every time it happened there was a ton of local buzz and everyone raced down there for unlimited sopaipillas and to watch the cliff divers. Kind of genius if you ask me, as long as Snopes didn't get wind of it.

When I was being questioned, Detective Campbell had mentioned Snopes, too. How would I get Snopes to prove my innocence? Oh, who was I kidding. Clearly, if my Facebook feed was any indication, nobody checked Snopes. Not often enough anyway, and never about such juicy stories. People believe what they want to believe, no matter how far-fetched. All I could do was fight for truth, justice, and the American way. Like Superman, but without any of the power.

I picked up my mug, uncovering the newspaper's masthead and tagline: *Voice of the Rocky Mountain Empire.*

Voice. My readers always mentioned how much they liked my writing voice. Writing is my medium, after all. I can be persuasive and eloquent there. I had to talk to that reporter. But not on the phone.

I logged into my email. So many messages. Most from the Contact Me page on my website. I clicked on the most recent one. The subject line read, "Melinda Walter."

"I always wondered how you got such creative ways of murdering the victims in your books. Now I know you practice them."

I gasped and deleted it with a trembling hand.

I read three more in the same vein. Dammit. Worse than I'd thought. I scrolled through all the emails to see if there were any names I recognized. About three-quarters of the way down, I saw that "Jonathan Crier" had emailed me through my website twice that morning. I scrolled some more. And on Tuesday. And even Monday evening.

Why hadn't he left a voicemail? Even just to say, "I emailed you." Better yet, "I'm going to run a story that's going to make you sound awfully suspicious regarding the mercury poisoning of your agent."

Wait. The article didn't say anything about finding mercury in Melinda's car. None of them did. That information wasn't out to the public yet. That meant only me, Lance, Ozzi, Q, my critique group, and my beta readers knew about the actual cause of death. Everyone but my beta readers knew about the royalties. Had someone been talking?

I composed the perfect 219-word email, outlining with intelligent reasoning what I wanted to say. I could have used twelve words: "I didn't kill Melinda and quit saying I did, you big meanie." I hit send and my phone rang immediately. I glanced at it. Unknown number. As I stared, the voicemail message lit up. I listened to it. "It's Jonathan Crier. Call me."

"Don't want to," I said to it.

I went back to my email messages and deleted all of them. Maybe there were some supportive ones in there, but I sure didn't want to wade through the others to find out.

As I stared at the screen, Jonathan Crier responded to my 219 words: *I just want to hear your side of the story. No way do I think you had anything to do with her death.*

"Then why did you write it that way, you slimy hellhound?" I yelled at my keyboard.

My finger trembled over the delete button. I'd said everything I wanted to say to him.

Another email from him popped up. *We can talk totally off the record. Please call.*

Off the record. A reporter's solemn vow. Reporters went to jail to protect their sources. It's an unbreakable bond. Their Hippocratic Oath. Their swearing on the Bible. Their Boy Scout Pledge.

I called him.

# Thirteen

*Y*ou promise this is off the record? I won't see anything in the paper about our conversation?"

"I can say 'anonymous sources' or 'sources close to Ms. Russo' if you like," Jonathan Crier said.

"What I'd like is for you to—never mind." I took a breath. "I don't have anything to tell you except that I had nothing to do with any of this. The reason I called is to find out who you've talked to and what they told you."

"I can't tell you that, Ms. Russo."

While I considered my next question, I heard the juniper bushes under my kitchen window scrape against the wall again. Peter O'Drool must have cornered another rabbit. I refocused on the phone call. Peter could wait.

"What if I asked you about certain people and you just say yes or no. Or if you can't even do that, maybe you cough once for yes, and twice for no. Like Queue Quaid. Did you talk to Q? Cough once for no, and twice for yes. Or was it the other way around?"

He laughed in a good-natured way that immediately made me suspicious. "There's no need to go all Deep-Throat-in-a-parking-garage, Ms. Russo. Yes, of course I spoke with Ms. Quaid. She was Ms. Walter's assistant."

"And what did she say?"

"Now that's a secret. But let me ask you a couple of questions. What's all this about embezzlement?"

"What the hell? Embezzlement?"

"My investigation has revealed that you've publicly accused Ms. Walter of stealing—or at least hiding—royalties owed you by your publisher. How much money are we talking about?"

"None! Melinda wasn't stealing from me!" *Have I used language like that in public?* I drew a blank. "Who told you that?"

"Can't tell you. But it's not that hard for me to find income statements. Public records are a wonderful invention."

"Who told you I said Melinda was stealing from me?"

"Ms. Russo, I'm very good at my job. Suffice it to say, I've spoken with everyone you know and everyone who knew Ms. Walter. Now, was the amount of these royalties large enough to warrant murdering your agent?"

I felt all the blood rush to my head. My mild hand tremor turned into a full-body vibration, like I was sitting on, holding, and brushing my teeth with industrial jackhammers. Lance was right. Reporters were tricky. Why in the world had I called him? If I said, "No, the amount wasn't large," he'd write that I'd murdered her for not much of a reason. And if I said yes ...

"I didn't kill Melinda." I pulled the phone from my ear, then brought it back. "And that's ON the record." This was one of the few times I longed for a sturdy landline I could slam down. Hanging up with attitude was simply not satisfactory on cellphones.

I put my head between my knees and tried not to barf. The whooshing in my brain slowed enough that I didn't think I'd faint in the next few minutes. I raised my head and slumped in my chair. I still vibrated, but it seemed with less horsepower.

Staring at my phone, I wondered who to call. Who could help me? Who would tell me what they told the reporter? And whether they told the police the same thing? But if the police suspected me, they'd have been here by now, wouldn't they? That's what happened on TV, anyway. Every murder was solved in an hour, less twenty-two minutes for commercials.

Life wasn't like TV, though, was it? Bad guys didn't always go to jail. People rarely broke out into song or tap dance numbers. Conversations weren't perfectly witty and accompanied by a laugh track. If Elmer Fudd wasn't a cartoon character, surely he'd have blown the stuffing out of that wascally wabbit by now.

Rabbit. I glanced toward the kitchen window, wondering if Peter was still outside. I stuffed my feet in my boots and pulled on a coat.

I kept to the sidewalk again, calling as I walked. "Peter … you out here?" I thought I heard rustling and stopped to listen, trying to determine its location. I walked a few more steps and saw footprints in the snow leading from the dry sidewalk over the decorative fence. Guilt flooded me as I pictured Barb or Don struggling over the fence to get Peter. I cleared the corner of the building and saw the juniper bush straight ahead. But I only saw tiny pawprints there.

I scanned the snow around the bushes. Just some straight pawprint paths, like doggy arrows shot into the junipers. No human footprints going toward the bush. My eyes studied the snowy expanse from the juniper bushes to where I stood on the sidewalk.

The footprints in the snow near the sidewalk didn't go toward the bushes. They stopped at my patio. A chill that had nothing to do with the weather raced down my spine. My feet were rooted to the sidewalk, my eyes following the tracks. Someone had tromped to my patio and stepped over the wrought-iron fence that surrounded it. It was one thing to step over the decorative fencing that ran along the sidewalk, but this was a much higher fence, almost a wall. With a start I realized they had peeked in the sliding door—maybe even tried to open it. Then I noticed more prints leading away from the edge of the patio, hugging the wall all the way to my kitchen window.

As I stared, trying to wrap my brain around someone peering in the corners of both my patio door and my kitchen window, a car alarm shrieked. I performed a clunky pirouette in mid-air and raced toward the apartment stairs. Chest heaving, I banged on Don and Barb's door.

When Barb opened it, I asked, "Did either of you come down to get Peter out of the bushes today?"

Barb frowned and shook her head. "I don't think so, dear." Turning into the apartment, she called, "Don? Did you go down for Peter today?"

I heard him say he hadn't.

"I don't think Peter's been out since you brought him back earlier. Which reminds me, he might want to go out now." Again, Barb faced the interior of the apartment. "Peter, do you need to go out?"

I stepped forward in time to see Peter in his sheepskin bed answer her by curling his nose tighter into his tail.

"Thanks for checking on us, dear." Barb began to close the door. "Now get back inside or you'll catch your death."

That's exactly what I was afraid of, too.

I raced down the steps, pausing near Suzanne's apartment. I raised my hand to knock but pulled it away at the last second, instead stepping into my apartment. I hurried back out carrying the banana bread still wrapped in plastic.

When Suzanne answered my knock, I held out the loaf. "Hey, Barb made this but I can't have walnuts. Do you want it?"

"You bet." She snatched it away. "Thanks."

"Hey," I said, trying to sound nonchalant. "Were you on my patio today? I saw some footprints ..."

"Yesterday, when I was trying to get your attention so I could give you those books."

My breath released in a whoosh. Of course. "And you walked along the wall to my kitchen window?"

Suzanne shook her head vigorously. "Nope. Not me."

My heartbeat jumped to double-time and I took a step backward from her. "Are you sure?"

"Absolutely." She squinted. "Why?"

"No reason. Just wondered." I tried to control the squeak in my voice, but wasn't sure I succeeded.

"You have a Peeping Tom?"

I gave her a tight smile. "I'm sure it's nothing, but keep an eye out, okay?"

She agreed and called out a thanks for the banana bread, but I had shut and locked my door by the time it reached me.

I dialed Lance and told him I thought someone had been peeping in my windows.

"It's your imagination. Right there in front? I doubt it. Now, at those buildings in back, where Ozzi's is, absolutely. Nobody goes back there. But you're right on the sidewalk, near the parking lot with all those lights."

"There are footprints in the snow right along the building from my patio to my kitchen window."

"You saw them go right up to your window, but not past it?"

"No. I didn't look that close. I stayed on the sidewalk." I began to feel foolish. Now I couldn't even say for sure the footprints weren't there earlier when I'd collected Peter O'Drool. Or even last week.

"Maybe maintenance came by to check something. You need to take a breath and chill, Space Case."

Hearing his childhood nickname for me was oddly comforting. I took a breath but was not anywhere near chill. He talked a bit more, being logical, trying to calm me down, but I quit listening to his words. Instead I let the sound and cadence of his voice wash over me.

Finally I interrupted whatever he was saying. "Will you come over?"

"Can't. Got a shift in twenty minutes. Go … eat some soup or something."

"I don't have any soup."

"Eat cereal. Watch TV. Have you been sleeping?"

"Not really."

"Well, that's it then. You're going bonkers from lack of soup and sleep. Just like you'd get during finals."

"Murderers and stalkers are hardly the same as college exams."

"True. But when you're tired, you tend to freak out over little stuff. Have Ozzi cook you a nice dinner tonight and drink that wine you've been saving. Call maintenance. Things will be better tomorrow after you're thinking straight."

Maybe. "Are you sure you can't come over?"

"I told you, I—"

"Fine."

"Call me if you need me." He quickly added, "But you won't."

He was probably right. It was my imagination. I thought about those footprints leading from the sidewalk to my patio. Yes, most likely made by Suzanne. She either forgot or just didn't want to say that she'd peeked in the kitchen.

Or it was a maintenance guy. Lance was probably right.

I sighed, wondering if he was right about Ozzi, too. I reached for my phone to call him but drew my hand back. I wanted to kiss Ozzi and have him wrap me in a hug, but it still hurt, remembering how he made me feel. Was I just being stubborn? Were we mismatched? This was our only big crisis so far and we weren't handling it very well. Besides, was it fair to drag him into my drama? He didn't sign up for that.

I couldn't afford to use any brain cells to figure out how to save my love life. I needed them to save my real life.

I wanted to talk to my mom. An adult. An adultier adult. I covered my face with my palms and remembered Jonathan Crier's words. He said he'd spoken with everyone I knew. My mom, too? Tears sprang to my eyes. The last I'd heard from her was that text message she'd left me on Monday before I heard about Melinda. She didn't know anything about any of this. Or at least I hoped she didn't.

I picked up my phone with shaky hands and dialed her number. Her message came on. She'd changed it since the last time I'd called.

"If this is some reporter, hang up now. I'm not talking. And if it's you, Bug, you be careful."

I clicked off. "I will, Mom. But I don't know what to be careful of."

# Fourteen

I needed to find out who, specifically, had talked to Jonathan Crier and what they'd said. No. I needed to find out who killed Melinda. I looked over my list of suspects. What kind of alibis did they have? I thought back to my research about mercury. I closed my eyes and watched my murderer in *Mercury Rising* prepare for and commit the crime...

Ordering the mercury online. Putting on gloves. Jimmying the lock on the car. Using Glu-Pocalypse to keep the heater on high and the windows closed. Spreading the beads of mercury under the driver's side floor mat.

I shook my head. I didn't know anyone who would do that. Maybe I was going about this wrong. What I needed to do was clear everyone. Prove they didn't do it. I pulled my list toward me.

The one name on there that I most wanted to clear was Ozzi. Even though his motive was nonexistent, I couldn't just pick up the phone and ask him about his alibi. I fiddled with a pen while I thought. The only thing I could think of that would make him get up in the middle of the night, shower, and leave my apartment would be if he got a call from his mom or from work. During our fight he'd told me that his sister had been with their mom, so even if there'd been some sort of emergency, Bubbles was there to handle it. Unless maybe they'd both been in a car accident. No, he would have told me that. I couldn't come up with any plausible emergency scenario involving his mother, so the only other option was a work emergency.

I thought about Jonathan Crier and picked up the phone. Instead of calling Ozzi's cell, I called his main office number. After threading my way through the automated jungle, keying in the responses I hoped wouldn't disconnect me, I was rewarded by a woman's Southern drawl. "Tech support. What can I do for ya'll today?"

Waiting for the automated choices to be announced, I wondered about a Denver-based tech company using a sweet Georgia peach on their recording.

"Hello? Darlin', I'm 'bout as busy as a one-legged man in a butt-kickin' contest, so if ya'll ain't got a question for me to answer, then—"

"Oh my gosh, you're a real person!"

"Real as apple butter. Who'm I talkin' at?"

I stammered, trekking back to the plan I'd made before falling into voicemail hell. "I ... I'm Jon ... abelle Crier from the *Denver Post*."

"Jonabelle?"

"I was named after my grandparents."

"Well, bless your heart. And what can I do for you?"

I took a stab. "I'm calling to ask about a recent server crash that your technicians responded to. Do you know anything about that?"

"I do indeed. It had everyone scrambling around like cats on a marble floor." She paused. "Wanna quote me?"

"Um, sure."

"Well, write this down. I'm Miss Lulaila—that's L-U-L-A-I-L-A—Philpott, of the Willacoochee Philpotts. Ever been to Willacoochee?"

"I don't believe so, no."

"Oh, you'd know it. It's hotter'n a billy goat in a pepper patch ten months out of the year."

"I'll make a note. So ... the server crash? When was that, exactly?"

"Hmm, let's see. We put out the all-hands-on-deck call round about eleven Sunday night—I remember because I was worried about the sweet tea brewin' and chillin' in time—and finally got the fox out of that particular henhouse Monday lunchtime. I remember because I was so hungry my belly thought my throat been cut. I tell you what, when all the fussin' was over, I felt like I was rode hard and put away wet. Slept clear through till Tuesday."

"Do you remember seeing Ozzi Rabbinowitz there?"

"I do indeed. He was madder'n a wet hen when he found out somebody threw a clod in the churn."

"'Scuse me?"

She lowered her voice. "I probably shouldn't be telling you none of this, but it wasn't no hacker like we thought. It was one of our own IT guys, dumber than a box of rocks. He been fired, but I shouldn't say who he is. His mama may read that paper of yours."

"Paper? Oh, yes, the paper." She'd been so entertaining I'd almost forgotten. "No names. It's not even an article about the server crash. Just some deep background for another story."

"I'd sure like to hear 'bout it, but I got calls backin' up clear to Canada. Anything else I can do you for?"

"No, ma'am. I'm good."

"Well then, you have a blessed day."

I grinned and hung up the phone. Miss Lulaila Philpott of the Willacoochee Philpotts had just cleared Ozzi's name.

In the alibi space next to his name, I wrote "At work" and then crossed him off the list.

My confidence was high, so I searched the list for the next person I wanted to clear. Sheelah. She'd been in the ER and went to the dentist in the morning. I chewed the pen cap. Easy enough to verify her alibi if I knew the name of her dentist.

I dialed her number. "Hey, Sheelah..." Suddenly I had no idea what to say.

"Charlee? What's the matter?"

"I...I...need to know the name of your dentist." It all came out as one word.

She didn't respond for a long time. Then, "Dr. Sayles in Castle Rock. His office manager is Monica. She can confirm my alibi."

"Sheelah, I'm sorry—"

"Don't worry about it. I know you have to check. I'd do it too, if I were in your shoes. It's just—"

At the same time we both said, "Weird."

After we hung up, I googled the dentist and found his number. I asked for Monica and explained what I needed.

"That's privileged information. We follow HIPAA rules around here. I'm sorry, but I can't help you."

"Will you at least call Sheelah and ask her permission to tell me? I'm sure she'll agree."

"No promises." Click.

As I was brainstorming other ways to verify Sheelah's alibi—none of them logical or easy—my phone rang. Dr. Sayles' number.

"Monica?"

"Miss Russo, I've spoken with Sheelah Doyle and I can verify she had a dental emergency last Sunday night when she contacted our on-call dentist. She was directed to the emergency room and was in our office first thing Monday morning."

She sounded like she was reading from a script, and maybe she was. I'd signed enough of those HIPAA forms to know patient privacy was a huge deal.

"Thank you so much, Monica. I appreciate it."

"I hope I wasn't rude, but you can't be too careful with the personal information you give out these days."

"Of course not. You're just doing your job. I get that. And you weren't at all rude. Thanks again."

With a relieved breath I crossed off Sheelah's name too.

Bubbles was next. Even though I'd shouted an accusation about Ozzi's sister the other night, I knew her motive was weak. If I could verify she was at their mom's house, then that would be three names crossed off in less than an hour. Plus, I knew my anger at Ozzi was fading and this would be an excellent way to broker a truce.

I called her, my heart feeling lighter than it had since all this ugliness began. "Hey, Bubbles? Do you have a minute? I was wondering what you were doing the night before Melinda was killed."

Silence.

"Bubbles? You there?"

"Charlee, did you just accuse me of killing your agent?"

"No, I—" *Probably should have thought this through better.*

"Because if you're looking for someone to throw under the bus— or in this case, the classic Corvette—then you better go look in your mirror. Don't call me again, and stay away from my brother."

"No, Bubbles ..." But she was gone.

I swallowed my pride and dialed Ozzi to try and mitigate anything she might say to him. Straight to voicemail. I called Bubbles back. Also voicemail. She'd beat me to him. I ran my hands through my hair.

That's what I got for being cocky.

I considered my options for checking Bubbles' alibi and could only come up with one. I dialed the phone.

"Hey, Mrs. Rabbinowitz, it's Charlee. How are you?"

"How many times have I told you to call me Bunny?"

About a million. But neither my brain nor my mouth would cooperate. It was hard enough to use her daughter's nickname. "Sorry."

"No, never mind. How's that son of mine?"

"He's fine, but I realized I haven't seen you in a while. Are you free for coffee?" I knew she worked just south of Denver in Castle Rock, a quick trip on the freeway.

"I am free, and I'd love company, but I'm not at work. Can you come down to Monument? I'll make you a home-cooked meal."

Monument was at least another half hour or so, almost to Colorado Springs. I checked the time. I could be down and back home before five and watch her face to see if she was telling the truth. "Sure, I can come down, but don't bother with dinner. I can't stay."

"Actually, that's good. I've had a procedure, which is why I'm not at work, and I'm supposed to stay off my feet."

"Nothing serious, I hope."

"No, just inconvenient. When can I expect you?"

"I'll leave right now. Forty-five minutes? An hour? Depends on traffic."

"That'll give me time to hobble to the door and unlock it for you. See you soon."

I hopped in the car and made it in record time. I forgot the speed limit was seventy-five down there. And the Traffic Fairy granted my wish.

I exited the freeway and wound through curving roads, most of the houses hidden by enormous spruce and pine trees. There was snow on the ground, and I was thankful the weather had cooperated today.

I located the correct street and turned into her driveway, skidding on hidden ice down the short incline before parking and catching my breath. I knocked and opened the front door to her house, calling, "Mrs. Rabbinowitz? It's me, Charlee."

"In here."

I followed the sound of her voice to a bedroom. She sat in the bed with her legs propped up on pillows. On either side of her there were two trays covered with everything a recuperating patient would need: tissues, water bottles, pain reliever, coffee carafe, hand lotion, cell phone, cordless house phone, several remotes, pile of paperbacks, Kindle e-reader, cookies, crackers, snacks of all kinds.

She watched me surveying her bedquarters. "Only thing I don't have is a bedpan!"

"Do you need help—"

"Nah, just went. I try to get up every so often and move around. Don't want bedsores." She saw the alarm on my face but waved away my concerns. "It's nothing. I'm just down for a couple days." She muted the sound on the TV and motioned me to a chair. "So, what do I owe the honor?"

"Nothing, really. Just wanted to visit. If I'd known you had surgery—"

"Just an outpatient thing. Didn't even need the full anesthesia. Ozzi didn't tell you?"

I looked at my hands. "We had a fight."

She pursed her lips and nodded. "So you wanted his mama's take on things. Let me tell you about Ozzi—"

"No, that's ... I know why—"

She talked over me and launched into a story about her late husband, Ozzi and Bubbles' father.

I didn't really want her to dig into my relationship, but I let her talk anyway. It was a much better reason for driving all the way down here than to ask about her daughter's alibi for a murder. She handed me snacks while she talked, which was great because she was talking up a storm. Clearly, she'd been by herself for a couple of days. I just had to find an opening to ask about Bubbles.

"... One thing you have to make sure of is that you're doing enough activities together. Even if it's just watching TV. Personally, I love TV. You young kids, though, always have to be moving and shaking..."

I let her voice drone over me while I ate another Oreo. If Bubbles was with her on Sunday night like Ozzi said, and she loved TV so much... "Do you watch Masterpiece Theatre on Sunday nights?"

Her eyes widened. "I do! Love that *Downton Abbey*. And the mysteries. I'm glued to PBS on Sunday nights."

"Did you see the last episode?"

She leaned forward. "Yes! Wasn't it great? That Maggie Smith is a pip. Bubbles and I were laughing our heads off."

"Bubbles was here?"

"Yes, we had so much fun. Since she was taking me to my surgery early on Monday, and I knew I wouldn't be mobile for a while, I made a *Downton* party. We drank brandy, wore fancy hats, and I made shepherd's pie, Yorkshire pudding, cauliflower soup, and even some spotted dick. There's still some in the fridge if you're interested."

"No thanks, I'll pass."

"Don't be a baby. It's just cake."

"Can't get past the name, but it sounds like you had fun."

"We did." She picked up her cellphone and pushed some buttons. "Pictures!" she sang out.

She handed it to me and I scrolled past dozens of photos of her and Bubbles wearing their Victorian-style hats posing next to the TV with *Downton Abbey* on the screen in all of them. The photos became less and less straight. I gave her the side-eye and handed the phone back.

She laughed. "We took a slug of brandy and a picture every time somebody said something British." She took back the phone and scrolled through some photos. "It was a particularly British episode." She settled back against her headboard. "And maybe we were both a little nervous about the surgery."

"But everything went okay?"

She nodded. "Bubbles was a peach. Got me drunk, spent the night, got me to my surgery bright and early Monday morning, and stayed with me most of the day." She stifled a yawn.

I took it as my cue and stood. "I'm so glad everything went okay. And thanks for the advice about Ozzi. I'm sure we'll work it out."

"Just a little glitch. Are you sure you have to go?"

"Yes, I have to get back. But it was great to see you. And thanks for the cookies." I bent to kiss her cheek.

"Sure you don't want to take some spotted dick?"

"Very sure."

"Be careful of the ice on the driveway. The trees keep it from melting."

"I will." I let myself out and locked the door behind me. In the car, I pulled my yellow notepad from my bag, wrote "with mom" under Bubbles' alibi, then crossed off her name. After I plugged my hands-free phone device in and called AmyJo, I eased from the driveway without mishap, now that I knew where the ice was.

"Hey, Ames. Guess what … I crossed both Ozzi and Bubbles off my suspect list. Five down, only a dozen to go."

"That's great. What are you doing? Want to get dinner?"

"On my way home from Ozzi's mom's house in Monument. I think I'll take a pass. I'm beat. I was at it crazy early this morning and I just left so it'll be a while." Traffic was much heavier now, still moving, but slow. I prayed there'd be no accidents or slowdowns. "I've been wondering something. When did everyone get to the critique meeting on Monday? I know Einstein came in right after me, but what about everyone else? Do you remember?"

"Not really. Why?"

"I don't know. It feels important to have as much of a timeline from all my suspects as I can."

"Makes sense. Let's see. Kell was there when I got there, duh. And Cordelia. Then after I got there, it was Jenica, then you, then Einstein."

"You're sure?"

"Sheesh, it's only six people."

I laughed. "You didn't write it down, did you? Isn't that the only way you remember stuff?"

"Hardee har har. I hope you've been writing stuff down, otherwise your investigation might dead-end."

I glanced at my yellow notepad. "Yep, writing stuff down."

"Seriously, though, Charlee. Be careful with all this. It just sunk in that we might know a real live murderer! Make a plan if you decide to call anyone. Don't just wing it."

After my conversations with the reporter and Bubbles, I had to agree that was solid advice.

"And stay safe, Charlee. Let somebody know where you are at all times."

"Yes, Mom."

"I'm serious. You don't know what—"

My phone beeped. "I got another call. I promise I'll be careful."

"Really?"

"Promise. Talk to you later." I clicked to the new call.

"How are you, kiddo?"

"Hey, Kell."

"I just wanted to know how you were."

I didn't want to tell him I was investigating all my friends, at least not until I could cross him off my suspect list. But I told him the truth. "I'm confusselized by everything."

"Sounds like a word Jenica would use in one of her picture books."

Jenica. I knew she and Kell were close, since he was the one who'd lobbied for her inclusion in our critique group, so I made a conversational plan right there on the spot. "Jenica seems a bit confusselized, too. So much darkness. Do you think she could have killed Melinda?"

"No! Because she's Goth? Isn't that a bit judging a book by its cover?"

"Just seems like she's hiding something."

"Of course she is. We all are."

My skin prickled. "About Melinda?"

"About ourselves."

I wasn't in the mood for any Deepak Chopra woo-woo philosophy lecture so I said, "AmyJo said Jenica was late to that meeting. Got there just before me."

Hastily, Kell said, "That's not right."

"AmyJo's lying?"

"Didn't say that. But she's … misremembering. Jenica was the first to arrive."

"Why do you say that? It's so different from what AmyJo told me." I was beginning to realize why Detectives Campbell-like-the-soup and Ming-like-the-vase kept asking me the same things over and over again. If you're lying, you'll trip up at some point.

Kell hemmed and hawed, trying not to answer.

"Ew," I said. "Are you two—"

"No! She's young enough—Her father and I—I've known her since—No!"

"Then … "

"Because we had a discussion before anyone got to the meeting."

"About what?" In for a penny, in for a pound.

"Confidential."

"Kell, someone's been murdered and I'm being framed."

"This has nothing to do with that."

"Let me be the judge of that."

After a pause, he said, "Fine. I had some business at Children's Hospital last week and I saw her there."

"Was she sick?"

"No, nothing like that."

"Then what?" I hoped the exasperation in my voice demanded an answer and not a disconnection.

"She swore me to secrecy. I'd seen her without her Goth look. She was there reading to kids."

"She doesn't want anyone to know she has a normal side?"

"You *can't* judge a book by its cover, Charlee."

"Of course you can. People do it every day. It's shorthand."

"Well, you can't judge Jenica that way."

"But you can't deny she's trying to hide something with all that black eyeliner. It's almost like a costume."

It was a silent standoff until Kell said, "I just wanted to see how you were doing. Call me if you need anything."

After we hung up, I realized he didn't tell me if he'd been questioned by the cops yet. Probably it was no big deal for someone in his position, head of a big company, gobs of money and power. Kell had probably been in courtroom situations a lot, lawsuits, depositions, statements. None involving murder, though. None that I knew of, that is. But he had a defense team available at the push of a button, so I was sure he wouldn't have been grilled like I was, anyway.

I'd call his secretary and see if I could get her to confirm that he was on that red-eye flight from Chicago on Sunday night.

I mused about the conversation, then realized what was bugging me. The Children's Hospital. Both Melinda and Jenica were involved with it and neither one had ever mentioned it. It had to mean something. And what business would Kell have there?

The traffic was much heavier now, but I was at the southern edge of the Denver suburbs so I took my time in the middle lane and let everyone else jockey for position while I mulled over what Kell had said about Jenica. I couldn't figure out why it would be such a secret about her volunteering. My curiosity got the better of me, though, so I used the voice-activated feature to call Jenica.

When she answered, I said, "Hey, do you volunteer at Children's Hospital?" Clearly I wasn't cut out for making a plan rather than winging it. I saw an image of AmyJo's disapproving face.

"No. Why?" Her voice had an edge to it.

"Kell mentioned that you did."

"He did." She didn't ask it like a question.

"We weren't gossiping or anything, it just … came up … in a conversation." The very definition of gossip. I took a breath. "It's just that I found out Melinda was on the board there, and you volunteer there, and Kell was there, and it seems … you know … weird."

"I'd bet money that lots of people volunteer there, but I'm not one of them. You got faulty information." Jenica disconnected.

I stared at the bumper in front of me. Maybe I'd misunderstood Kell. I called him and asked for clarification. He was equally adamant that she volunteered.

One of them was lying.

I guessed it didn't matter as long as Jenica's alibi checked out, which, of course, I'd forgotten to ask her about because I couldn't be bothered to make a plan.

The thought of calling her back set my teeth on edge, and I needed impartial information to check her alibi anyway. She'd told AmyJo that she and her boyfriend had won tickets to the concert at the Fillmore that night and hung out afterward with the band. I could talk to her boyfriend, Dooley, but I didn't have his phone number. As well as working as a tattoo artist by day, he took art classes at the University of Denver in the evenings and worked on campus, but I didn't know where. I checked the time. Classes probably went until nine or so; plenty of time to get over there and track him down if he was around. It had been a long day without much sleep, but I was in the car, heading north, and maybe I could cross another name off before I crawled into bed.

Maybe Einstein was on campus teaching tonight and I could find out his alibi, too.

This all seemed like a plan. AmyJo would be proud.

I was completely unfamiliar with the DU campus and after considerable cursing finally found a place to park. The campus wasn't as well-lit as I'd have liked given all the random spots of ice. I carefully picked my way toward the Art Department after consulting the *You Are Here* maps and asking everyone I passed. The building was quiet, though I did hear the indistinct hum of voices, probably in classrooms and studios. I wandered the halls, poking my head in wherever looked promising. But nothing was, until I stepped into a large open room with canvases hung around the perimeter, a display of every style and medium of painting in a riot of subjects and colors. A knot of twenty-somethings stood leaning on unoccupied tables. They straightened as I walked in.

"Hi. Do any of you happen to know someone named Dooley? I think he's an art student here," I said.

They shook their heads, but one of the girls said, "The department secretary is in the back. She might know. Want me to ask?"

"Would you? That would be great."

The others went back to their conversations while I browsed the paintings on the walls. They were all for sale. I assumed they were from a student show. One particular watercolor caught my eye because just by looking at it, I felt calmer, more at peace. It was a seascape with a lighthouse, not quite realism, but not quite impressionist, either. Something different, perhaps a cross between the two, a style I'd simply never encountered before despite my many trips to the art museum. I couldn't make out the signature.

I pointed to it. "Do any of you know who painted this?"

A lanky student with his long hair in a man-bun strolled over. "Want to buy it?"

"Is it yours?"

"It can be." He grinned at me. "Give me thirty-five bucks and I'll never tell."

"Nice try," I said.

He leaned forward, reading the signature. "Oh, that's one of Black's."

My ears perked up. "Dooley Black?"

He shrugged. "I don't know. We call him Black."

"Bunch of tattoos? Skinny?"

"Yeah. When he's not in the studio he works over at the sandwich place past the library."

The girl came back. "She says she can't give out any student information."

"Thanks anyway, I think I found him." I glanced at the seascape on my way out and thought about AmyJo remarking at critique group that things weren't always as they appeared.

I'd only met Dooley a couple of times when he'd picked up Jenica from critique group, but this was not even close to the kind of art I expected to be in his portfolio. I'd only seen his wild and angry tattoos, which he told me he designed, and his big-boobed illustrations for Jenica's picture books.

I exited the art department building and immediately slipped on a patch of black ice, landing on my tailbone and my left wrist. My butt hurt as much as my pride—maybe more—and I wasn't sure whether to be happy or sad nobody was around to witness and/or help me up. I gathered myself and limped in the direction they'd indicated for the sandwich shop, rubbing my wrist until it felt better. I bent it in all directions to make sure it wasn't broken. Not so sure about my tailbone. Rubbing it seemed unladylike, but I did it anyway. Didn't help the pain at all.

I was happy to find Dooley behind the sandwich counter and even happier to find no one in line. In fact, the place was deserted except for one scruffy-looking guy with earbuds in and his back to us.

"I don't know if you remember me—"

"'Course I do." Dooley's smile lit up his face. "You're in Jen's critique group. What can I get you?" He waved vaguely at the menu written on an oversized chalkboard above his head.

"Actually, I just wanted to talk to you." I grimaced. "You don't mind if I sit down, do you?" I eased myself into a molded plastic chair. "I just wiped out in front of the art department."

"I know exactly where you mean." Dooley plucked a paper cup from a stack. "You could probably use coffee." He filled it and brought it out to me.

I accepted it. "I'd rather have a new tailbone, but this is nice, too." I glanced at the menu. "On second thought, could I get a grilled ham and cheese?"

"Sure." He started moving fast behind the counter. "What did you want to talk about?" he asked while he worked. "Everything okay with Jen?"

I blew across the top of my coffee to cool it. "Yeah, everything's fine. I heard you and she went to the Fillmore Sunday night."

He stared at me. "Checking alibis?"

"No, nothing like that. Besides, I'd think the police have already done that." He nodded. "I was wondering if …" I couldn't think of one thing that sounded plausible. Must have been the pain, because I'd already forgotten AmyJo's advice to have a plan. I also had forgotten to tell anyone where I was. "Yeah, okay. I'm checking alibis. You two were at the Fillmore?"

"Wouldn't have missed it. Nobody beats Pleasure Center for Armadillos in concert." Dooley got a wistful, faraway look as he flipped the sandwich.

"How long did the concert last?"

"You don't waste free backstage passes. We got there before the sun even went down and then partied with the band afterward at the hotel. Got our picture taken with the band by the official photographer and everything. Still there when I was supposed to be taking an exam on Monday morning."

"But Jenica was at critique group Monday morning."

"Barely. I dropped her off and then I went home to crash. Totally spaced my test." He slid my sandwich onto a paper plate, cut it diagonally, and piled a handful of chips next to it.

"Jenica wasn't tired?"

"Probably. But she doesn't like to let you guys down. Serious about her writing, that one." He placed the plate and some napkins in front of me and plopped into the chair across from me.

"It seems like you're serious about your art, too, other than blowing off a test," I said, smiling. "I saw your watercolor hanging in the art building." I took a big bite of the grilled sandwich. Not quite as crisp as I like, but it was good.

A blush flashed across his cheeks. "Yeah. I'm serious enough, I guess, but I don't have people like you do. I just have assignments." He used his thumbnail to scratch at a dried blob of mustard on the table.

I shrugged, then winced. The tailbone pain was migrating upward. "Maybe you should find some people, too. You've clearly got talent. I'm sure there are people in the art community who would love to mentor a promising young artist. Go find someone you trust."

"Maybe I will." He cocked his head. "This must be why Jen looks up to you so much."

*Jenica looks up to me? News to me.*

A customer came in and Dooley got up to take his order. "No charge," he whispered.

"Thanks," I whispered back. "Oh, one more thing," I called to him.

He turned toward me but kept walking.

"Did Jenica mention having to get to writing group early for any reason?"

"Not that I can remember."

I sipped my coffee and finished my sandwich and chips, expecting to chat more after he served the customer, but a rowdy group of five students came in so I knew he'd be busy. I struggled to stand, and when I did, I gave myself a little standing cat-cow yoga stretch. I didn't break in half, so I figured I'd live. I picked up my coffee, took a final sip, and threw the cup and my plate away. I waved at Dooley, who hollered a goodbye over the noisy group.

I still didn't understand the mysterious secrets involved in the Children's Hospital, but it seemed Jenica had a solid alibi. Just as I reached for the door, my phone chirped a text message from AmyJo. *Be careful if you go out. I hear it's really icy.*

Gee, thanks, Ames.

I shuffled outside, carefully studying the sidewalk for any icy patches I hadn't seen earlier. It was dark but everything seemed dry. When I looked up, I saw Einstein Eichhorn walking about fifteen yards away, on a sidewalk angling toward me.

I waved. "Einstein!"

He looked right at me, pivoted, and headed the opposite direction. I was sure he saw me. I tried to follow, but with my pain, I couldn't keep up. I asked every person I met where the physics department was and nobody seemed to know, pointing in all sorts of contradictory directions. When I finally got to the building, my back throbbed. I checked the directory and found his name. Great. Third floor.

I hobbled up the stairs, clutching the railing and resting every so often. When I reached his office, it was dark and the door was locked. All that effort for nothing. I struggled back down the stairs, gripping the handrail with two hands like my life depended on it, because it did.

I reached the bottom and turned to the right instead of the left, the way I'd entered the building, and came face to face with the elevator.

# Fifteen

It was pitch dark by the time I limped across campus toward my car, the moon obscured by heavy cloud cover. The food, the pain, and the lack of sleep the night before were making me drowsy, and I stumbled more than once. I lost my way a couple of times, my instincts on the fritz. Couldn't wait to crawl into bed. It seemed a lifetime ago that I'd visited the mechanic's, but it was just that morning.

My breath came out in an unladylike *oomph* when I collapsed into the driver's seat. I took a moment to rest and collect myself, then pulled out my yellow notepad. My pen hovered over Jenica's name, ready to cross her off as a suspect, but a half-formed notion gnawed at my muddled brain. Jenica and Dooley had been together that night. He wasn't impartial at all. Concentrating through my fog, I finally grasped that I couldn't take Dooley's word on her alibi. My gut told me he was telling the truth about her, but I needed corroboration. I couldn't figure out how to get it, though, as the fog closed back in.

I stuck my key in the ignition but remained in the parking spot while I set up my hands-free phone and dialed AmyJo. Voicemail. I tried Sheelah.

When she answered, I said, "Thank God."

"Charlee? What's wrong?"

"Nothing. Well, everything. But nothing. I just need you to talk to me while I drive home."

"You're not making sense. Where are you?"

"At DU."

"I'm coming to get you."

"No. I've had a long day and I'm pooped, so I need you to keep me awake. I'll stay off the freeway and go across on Evans. There won't be much traffic. Just talk to me for twenty minutes until I get home."

"Of course. What shall we talk about?"

I pulled out of the parking lot and pointed the Kia toward home. "Anything."

Sheelah chattered about her day and her tooth and the chapter she'd been working on, but I barely made sense of her words. I asked what I hoped were clarifying questions and made witty banter even as my eyes were drooping. Stopped at a red light at the next major intersection, I opened the window and stuck my head out so the cold air would slap me awake. I felt a bit perkier by the time the light changed, and I hoped it wasn't just my imagination or wishful thinking. As I picked up speed, though, it became hard to hear Sheelah so I rolled up the window.

"You're cutting out," I told her. "Can you hear me?"

"Not very well," she said.

I checked my phone battery. "My battery's dying. But I opened the window and feel better now. Wide awake." Not quite the truth, but I didn't want her to worry. "Sheelah? You there?" The call had been disconnected; probably not enough juice. I considered plugging into the car charger, but I felt less sleepy now and reasoned I'd be home soon, so I disconnected and threw everything onto the passenger seat.

Traffic remained light, for which I was glad, but I would have been happier closer to home and off the major streets. After a few blocks the lack of traffic and warm car lulled me into drowsiness again. A horn honked and I jerked awake, hyper-aware now of heavy traffic surrounding me. As the traffic ground to a halt, I gripped the wheel and blinked several times to clear the black dots dancing in my vision.

The lights of a gleaming multiplex cinema flickered across the large parking lot of a shabby shopping center to my right. The nearby marquee showed several new movies playing, many of which were well-reviewed. Looked like everyone thought Wednesday evening was the time to see them.

The intersection and shopping center were inadequate and poorly designed, maybe not when they were originally built but certainly now with the addition of the huge theater. The stop-and-go traffic combined with my already drowsy state soon hypnotized me and before I knew it, my slow reflexes forced me into a right-turn-only lane heading into the shopping center. If the concrete barriers hadn't been right in front of me and if I'd had less muddled thinking, I would have simply waited with my left turn signal blinking until someone let me back out into traffic.

Unfortunately, even small concrete barriers and a touch of muddled thinking can create a change of plans, so I veered right, the opposite direction from the traffic streaming out of the parking lot. I drove slowly, squinting at the road, trying to find a break in the crumbling concrete divider so I could turn around. But there was none. Someone with a very anal-retentive personality probably slept soundly, knowing all cars would drive exactly as pre-determined around the shopping center.

I gave up and decided to simply circle the entire shopping center on the ring road. By the time I got back to where I was forced off the road, the movie theater traffic would have loosened up, I figured. Everything else in the shopping center was already closed and dark—breakfast café, dry cleaners, meat market, nail salon, DMV—all daytime businesses.

The road took me behind the cineplex, which was such a monolith, it hid the lights from the parking lot. My headlights swept across a bright orange sign that screamed in all caps, *Warning! Keep Out! Hazardous Area! Danger of Drowning! Private Retention Pond.* There was no fence or wall and I shuddered to think of kids playing near here.

I drove slowly and dodged potholes big enough to swallow the Kia. I saw that the concrete lane divider was gone and considered turning around. But since it was probably an equal distance from where I'd been forced into the parking lot and where I expected to exit, I decided to keep going rather than turn around. I knew how torn up the road was the way I'd come; maybe it was better going forward.

The road curved in front of me. I saw the dumpsters for the cineplex at about the two o'clock angle, so I didn't think the road would go much further, and it certainly couldn't get any worse.

But it did. After almost breaking an axle in one of the holes, despite my squinting and straining to avoid just such a thing, the black dots danced in my vision again and I stopped to close my eyes. My body must have thought I'd finally fallen into bed and took the opportunity to relax completely. I dropped my head back. So much pleasure. In a Kia. Who would have guessed? I could sleep here. All night. All niii—

BAM! My car jerked in the dark and I felt it moving. By the time I was remotely aware of what was happening, the Kia had traveled at an angle across the road toward the retention pond. I slammed on the brakes and skidded across the earthen easement. When I'd stopped completely, my front wheels were at the edge of the retention pond and I stared, dazed, into a small lake.

I must have fallen asleep, but what was that noise? I looked behind me. Nothing. The dark and the curved road could have hidden anything. Or anyone. Suddenly I snapped fully awake. Visions of Melinda's wrecked car flashed past my brain. I shoved my car in reverse, kicking up gravel and dirt. I slammed it into drive, overcorrected, and scraped one of the dumpsters as I bounced out of a pothole and careened past. Dodging potholes like they were slalom flags, I raced along the ring road until I got to the arterial road that bordered the shopping center. I skidded to a stop, checked for cars, turned right, and gunned it. Another right turn in front of the shopping center and I was back on the main road.

All the traffic had cleared. The dashboard clock read 9:32. I must have fallen asleep. For how long? Fifteen minutes? Twenty?

I slowed to the speed limit and took deep breaths to calm myself. My head was on a swivel the entire drive home. When I reached my apartment complex twelve minutes later, I felt foolish. I told myself I must have fallen asleep behind the movie theater without putting the car in park. The noise could have been a bird landing on my hood, or a car backfiring a mile away, or even some creative snoring on my part. But whatever it was had startled me and, without fully waking up, I'd put my foot on the gas. Luckily I'd stopped before plunging into the pond.

I pulled into my parking place and inspected the side of the car where I'd sideswiped the dumpster. An eighteen-inch-long scrape now decorated the side of the Kia. I ran my hand along it. Dammit. Deep enough to rust.

I wanted to check the rear bumper, too, because I couldn't quite shake the sensation that I'd been pushed across that road. I gasped when I saw the back of the car.

Someone had written in the grime, *Wash me ... OR ELSE.*

How long had that been there? Wouldn't I have noticed it before? I racked my weary brain trying to retrace my steps around my car that day. Surely I'd walked around the back at some point earlier. But I couldn't be sure.

And the message? I've seen plenty of finger-scrawled "wash me" notes on cars, but never with an "or else." Was that someone's idea of a joke?

If so, I didn't get it.

# Sixteen

It seemed I'd just drifted off to sleep when the phone woke me. I groped for it like an octopus on Valium. The charging cord was too short to allow me to see the caller ID. Didn't matter, since I was too groggy to see it even if it was a mile long. Slumber had allowed me to forget about my back pain, but now it came screaming back. "Mrph?"

"Charlemagne Russo?"

"Mrph."

"This is William Rosenthal of Rosenthal, Rosenthal, and Squib. We represent Penn & Powell Publishing."

"Squid?"

"Squib."

"Penn & Powell?"

"Your publisher."

Back pain and the sharp tone in the man's voice roused me. Was I dreaming? Yes. No. That pain was all too real. I yanked the cord and brought the phone to my face. *212.* Manhattan area code. I rolled and wiggled and heaved and maneuvered myself up to the headboard, wincing with each movement. "Sorry. I haven't been sleeping well."

"I can imagine." He cleared his throat. "It has come to my attention that you are spreading false and malicious gossip about my client via the print media."

Defining all those words and putting them in context took me longer than normal.

"Ms. Russo?"

"Yes, I'm—"

"While we look into this matter further, your contract is being reviewed. You are on notice to cease any defamatory language. We'll be in touch."

"Can I speak with my editor?"

"No. There will be no communication with Penn & Powell in any form whatsoever until further notice. If you need to discuss anything, you will do so through me. Expect a certified letter."

Rosenthal hung up. I stared at my phone until it went dark. This was bad. Very bad. I knew it, but had no idea how to fix it.

My phone lit up while I sat there staring at it. For a split second I thought it might be Lance or Ozzi calling to say, "Gotcha! You really fell for that one. Let's go get some pancakes."

But no. The caller ID told me it was Jenica.

"Did I wake you?"

"No ... I was ... up."

"Are you sure? People are weird when the phone wakes them up. Like they don't want to admit they ever sleep."

"Yeah ..."

"So I hear you were checking up on me and Dooley."

I shook my head to clear it, but that must only work in cartoons because I still felt fuzzy. Did an attorney just threaten me? I checked the call history. Yep. Area code 212. Defamation. Newspaper articles. Reporters. Detectives. Murderer. Wash me ... or else.

I leaned forward, inhaled through my nose, and exhaled through my mouth. An acute sense of purpose and determination calmed me. I *had* to find out who killed Melinda and determine if I was in any danger myself. I shifted further over onto my butt cheek until the pain lessened.

"Jenica, why wasn't Heinrich at the critique group meeting the day Melinda was killed?"

"What? You need to wake up. Are you dreaming?"

"I'm wide awake now. Where was Heinrich that day? You guys go way back."

"Charlee, just because he was my English teacher doesn't mean I keep track of him."

"I know you guys talk. Do you know where he was?"

"No. But just like me and Dooley, he wasn't out being a homicidal maniac, if that's what you're getting at. I think you'd know that after that thing with your brother."

"What thing?"

"At the school a few years back?"

One of Lance's first calls as a rookie was an altercation. He got there and made it worse. Way worse. "How do you know about that?"

"I was there. So was Heinrich. It was our school. Those were Heinrich's students."

"I didn't know you knew my brother."

"I don't. But Heinrich does. He had to go to the hearing."

"Neither of them said anything to me."

"Why would they? Your brother knows your critique group?"

"No, I guess not. But Heinrich knew, and he never said anything."

"Maybe he thought it would embarrass you."

"Maybe." The Cosmic Sibling Scorecard, I was fairly certain, would show that I embarrassed my brother exponentially more often. But why would Jenica cover for Heinrich? *Was* she covering for him, or did she really not know where he'd been? Did she really go to that concert at the Fillmore or was it yet another lie?

Jenica's voice became louder in my ear.

"I'm sorry, what?" I said. "My mind wandered."

She said, "Since you practically accused me and Dooley of murder, I need a favor. I wasn't going to ask, with everything you have going on, but now it seems you owe me. Could you take a look at my rhyme? You're the best at it. Something's wrong, and if I could fix it before our next meeting, I wouldn't lose so much time with it. If you looked at it today, then I'd have—no, never mind. I shouldn't have asked."

She paused and I pictured her playing with her spiked collar like she did when she was embarrassed.

"No, it's fine. I'm happy to. It'll take my mind off my problems for a while. And for the record, it seems like I'm accusing everyone of murder, so you guys are in good company." Plus, maybe to thank me, she'd tell me what she knew about Heinrich's whereabouts. And maybe even come clean about the Children's Hospital question. "Email it and I'll see if I can help."

We disconnected and I struggled out of bed and into the shower. The hot water felt like a miracle cure on my screaming soft tissue. I stayed in until my fingers and toes were pruney and the water started to run cold.

After I smelled like pomegranate/mango (body) and coconut (hair) and peanut butter (breath), I sat on a fluffy pillow strategically placed on a kitchen chair and opened my computer to troubleshoot Jenica's picture book verse.

My heart seized when my computer desktop faded away and was replaced with a cartoon Ozzi dancing an animated jig. He had a huge head on a tiny body that wouldn't stop moving. His face remained rigid with just his mouth opening and closing like ... well, like bad animation. He sang a ridiculous song consisting solely of the words "I'm sorry" to the tune of *Stars and Stripes Forever*. A couple of "very verys" were added in a useless attempt to fix the cadence.

"That's gotta be some form of treason." But I couldn't help chair-dancing to the piccolo part, at least until it hurt. It was oddly hypnotic to see Cartoon Ozzi dancing. How long had this taken him to animate?

Of course, my boyfriend denied he was a hacker, even though whenever he explained his job, it sounded exactly like hacking to me. And here was proof. I muted the sound, but Cartoon Oz kept dancing. I frowned at the screen. Did Ozzi know my passwords? I'd never been careful with them around him—why would I be? Maybe he didn't hack me at all.

But maybe he did. Even if he had hacked me, though, it didn't mean he'd hacked into Melinda's computer like I'd suspected earlier. But what if he had? What if he got tired of me whining about my issues with my royalty statements and decided to help me out? Or shut me up. Sure, he might have found financial information, but that wouldn't have made him kill her. I mean, he still had his childhood Winnie-the-Pooh. It was difficult to picture.

I once saw him lose his temper, that day a jerk said things to me and Ozzi chased him down the street. Thank goodness Lance was there to stop him. It wasn't like Ozzi. Was it? Just because I hadn't seen him that mad very often didn't mean he'd always kept his temper in check.

I didn't really think Ozzi had killed Melinda, but if TV and mystery novels had taught me anything, it's that it's always the last person you suspect. If my life was a cop drama, the killer would show up briefly before the first commercial. Unassuming, perfectly nice, helpful, reasonable.

Which, of course, described everyone in my little drama.

Besides, Ozzi had been at work that night. Miss Lulaila Philpott had verified that. But just because he was at work didn't mean he couldn't have been involved. If he could hack into my computer remotely, could he have hacked into the electrical system of Melinda's car? I knew that the mercury was the cause of her death, not the car crash, but still, it nagged at me.

I called the number for Melinda's mechanic.

"Bob Dunphy."

"Mr. Dunphy, it's Charlee Russo. Can I ask you something?" When he didn't respond, I added, "It's about cars."

"Okay then."

"Melinda's car."

I heard him sigh.

"I just need to know if somebody can screw with the electrical system or the engine or something—"

"I told you before, we did not sabotage Melinda Walter's car. And if that's—"

"No, not you guys. Somebody like a hacker. Could a hacker take control of her car?"

"Of course not. If it was one of those newfangled driverless cars, then sure. But this is a classic car, restored to its former glory. Hand-crank windows. Manual locks. There's no computer in there."

I laughed, relieved. "Of course there's not. How stupid of me. That's all I needed. Thanks for your time."

Ozzi's name remained crossed off my suspect list.

My detective work was interrupted by a knock on my door. Every nerve and muscle clenched. Again. If this kept happening, I'd have the tightest abs and tush around. I knew it was absurd, but the only people I expected to knock on my door these days were cops and murderers.

I wasn't sure which I'd rather see.

They knocked again, louder and more insistently this time, jarring me from my paralysis. I shuffled to the door, sneaking up on the peephole. Relief flooded me and I opened the door to two perky twenty-something women wearing matching, but not quite rhyming, *Green Clean Team* polo shirts.

"Hey, Charlee. Did you forget? Second Thursday of the month. Cleaning day."

"Hi, Marta. Hi, Blanca. I'm sorry, I did. Just give me five minutes."

Once a month, I secretly paid to have Don and Barb's apartment cleaned. I quickly wrote the house cleaners a check and handed them the Singers' key before climbing the stairs and knocking on the couple's door. I peeked over the balcony to make sure no bad guys were lurking, even though I wasn't entirely sure what a bad guy might look like. I guessed if I saw someone wearing a black Stetson or trussed up like Hannibal Lecter, I would probably run away.

When Don opened the door, Peter O'Drool raced around my ankles the requisite number of times before racing back inside to fetch his squeaky toy.

"Hey, Don, I need to get away from my computer for a while. Will you and Barb go with me to the art museum?" I knew they'd say yes because it was one of their favorite outings.

Barb plucked her coat and purse from the back of a chair while Peter pranced around me, displaying his toy. "We were just wondering what we were going to do today."

I picked up Peter and booped his nose with mine. "You should be very proud of your toy, but you're going to have to play with it by yourself for a while." If a dog could say "Okey-dokey," that's what I would have heard when I deposited him in his well-worn doggie bed. I knew Marta and Blanca brought him treats and showered him with attention while they cleaned.

As Don closed and locked the door he said, "See you later, Pete. Don't do anything I wouldn't do."

"Be really careful, okay?" I said to them. "I slipped on some ice last night. Not as fun as it might sound."

"Oh, you poor dear," Barb said, patting my hand.

I followed them down the stairs, all of us limping and favoring certain limbs. I wondered, as usual, how long it would be before their knees and hips couldn't negotiate the stairs anymore. When that day came, I already knew I'd switch apartments with them. Spry as they were, I suspected that day wouldn't come any time soon.

They held each other and took slow, shuffling steps over the snowy and icy spots while crossing the parking lot. I hovered behind them doing the same, hoping I could catch them before they fell, nervously reminding myself that I hadn't even rescued myself from the ice last night.

Don raised his eyebrows at the message on the back of my car. I shrugged in response. I gathered a handful of snow and erased it as best I could while they settled into the back seat of my car, where they liked to sit. Don said it was because they liked to hold hands and smooch, but I suspected it had something to do with the pile of crap that always seemed to live on my front passenger seat. Or maybe it was my driving and they felt safer back there. Regardless, I was always happy to chauffeur them around.

Twenty-five minutes later we'd made our way through Aurora and into the heart of Denver, where we pulled into the museum parking structure. Trolling for a spot, I spied an open one far from the elevator and asked if they wanted me to drop them off a bit closer.

"Landsakes. We're not invalids. The exercise will do us good," Barb said.

"Alrighty."

I parked and we made our way back the way we'd come, heading for the elevator in the corner. Parking garages always gave me the spooks, but now I was positively jumpy. There were no other people that I could see, but so many weird noises I was sure there'd be an ambush somewhere between my car and the elevator. I held my breath and tensed, ready to let loose with a well-placed karate chop or roundhouse kick, assuming I could perform either. Deep down I knew if anyone jumped out, I'd probably just scream. I liked to think I wouldn't grab Don or Barb and use them as a shield, but I couldn't be certain.

I drew a deep breath when we got to the elevator without mishap. No scary characters sighted either in the elevator or walking across the plaza to the museum. I ushered Don and Barb inside the building, where I felt I could completely relax. I don't know why, except there were uniformed guards there and they made me feel safe. Nothing bad can happen in an art museum, right? Except for being confronted with the sight of modern art. That's an unnecessarily brutal assault on your sensibilities.

Don and Barb headed straight for the café across the gift shop. I got a Houdini panini and they split a Ty Cobb salad.

After we ate, we browsed the "gift shop exhibit," the only one we ever saw. They could look at all the famous works of art in postcard and art book form, as well as the special products the museum brought in for the traveling exhibits. "Like a guided tour without all that walking," Don always said.

It served our purposes quite well. We didn't have to pay admission, we didn't get exhausted after executing the slow shuffle through all the galleries, and nobody cared when Don inevitably dragged an oversized art book to a café table to leaf through the pages.

I picked up a brochure about the traveling exhibit on display upstairs. It featured the art stolen by the Nazis in WWII, the organized looting by the Third Reich. Some of the paintings had been identified and reunited with the rightful owners, but many hadn't. The brochure explained how all the museums and collectors in the world were being encouraged to research and determine the provenance of all the art in their collections.

I folded the brochure and shoved it in my bag, turning toward the sandpictures Ozzi and I loved so much. I picked up a small one and turned it upside down to watch the cascade of sand in motion. The muted colors rose and fell, slowly waltzing to unheard music. The grains twisted and turned, meeting new partners and rejecting old in a spectacle that could never be performed exactly the same way ever again. Watching slow-motion mountains and valleys form and reform with every turn of the frame was hypnotizing.

"Like me and Ozzi," I murmured to the sandpicture. We were perfectly fine while sitting on the shelf, both of us happy and content with our lives. But then some unseen hand had picked us up and turned us over and everything had changed, perhaps never to be the same.

I jumped when Barb touched my elbow. "Ready to go, dear? Go pick out something."

Each time before we left, Don and Barb insisted on buying me a souvenir so I'd learned to be careful about what I expressed interest in. They'd offered to buy me one of the sandpictures many times, but I didn't want them spending that much money on me. I told them I didn't have room for one and they seemed to accept my explanation. And if I wanted to admire the silk scarves, I made sure they weren't looking.

I headed over to the wall of postcards, most of them reproductions of the art in the building or from past traveling exhibits. A double postcard of two of the plundered works of art caught my eye. Both were stylized couples. One, in fact, was titled *Couple* by Hans Christoph, and the other was titled *Man and Woman in the Window* by Wilhelm Lachnit. I showed it to Don and Barb, saying I liked the colors, but I realized even as I said it that maybe the postcard had caught my eye because it reminded me of me and Ozzi. It reminded me of a vague something else, too, but this remained out of reach.

On the way home, the Singers always insisted we stop at the craft store near our complex so I could run in and buy a pre-cut art mat or cheap frame for whatever I'd chosen. Adorably, Don once again pressed a five dollar bill into my hand from the back seat.

I delivered Don and Barb back to their apartment and was rewarded with another inspection of Peter's squeaky toy and a plate of brownies already wrapped up in cellophane and tied at the top with a ribbon. I was beginning to suspect my secret monthly cleanings weren't such a secret after all.

When Barb gave me the plate, she placed her hand gently on my arm and gave me a little squeeze. "I'm sorry, dear, but these don't have walnuts. I ran out after the banana bread."

"Oh, that's perfectly fine." I struggled to modulate my tone and rein in my glee. "I just love that you think of me so often, baking me such delicious goodies. I wish I could repay you."

Barb waved me away.

Balancing the brownies on my palm, I made my way back to my apartment. I stopped twice on the flight of stairs, ears perked, trying to discern unusual noises I heard. Both times, I realized it was the rustling rhythm of the cellophane, the hobby store bag, and the bag from the museum gift shop. My twitchiness at the prospect of a murderer after me had not been eased by our field trip.

At my door I bobbled the plate of brownies with the bags, trying to find my keys in my messenger bag. You'd think that after watching all the crime dramas on TV I'd know enough to have my keys in my hand, maybe even poking out between my fingers to double as an eye-gouging weapon. But no. The prospect of walnut-free brownies had overwhelmed my good sense.

I put everything down and slowly squatted to dig through my bag. You'd also think a clever and accomplished college graduate such as myself would be smart enough to put her keys back in the same place each time.

Quiet footsteps sounded behind me and I froze. My hand slowly wrapped around my set of keys and I maneuvered them between my fingers. The footsteps stopped. I stayed down, hand in my bag, thighs and back screaming for release. Feet shuffled on the concrete. I inhaled, held my breath, and counted in my head. *One … two … three.*

I stood and began to twist, elbow raised, keys in my fist. At that precise moment a hand clasped my shoulder. I lost my balance and toppled, shrieking. I flailed my eye-gouging keys wildly in the air around me, striking nothing.

"Geez. Chill out."

Suzanne.

"Cripes! What are you doing, sneaking up on me that way?" I looked down at my knee, solidly centered in the plate of now squished brownies.

"I wasn't sneaking. I was just walking. Not my fault I'm naturally stealthy."

"Everything okay down there, Charlee?" Don's voice called out.

"Yeah, Don, everything's fine." Except the brownies. I struggled to my feet, relieved nothing hurt worse than it had before. I unlocked the door and gathered my things, staring forlornly at the brownies.

"Sorry about that," Suzanne said.

"Easy come, easy go, I guess."

She made no attempt to leave.

"Is there something you wanted?" I allowed the slightest tinge of annoyance to creep into my voice.

"The cops came yesterday."

"I know. I saw when Barb brought me the flowers." I gestured at them on the table.

"They tricked me into opening the door."

"How?"

"They knocked—"

"Not really a trick. That's how most people do it."

"—and then pretended to leave. Probably surveilled me." Suzanne's eyes darted around. She seemed more paranoid than normal.

"What did they say?" I asked. A good sleuth would have asked her this during our banana bread exchange, but I'd been too worried about my potential Peeping Tom and/or murderer.

"They asked about my alibi, but I told them I couldn't remember because Mercury was in retrograde. They scolded me for joking about the murder, but I couldn't tell them the truth about where I was because then they'd arrest me for sure."

Now my eyes darted around. I backed away from her into my apartment.

But not before she muscled her way past me.

# Seventeen

I returned my eye-gouging keys to their position between my fingers and widened my stance for extra stability. Suzanne retrieved the brownies and then sat on my couch. I stayed where I was, messenger bag on my shoulder, plastic bags looped on my still-sore wrist.

"So, why would the police arrest you?"

"Because I refused to tell them my alibi."

"Which is ... "

"That the night before your agent's murder, I couldn't have tampered with her car because I was breaking into the bookstore."

"What? Where ... which ... why?"

Suzanne's face hardened. "How do you think I got all those books? Do you know what a freelance health care worker makes?"

I pictured my beloved bookstores around Denver—the Tattered Cover, BookBar, Capital Hill Books, the Broadway Book Mall. The idea of someone breaking into them felt like breaking into the very depths of my soul.

I was afraid to ask but did anyway. "Which store?"

"Espresso Yourself."

"Across the street?" I waved vaguely toward my front door. "The one Lavar and Tuttle own? How can you steal from them?" I felt my face getting hot and fought to control my temper.

Suzanne shrugged. "Never met 'em. They're never there when I do my … shopping. And I don't drink coffee."

"Yes, you do."

"Let me rephrase. I don't drink coffee where I steal."

"What are you thinking?" I dropped my keys into my bag, then dumped all my bags on the floor. "You can't just go around stealing books. They'll put you in jail for that."

"Nah. Those flimsy locks over there just make it so easy. It's almost as if they want me to break in."

"Pretty sure they don't." I rubbed my injured wrist, glad I hadn't made it worse.

"It's not that big a deal. I go over there Sunday nights and pick out three books I'd like. They must not miss them. Haven't changed the locks. Have they ever said anything to you? You guys are friends."

I couldn't recall them ever mentioning a break-in. But would they? It wasn't information you'd want to get out, it seemed. "What you're doing is—"

She raised one palm to me. "Not the point right now."

"What is the point, then?"

"That I don't have an alibi for the murder."

I shrugged. "Neither do I."

Then I cut my eyes at Suzanne. "When did you break into the bookstore?"

"You know, it's more of a coffee place than a booksto—"

"When?"

"Like, midnight Sunday."

I stared at her.

"I didn't kill her."

I kept staring. Could she have killed Melinda? She was being awfully forthcoming if she had. On the other hand, if I'd killed someone, I'd prefer the lesser crime of breaking and entering too. Suzanne had all those books about murder in her apartment. But she'd read them all and would know she'd be a prime suspect. And why would she kill someone exactly like I wrote? Surely she'd read about better ways, ones that couldn't be traced back to her reading my manuscript. And motive. What was her motive?

"Stop staring," Suzanne said. "You're giving me the creeps."

"It's only fair. You're giving me the creeps, too. And those books you gave me. They were stolen, weren't they?"

We continued our stare-down until I blinked.

"Charlee, you know I didn't kill her."

I glanced at the plate of smushed brownies on the coffee table. I untied the ribbon at the top of the cellophane and peeled back the wrapping. I scooped up a hearty fingerful of fudgy confection with my finger, then licked it off. I didn't know who or what to believe anymore but hoped brownies would enlighten me.

"Gross." Suzanne stood and walked toward the door. With her hand on the knob, she leveled her gaze at me. "I didn't kill anyone."

I had another fingerful halfway to my mouth. It hung there while I considered Suzanne's secret life of crime. "Wait."

She let go of the knob and stood, looking puzzled but hopeful.

Keeping my eyes on her, I dug in my bag until I found my phone. "I'm calling my brother. The cop."

She started to protest, but I raised one finger as he answered. I continued to stare at her while I said, "Lance, hey, I know I said I'd be there soon but I have to do something real quick. If I don't call you in fifteen, come over here. Fast. So we're not late. If I'm not home, I'll be at my next door neighbor's."

I clicked away before Lance could ask questions, but I hoped he could understand subtext. At least if Suzanne was really a murderer and decided to do me in, Lance would be on it. I was hoping that one, she wasn't a murderer, and that two, my phone call would be insurance.

Keeping my phone in my hand, I ushered Suzanne out the door. "I want to see these books you say you stole."

I followed her into the second bedroom of her apartment. The only furniture was an easy chair next to a small end table in the center of the room. Every wall was now floor-to-ceiling bookshelves, mostly filled with books. I'd been in here briefly a couple of times over the years, borrowing from her vast library. But this time, I crossed to the far side of the room. "You stay there." I pointed to the doorway.

She leaned against it, a bemused smile making her lips disappear.

Keeping one eye on her, I began pulling books randomly from the shelves. All of them had price tags from Espresso Yourself. I didn't know anything about kleptomania, but wondered if this was a manifestation. It didn't seem logical, but was there a subset of kleptomania where someone only steals one thing from one place?

"What else do you steal?"

"Nothing. Well, sometimes I get hungry when I'm there."

I inspected practically one entire wall of books. All were from Espresso Yourself.

"Believe me now?" she asked.

"I don't know what to believe." I brushed past her into the living room, and a calendar thumb-tacked to the wall caught my eye. All of the Monday squares were colored in neon orange marker. Each square had *Senior Center 4 a.m.–noon* written in it. Was Suzanne breaking in there, too? And would she be so blatant as to calendar it?

She sauntered past me and flopped on her couch, raising a pillow behind her neck.

"Since when is the Senior Center open at four in the morning?"

"It's not. But the residential side needs caregivers. Namely, me. On Mondays for the last three years, anyway."

I watched as she adjusted the pillow. I had to admit, Suzanne did not look like a killer. She seemed calm and at ease with me asking her questions and inspecting her life. But still. "You mean to tell me you break into the coffee shop every Sunday night at midnight, then go to work at 4 a.m.?"

"I don't sleep much."

My brow furrowed, and she realized I'd need more information.

"They get new books every Friday but don't get around to putting them out until late Saturday. I don't like 'em picked over."

"Then why not break in on Saturday night?"

"Because after the Sunday rush, they get their pastries ready for the week. I told you, sometimes I get hungry. Have you ever had their butter braids? Magnificent."

It all sounded ridiculous enough to be true. And the butter braids were magnificent, and usually scarce, which is why I always got a muffin. I didn't know what to believe. I stared at my neighbor lounging on the couch, looking relaxed, perhaps even relieved to have confessed. She certainly didn't look like a murderer. But my gut feeling wasn't proof. I needed more.

I pulled my phone from the pocket of my jeans and, without looking, pushed the power button and flipped the silencer on the side. "What was that?" I pointed toward the kitchen.

As Suzanne tilted her head and glanced that direction, I snapped a series of photos of her.

She never knew.

"I didn't hear anything."

"Must have been my imagination." I turned to leave. "I need to think about all of this." Before the door closed behind me, I reminded her about my brother, the cop.

I ran into my apartment long enough to grab a coat. As I walked to Espresso Yourself, I called Lance.

"Finally!" he said. "I was two seconds out the door. What was that all about?"

"Stand down, Officer." I didn't want to explain about Suzanne until I knew more. "I was just talking to somebody I felt iffy about, but it's okay now. They're gone."

"Sounds like you're being stupid."

"If by stupid you mean the opposite of stupid, then yes." I expected at least a chuckle from him but didn't get it. "Remember how Mom and Dad used to say we could use them as an excuse if we didn't want to go to a party or something that made us feel uncomfortable?"

"No."

"Oh. Well, I do, and that's what I was doing with you."

"Does this have anything to do with Melinda's murder?"

I stopped walking and jiggled my knees in frustration. "Lance, I need to prove my friends aren't killers. I need to put this behind me, get some closure, and get back to my writing."

"What you need is to let the police solve this."

"You're the police, so who did it?"

He ignored my snark. "I'm not working this case. In fact, I'm not even supposed to be talking to you about it."

Before I could ask why, he said, "Leave it to the professionals, Charlee. I mean it," and then he hung up.

"Oh, he *means* it," I mocked, dropping the phone in my bag. "Easy for him to say."

A few minutes later I saw the coffee shop sign. Wooden, hand-lettered, with bright colors announcing *Espresso Yourself—Coffee and Books,* with a tagline underneath: *For when you have a latte on your mind.*

The sign wasn't the only thing about the coffee place that I loved. Even when it was crowded, nobody was surly. The coffee wasn't great, but it was more than serviceable. Cheap and plentiful, too. And someone else made it, which increased deliciousness a hundredfold. Suzanne was right about the pastries. Everything was always magnificent. The muffins were covered in mysteriously marvelous streusel, made with prodigious amounts of butter, brown sugar, and what I theorized must be crack cocaine, ensuring my loyalty.

So I walked into Espresso Yourself, completely dead at 4:30 on a Thursday afternoon. The proprietors were two gay ex-Marines— Lavar the crazy Christian and Tuttle the crazy atheist—both with physiques that would put a recruiting poster to shame. If it wasn't too busy, they'd argue, tease, and score philosophical points with the other to pass the time. Regardless, it was clear they loved each other, and they made everyone feel welcome, no matter what.

Lavar sat at a table with an empty plate crisscrossed by a knife and fork in front of him. Tuttle perched on a stool behind the counter, reading a book. They both jumped up to hug me when I walked in.

"Girl, what you doing here? Got a case of writer's block only my coffee will dislodge?" Lavar asked.

"Nope, not writing much the past few days."

"Tut and I are both praying for you."

"Speak for yourself, Lavar. I ain't praying for nobody." Tuttle's face softened. "But I do hope they find out what happened to your friend, Charlee. Shameful business."

"Thanks, guys. I wanted to see if you know this woman." I held out my phone to Lavar and scrolled through a few of the photos of Suzanne. I didn't want to say anything about the break-ins until I knew more.

Lavar shook his head and handed the phone to Tuttle. "Doesn't look familiar."

"To me neither." Tuttle handed the phone back to me.

"Do you guys keep a customer database?"

They both laughed.

"Aren't you precious," Lavar finally said.

"So, no?"

"No."

"Why? Who is she? Wait—you're investigating!" Tuttle's hand flew to his throat. "Is she the murderer?"

"That's an unpleasant thought." I didn't tell them it had crossed my mind more than once.

"You know what I mean," he said.

"She's my neighbor."

"Did something happen to her? Is she okay?" Lavar asked.

"Jury's still out, but I'll let you know."

# Eighteen

I finally got a solid eight hours of sleep, but only because I dosed myself with some expired nighttime cold-and-flu concoction I found in the medicine cabinet. Friday dawned cloudy in all the imaginable ways. Don't tell the FDA.

Wedging myself in the corner of the shower until the hot water ran cold helped brush away the majority of the cobwebs in my brain. I made a plan for the day. It had two things in it: make coffee, and verify the alibi of Dave and Veta Burr.

I padded out to the kitchen in my ratty chenille robe and stared into the empty coffee container. I pulled the carafe out from the coffeemaker. Empty. Revising my plan to "obtain" coffee and clear Dave and Veta, I padded back to my room to get dressed.

Espresso Yourself was crowded, so no time to chitchat with Lavar or Tuttle. I did ask about the deliciously sweet berry and butter aroma, but that could hardly be considered chitchat.

"Blueberry butter braid," Lavar said while he poured my coffee. "But it's gone already. We never seem to have enough of that stuff." He tightened the lid of my plastic travel mug, then handed me a streusel muffin.

I pulled out my wallet but he waved it away.

"How do you guys stay in business?"

"Power of prayer, baby. Power of prayer."

When he turned to the next customer, I crammed a twenty in the tip jar. As I walked to my car I wondered if that was their nefarious business plan. Did they convince everyone to pay twenty bucks for a five-dollar order? If so, they were geniuses.

Everything was cold, inside the car and out, so I kept my gloves on even though it made it more difficult to pull my mug from the cup holder. In the half hour it took to get to Dave and Veta's neighborhood, I was only able to sip half my coffee before it got tepid and uninspiring.

I had just turned into their Westminster subdivision of cookie cutter houses when a black SUV with darkly tinted windows almost T-boned me from the left, forcing me into a cul-de-sac on the right. I slammed on the brakes and let loose a stream of profanity, directed its way, that fogged up my windshield. I assumed they simply hadn't seen me in their rush to get to work or school or the hospital to have their baby. But as I rolled down my window to help defog the car, I was surprised to see that instead of leaving the subdivision, the SUV turned and went deeper into the development.

I used a sleeve to clear the windshield the rest of the way and rolled my window up. I pulled up a mental map of Dave and Veta's neighborhood but couldn't picture another way out. Like most large subdivisions, there probably was one, but why wouldn't the SUV take the closest exit, especially when they were obviously in a hurry?

Oh well, what did I care, as long as they didn't hit me.

I hoped I remembered the series of quick turns required to find the Burrs' address. The streets were all short because there was an elementary school in the center of the development. I didn't know why that mattered, but it did, and I had to get to the other side. I'd forgotten about the school and was glad it was after nine so the streets weren't packed with carpoolers. Alone at a four-way stop, I began to cross the intersection when a black SUV—was it the same one that had almost hit me?—slowed, then rolled past. I tried to see who was driving but the tint was too dark. Hadn't Lance told me one time that it was illegal to have such a dark tint?

Again, what did I care? That is, until they pulled a U-turn behind me.

My eyes kept darting from my mirror to the road in front of me. Was it the same car? Were they following me?

The road curved past a small pocket park and I turned right on the street just past it. The SUV slowed but kept traveling straight. I unclenched my grip on the steering wheel and made a quick right onto Dave and Veta's street. I passed their house and parked at the curb four houses down. I sat there for a bit, sipping my gross tepid coffee to settle my nerves and make sure the SUV didn't come back.

I called Lance. "The weirdest thing just happened."

"You didn't fart in public?"

"Ha. And no." I explained what had happened with the SUV. "Isn't that weird?"

"That you saw two of the most popular cars in the most popular color in Colorado?"

"Is that true or are you just making stuff up?"

"That's for me to know and you to find out, Space Case."

"Lance." I tried to use my mother's voice. "I'm serious."

"It was your imagination. Why would a car that almost hit you also try and follow you? You're jumpy lately. Remember those footprints under your window? Routine maintenance check of the gutters."

"How do you know that?"

"I'm a cop with a phone. It ain't rocket surgery."

"You called them? Because you were worried about me? Even when you'd told me not to worry? That's sweet."

"Shaddup. Why are you at Dave and Veta's?"

"Social call."

"You sure? It's not part of your investigation?"

I was fairly certain he knew I was lying, but I said, "I told you. It's a social call." What he didn't know wouldn't hurt him.

"Riiight." He paused. "Be careful, Space Case." Another pause. "Call me later."

"Only if you promise to tell everyone how very much you love me," I said with a smile.

"Bye."

I dropped the phone into my bag, but my smile disappeared. Why would maintenance have been sidling along the wall of my apartment to check the gutters on the third floor? Why wouldn't they have used the grassy area between the buildings? And didn't they have an easier way to access the roof? But I had to believe Lance asked the right questions. I was a bit chagrined I hadn't thought to call the management office myself.

At least it made me more confident in my decision not to tell Lance everything that was going on. If I did, he would start looking into it, and he'd told me he wasn't supposed to be involved.

A man walking a golden retriever slowed and stared hard at me as he passed, derailing my thoughts, obviously trying to ascertain why I was just sitting in my car.

He wouldn't believe me if I told him.

I waved at him, then reached into my bag and pulled out a clipboard with some papers and a pen attached. The top sheet was a form I'd made that morning, all part of my plan. I buried my Peeping Tom worries and concentrated on the issue at hand. The SUV hadn't returned, and I hoped Lance was right that it was just my imagination.

I got out of the car and walked down the sidewalk toward Dave and Veta's house. But I stopped at their next door neighbor's and rang the bell.

A woman who looked to be in her sixties opened the door. "Yes?"

"Hello, I'm conducting some research about—"

"Not interested." She started to close the door.

"It'll just take a minute. I'll make it worth your while." I mentally pawed through my bag, trying to determine if I did, in fact, have anything to make it worth her while.

"How?" She narrowed her eyes.

"Um ... " Now I actually pawed through my bag. "Starbucks gift card!" I thrust it triumphantly in the air.

"How much?"

"Ten bucks." It was a token thank you for speaking to a writer's group a couple of months before. How could they have known I always went to Espresso Yourself?

"Okay, but make it snappy. And you might want to lead with that in the future." She held out her hand and I dropped the card into it.

"You're right. I'm new at this." I pulled the cap from the pen and dug the clipboard into my ribs.

"What's this about again?"

"Your TV habits."

"Are we going to be a Nielson family? I've always wanted to do that." The woman slid the Starbucks card into the pocket of her sweater.

"First, do you have cable?"

"No, it got too expensive and it was all crap on there anyway." She nodded at the clipboard. "You tell them that."

"For sure." I wrote *expensive crap*. "Next question, do you have Netflix?"

"We get movies in the mail, but next door they have the whatdo-youcallit … George?" She turned and yelled into the house, "What do you call it when we go to Dave and Veta's to watch TV?"

A rumpled gray-haired man came to the door. "Sunday?"

"No, that Netflix thing."

"*Breaking Bad?*"

She let out an exasperated breath. "No, when you don't get the movies in the mail but it comes straight through the air."

George shrugged.

"Streaming?" I suggested.

"Yes. Streaming." She shooed George away. "He's not the techie in the family, but he loves going next door for our weekly *Breaking Bad* watch party. Dave's an ex-science teacher, so we do it like a book club. We watch and discuss. Sometimes he pauses it to explain more about cooking meth."

The idea of four retirees talking about cooking meth made me giggle. "And you do this every Sunday?"

"Yep. Before that we watched all of *The West Wing* because George used to teach civics. Same thing." She leaned in close. "But just between you and me, I like *Breaking Bad* better." She grinned. "They should have called it *Breaking Best*."

"Sure," I said, jotting some notes. "And just to clarify, you were next door at Dave and Veta's this past Sunday night watching?"

"Yep."

"What time?"

"Hmm, let's see. They come over here around six and I cook dinner. We're usually over there around eight."

"And how long did you stay?"

"We're probably home ten or ten thirty, most nights."

I winced. That didn't create much of an alibi. I didn't know what I was expecting, but corroboration for just a few hours of the time in question wasn't enough. It was too bad they didn't turn their viewing parties into slumber parties.

"Wanna write down the other shows I like?"

"Um … no, I think I have everything I need."

"Not much of a questionnaire."

She was right. I needed her to think I was really doing research. I flipped the page, hoping she wouldn't see it was blank. I angled the clipboard up higher. "Oh, silly me. I forgot the second page. And yes, they want to know the other shows you like."

She began rattling off titles, many of which I'd never heard of. Occasionally she'd launch into lengthy and disjointed synopses that I pretended to listen to. But my mind was elsewhere, trying to figure out how I could account for Dave and Veta's time past ten thirty when their neighbors went home.

Suddenly a metallic shriek rocked the neighborhood, and I flinched.

"Oh, don't worry about that. That's just Dave and Veta's garage door." The woman craned her neck toward their house, but I made sure to keep my back to it. "It's off its tracks or something but they won't get it fixed. Used to scare the daylights out of me and I'd come running." She waved. "Dave must be heading off to work."

I tapped the pen cap against my cheek. "Do you hear it at night, too?"

She laughed. "They don't drive at night. That car is locked up snug as a bug in a rug from sundown to sunup."

"Are you sure?"

"Yep. And I'd know it if it wasn't. The first time I heard that door, around Christmastime, I was taking a nap. I almost fell off the couch. And then I went over and gave them a piece of my mind."

I smiled and tucked the clipboard into my bag. "I think that's everything I need, Mrs. ...."

"You never asked my name." She narrowed her eyes at me.

"It's supposed to be anonymous, but if they need anything further, they can contact you through your Netflix account." I inwardly cringed, knowing that made absolutely no sense.

"They better have more Starbucks for me, then."

"You can be sure of it. Thanks for your time."

She shut the door without a goodbye and I hurried away from Dave and Veta's house, toward my car. When I got there, I dialed the phone.

"Hey, Veta? Can you and Dave come over for dinner tomorrow night?"

"No, we had to quit driving at night, dear. Our eyes got old when we weren't looking. But I could do lunch."

"Are you sure? You never drive at night? Not even to do something fun?"

"Did you go to cooking school or something, dear?"

"No, nothing like that."

"If it's that important to you, we could call one of those Uber cars I've been hearing about."

"No, never mind. What are you doing right now?"

"Nothing. Dave just left for work."

"How 'bout I get some sandwiches and come over?"

"That would be lovely, dear!"

"I'll be there in ten minutes."

After sandwiches and leftover pecan pie, I waved goodbye to Veta, thrilled to know I could cross both her and Dave off my suspect list. I'd quizzed her a million different ways and felt entirely confident that they never opened their squealing garage door at night, they always parked in their garage, and they truly never drove at night anymore.

As I drove home, giddy with my success, I considered each of the remaining suspects on my list. How to cross them off?

I'd been playing phone tag with Kell's secretary to see if she'd confirm that he was on that red-eye flight, but I wasn't sure how to verify Cordelia and Byron's alibis, or Henry's, or what Dooley had said about Jenica's.

And I didn't even know what Einstein and Heinrich claimed to be doing that night.

I did feel confident that Suzanne went to work at the Senior Center, so she was clear after about three thirty a.m. on Monday, but I only had circumstantial evidence that she'd broken into the bookstore before that. Was half an alibi good enough?

And technically, I hadn't crossed off Melinda herself yet. But that was ridiculous. Nobody would commit suicide by poisoning themselves with mercury. Unless they were beyond evil and really wanted to frame me.

Okay, she stayed.

A couple days ago, I'd almost crossed Q off because of her alibi with the timestamps on those postings on the *Dear Horrible Writer* forum. I wished I knew more about computer stuff.

I braked hard and whipped into a shopping center, parking in an outlying spot. I needed to ask Ozzi. I dug for my phone. I was ready to make up with him. Wasn't I? I fiddled with my phone and tried to decide. He thought I was a murderer. I'd thought the same of him prior to my conversation with Lulaila Philpott, but I'd had to. It was part of my job while investigating this. He'd thought it about me immediately. I remembered him backing away from me during my booty call. He'd called me ridiculous.

I dropped the phone back in my purse and drove home, thinking about computers and timestamps.

When I got there, I went straight to my computer. Dooley had mentioned something about a photographer for the Fillmore Theatre snapping pictures at that concert. Maybe the photos would have time-stamps, like Mr. Dunphy's did. I pulled up the Fillmore website and clicked the link to the Pleasure Center for Armadillos concert, and then another link that took me to the band's website.

My screen filled with thumbnails of photos from the concert. I scrolled down. Four pages of thumbnail photos. I clicked on the first one, which was of an empty stage, and it filled my screen. Below it was a small date and timestamp.

"Yes!" I pumped a fist in the air.

I studied the photo, searching for the name of the photographer who might be able to corroborate Jenica's alibi. Nothing. I tried the next picture. And the next. And several more.

I didn't find the photographer's identity, but I did find something else. All the photos had yesterday's date. Which meant these timestamps recorded the time of the upload, not the time the photos were taken.

I groaned, then minimized the page of thumbnails and squinted until I spotted some of Jenica and Dooley. I paged through all the photos. So many of the two of them, partying, dancing, hanging with the band. At least Dooley had been telling me the truth about being there early and staying late.

I scrolled all the way to the bottom of the home page on the band's website until I saw *Photography copyrighted by Josh Argus. For rights, click here*. I did, and ended up on the contact page of his website.

I dialed the number. When he answered, I said, "I'm interested in the photos you took at the Pleasure Center for Armadillos concert in Denver recently."

"What's your email and I'll shoot you a price list."

"Oh. Not to buy them. I just need some information."

"Story of my life."

"I'm more of a show-tunes girl, myself."

"Are you trying to make me cry?"

I thought for a minute. "I like Green Day. That Billie Joe Armstrong ... got any good ones of him?"

"Yeah. No. You are aware I take pictures of Pleasure Center for Armadillos. But next time Billie Joe opens for them, I'll snap a couple for you."

"And I'll pay you."

"You'll be the first." Josh Argus paused. "I like you. If you don't want pictures, what do you want?"

"Information. I'm trying to find out if you remember the contest winners that night. You have a bunch of pictures of them."

"Dooley and Jenica? Of course I remember them. They were a hoot."

"Can you tell me when they got there and when they left?"

"Are you a cop?"

"No. But I need to know. I'm like Jenica's big sister."

"They were there before I got there around four o'clock on Sunday afternoon, and they were still at the after-party when I left around seven Monday morning. Ah, to be young again."

"Seems like you held your own. Those are some great shots you uploaded."

"Thanks."

"Can I ask you one more thing? I see all the uploads are time-stamped. In theory, could you change those if you wanted to?"

He thought for a minute. "I don't know. Maybe I could change the date and time settings of my computer."

"What if you were uploading them to someone else's website or, for instance, posting in a forum you were the webmaster of?"

"I suppose anything is possible, but you'd probably need to have done the coding for the site to begin with, or at least have complete access to it. And for this many photos, it would be hella time consuming. Most people only know how to do the little bit they need to do on their computers. What do you do for a living?"

"I'm a writer."

"What happens when you have a problem with your word processing program?"

"I shout and cry and pour myself a drink until it magically repairs itself."

"Same thing I do with my editing programs."

"So you think it's the same with timestamps on message boards and stuff? Would you have to be a total techie?"

"You mean like to change the stamp on every single message?"

"Yeah."

"That would take forever. If it was even possible. Some websites get hundreds of interactions every hour." He paused. "Why do you want to know?"

"I'm a lot of people's big sister. Thanks for your time, Josh."

I dug for my suspect list and drew a satisfying line through Q's name and Jenica's.

Closing the lid of my computer, I leaned back and rolled my shoulders, visions of timestamps dancing in my head. Suddenly I snapped up straight in my chair.

I dialed Cordelia's number. "Are you home? Give me your address and I'll be right over."

I drove my Kia onto the cleanest, most pristine driveway I'd ever seen and prayed fervently that I wouldn't drip oil on it. If I'd expected to stay long, I would have reversed and parked out on the street. I hurried up the walkway to Cordelia's dignified mansion, cream-colored with dark slate tiles on its steep gabled roof. I stopped and took two steps backward, looking to my left. "A turret. Wow."

She answered the door almost before I rang the bell. "What's going on, Charlee? What's the matter?"

"Nothing! Show me your burglar alarm."

Cordelia pointed to a plastic-covered box mounted on the wall behind me.

"We can check your alarm." I spoke fast and breathless. "When you set it on Sunday night and when you turned it off. There's probably a timestamp on it." I studied the small printed directions and punched some numbers. "Ta da! I just proved your alibi." I stepped back and offered her a closer look with a Vanna White wave of my hand.

Cordelia rubbed the pearls around her neck but didn't move. Instead she wrinkled her brow and said, "Yes. Well, that and our security cameras showing we never left the house. We figured that out and told the police already."

I allowed the combination of humiliation and exhilaration to flow through me. It was odd. Like broccoli with chocolate sauce. Or a brick bed with a feather pillow. Or an all-expense-paid vacation to a rendering plant.

"I'm sorry, Charlee. It didn't occur to me to tell you."

"Of course not. Why would you?" I smiled at her. "I'm just glad your alibi is official."

And I was. Another name crossed off. Actually, two, because her husband had been there with her.

Eleven down, six to go.

# Nineteen

Saturday dawned overcast and extra cold. Yesterday's sun had melted the snow from our last storm, except for the iciest and most hard-packed on the perpetually frozen north side of the buildings. But because it was March, Colorado's snowiest month, our clear roads were threatened once again as the next storm being hyped looked like it would finally arrive.

The unpredictability of March snow always causes mob-mentality panic at local grocery stores. The slightly empty shelves are nowhere near Russian-breadline empty, but panicky shoppers still grab emergency supplies as if the Bolsheviks are closing in. However, even after our worst blizzards, with record snowfall amounts, within the next day or two the blue sky smiles down upon us. Schools reopen, dogs get walked, roads become passable. In Denver, you'll never be inconvenienced for long unless you're having a baby or a heart attack, both of which log higher rates during blizzards.

Stress-related, I suppose. But there's always a tinge of low-grade stress just before the storm hits. I will admit to getting sucked into the Grocery Store Apocalyptic Groupthink Drama once, the day before a blizzard. I saw there were only two pounds of butter on the shelf and I grabbed them both. I didn't need butter, and certainly not eight sticks of it, but I felt the pull of that panic. What if I did need it? What if I ran out? How would I survive for two whole days with only the single stick of butter I'd had in my refrigerator for the past three months?

But on this morning the clouds only spat random flakes, trying to work up the enthusiasm to match the weather forecasters' hype. I had bigger worries than my pantry situation, although it occurred to me that I was low on practically everything, including cold medicine. The thought of going to the grocery store on a Saturday exhausted me, however. Better to starve to death.

The apartment complex was quiet. Most people were off work and school, sleeping in or puttering around home. I suspected everyone had coffee in the house except me. I pulled the corner of my drapes back and looked with longing across the parking lot toward Espresso Yourself. I sighed and wrapped my robe tighter around me. At least my wrist and behind weren't as sore today.

Maybe I could run upstairs and ask Don and Barb to borrow enough coffee to make a pot. Maybe they'd even have some already brewed. With pancakes. And bacon. And scrambled eggs. Maybe if I called, they'd bring it all down to my apartment.

A knock on the door made me smile, then frown. The fantasy of the Singers bringing me a hot multi-course breakfast faded away. I tiptoed to the peephole and saw Detective Campbell-like-the-soup filling the space like a human Pike's Peak. He held two cups of coffee, one raised in the air as if he knew I'd peek out. He wore a parka and a look on his face that said, *You know you want it.*

I ducked down and squat-walked toward the kitchen. Halfway there I turned and squat-walked back to the door. "I'm not dressed," I called through the door. "Leave the coffee and come back in an hour."

"No can do."

I debated for as long as a hungry lion debates whether to pounce on a wounded gazelle.

I opened the door a crack and held out my hand for the coffee. "I just got up, I'm not dressed, I smell bad, my back hurts, and I haven't brushed my teeth. I wasn't really expecting company."

"That's what I was hoping for. I was also hoping you wanted coffee."

"More than life itself."

He handed me the cup but didn't let go, so I reluctantly stepped aside so he could enter. I glared at him until he released the coffee. We sat at the kitchen table, where I removed the lid from my cup and stuck my nose millimeters from the earthy aroma of its contents. Was that a hint of cinnamon? I let the heat tendrils crawl up my nostrils and into my good graces. Twice. Then I faced him.

"Where's your partner?"

"I'm on my own today."

I blew on my coffee and took a fortifying sip. He wouldn't bring me coffee if he was here to arrest me. Would he? Is that how they did it at the fancy precincts? "What can I do for you, Detective?"

"I wanted to ask you about your neighbor, Suzanne Medina."

I smiled. "So I'm not a suspect anymore?"

"Did I say that?"

The smile slid off my face. Did he think Suzanne was a credible suspect? I thought about her burglaries and all the times she'd snuck up on me, but that didn't make her a murderer.

"Okay. Let's talk about Suzanne."

Detective Campbell flipped open his notebook just like they do on TV. "We know Ms. Medina had access to your manuscript. You can confirm she read it?"

"Yes. Well, I think so. I mean, she gave me notes, but I didn't sit there and watch her read it."

"So, yes. Good." He riffled some pages before stopping at one. "Did you know Ms. Medina prior to living here?"

"No."

"Were you aware she previously resided at the Mental Health Institute in Pueblo?"

"The psychiatric hospital?"

He nodded.

"Why was she there?"

"Let's just say this isn't her first brush with the law. She has a history of disruptive behavior."

I was flabbergasted. Sure, Suzanne was eccentric and odd, but this seemed beyond the pale. "Disruptive how?"

Campbell glanced around as if to make sure we were alone, even though he knew very well we were. "She liked to sing in public."

"Sing? Like the buskers on the 16th Street Mall?"

"No. Like skipping down the middle of the street at two in the morning screeching Pink Floyd." He closed his notepad and sipped his coffee. "Ah, good brew. Nice and dark. When I'm retired I'm going to drink good coffee every day, not that swill they have at the station."

So regardless of the tax base, workplace coffee sucked. I'd have to tell Lance it wasn't just his crappy precinct.

"You're retiring?" I asked.

"Yep, six days"—he glanced at his watch—"five hours and eighteen minutes."

"Looking forward to it, I see."

"This'll be my final case. Hopefully it won't be like my last one." A storm passed in front of his eyes. "Really put in the work on that one but the DA wouldn't pursue." He stared into his cup, then looked up and smiled. "This one'll be different."

He sipped his coffee again, so I forced myself to sip mine too, wondering why he was really here. It didn't seem proper police procedure to tell me about Suzanne's history, plus he hadn't asked me anything new. And he'd brought me coffee. My eyes widened and I looked at the floor. Was he hitting on me? I covered my embarrassment by taking too big a drink.

"So, why'd you lie about your whereabouts the morning of Ms. Walter's murder?"

I choked on my coffee, finally managing to sputter, "I never lied!"

Detective Campbell raised his eyebrows at me while he took another sip.

I racked my brain. Damn. I'd forgotten to tell them about stopping for coffee, like Lance had reminded me to do. "Ohmygosh, I forgot to tell you I stopped for coffee at Espresso Yourself. It's over there, across the street." I pointed in that direction.

"Is that all?"

"Yes! No! I got a muffin."

He stared at me.

"A blueberry one."

Still stared.

"With streusel."

He kept staring and I felt a trickle of sweat run down the middle of my back.

"Why'd you get a muffin if you were having breakfast with your agent?"

I groaned. "I lied about that to my critique group because with my tremor, I always spill on myself and they tease me because I have to change clothes so often. I spilled that morning but I wasn't up for their jokes."

"And what about that loud argument at Mr. Rabbinowitz's apartment the night of the murder?"

The booty call fight. I tensed. "What does that have to do with anything? People in a relationship fight."

"Especially if their murder plot goes wrong."

"What?" The trickle of sweat turned into rushing snowmelt. Was this an ambush?

Campbell again stared at me over the top of his cup. Then he grinned. "Listen. I don't think you killed your agent. I'm sure it's probably Ms. Medina."

Probably? Was this guy for real? He was clearly just punching the clock, counting down the minutes until his retirement. And why was he here without his partner? Again, I felt my face redden and fought to keep my temper. Was Campbell trying to railroad Suzanne? He was burned out on this case and she was the path of least resistance. I thought of my brother and all the good, diligent cops in the world. They'd never think of picking the low-hanging fruit. Sure, Suzanne was eccentric and broke into bookstores, and maybe even had done a stint locked up in a loony bin. But since when did that mean she killed Melinda? She didn't have a motive before, and she still didn't have one now. And if they arrested her for it, then there would still be a murderer out there, perhaps stalking me.

I finally managed to speak. "So you've cleared everyone else who read my manuscript?"

"Sure. Yeah." He waved away my question like it was an annoying gnat.

"You talked to Sheelah's dentist, AmyJo's sister, and the photographer at the Pleasure Center for Armadillos concert?"

"Absolutely." Campbell slid his pen through the spiral of his notebook. "Everything checked out."

I offered him some of Barb's walnut-laced cookies to buy myself some time to think. "That photographer was something else, right? What was her name? Guadalupe Hernandez? I could barely understand her, that accent was so heavy." Guadalupe Hernandez was a girl I went to high school with. She spoke with perfect diction and had no hint of an accent. Why her name popped into my head, I'll never know. But it was a little bit genius.

"I used a translator. Don't want anything amiss when it goes to the DA."

I slid my hands under my thighs. He was outright lying about investigating Melinda's murder. This was way beyond withholding a few facts or keeping your cards close to your vest. This was laziness. Fabrication. Dereliction of duty.

My pulse quickened, as did my breathing. "Remind me what time frame you're concentrating on?"

"Ms. Walter parked her car late Sunday, left her house around seven Monday morning, and was found dead soon after that."

"Well, then, it can't be Suzanne. She was with me." Reputation be damned.

"Weren't you with your boyfriend? Kinky."

"After he left, I couldn't sleep. It was only around midnight. I heard Suzanne next door, so I asked her to ... help me move some stuff to my storage unit. I'd been putting it off, and since we were both wide awake, it seemed like as good a time as any to do it." I tried to picture the inside of my unit. *Please, please, please don't ask me what we moved there.* I added, "That's when I spilled on myself. At the storage unit. With Suzanne. We were there all night." Oh, why did I say all that? It was so easily checked. And would they really believe I'd worn the same clothes the next day? I glanced down at my shirt. Probably.

"Why didn't you tell us this before?" Campbell pulled the pen from the spiral loop on his notebook.

"I forgot. It's not every day that I get accused of murder." Which was, of course, all the more reason to have mentioned it. I hoped he would overlook that.

"Why didn't Ms. Medina tell us?"

"You said yourself she was crazy."

The detective stood and pocketed his notebook and pen, leaving his cup on the table. "I guess this requires a follow-up conversation with her."

I was eighty-seven percent sure Suzanne didn't kill Melinda, but one hundred percent sure Campbell was not doing his job. I couldn't let him keep doing this to her simply because he wanted to create a slam-dunk before his retirement swan song.

"What was Suzanne's motive?" I asked.

He shrugged. "Why does anyone kill anyone?" He zipped his parka and left my apartment. I heard him knock on Suzanne's door.

He knocked again, louder.

I looked out the window and saw him walking toward the parking lot. I was relieved that Suzanne wasn't home, because if she didn't corroborate the alibi I'd created for her, Campbell would probably be marching both of us off in handcuffs right now.

When he reached the edge of the building, an eddy of snow swirled around him and walked him to his car. The dark sky belied the daytime hour, and the snow fell harder. Shadows danced around the corners of the buildings, but I didn't know whether it was the wind playing tricks or something—or someone—else.

Watching Campbell drive away created a knot of both relief and anxiety in the pit of my stomach. There was an immediate knock on the door. I opened it to Suzanne.

"I thought you weren't home."

"I'm a klepto, not an imbecile. I know when to dodge a cop. Especially one who wants to verify a fake alibi."

"You heard?"

"I hear everything that goes on in your apartment, love. I know you pay for Don and Barb's housecleaning. I know you have a bit of a problem with lactose. And I know that you and Ozzi don't really watch late-night TV even though it's on."

I blushed. "I never hear you."

"I don't have a hot boyfriend." Suzanne plopped herself on my couch. "And now you know my secrets. So tell me. What did we put in your storage unit and how long did it take us?"

I put my hands on my hips. "Suzanne, I'm only going to ask you this once. And you better tell me the truth."

"Or else what?"

"I don't know. But you better tell me the truth." I took a deep breath. "Did you have anything to do with Melinda Walter's death?"

"Don't be a ninny. Of course I didn't." She eyed the chocolate oatmeal cookies on the table. "Can I?"

I stared at her, then collapsed into the chair. "Be my guest." I watched her take enthusiastic bites. "I believe you."

"Duh."

"Now go away so I can think."

She gestured toward the plate.

"Yes. Fine. Take them."

When she closed the door behind her, I called Lance. While I waited for him to answer, I glanced uneasily at the vent and wondered how well Suzanne really heard what went on in here.

"Charlee, I can't talk."

"Not an option right now. Detective Campbell came to see me."

"And?"

"And he's not doing his job. I've investigated Melinda's death more than he has. He's convinced my neighbor Suzanne did it."

"And?"

"And she didn't do it. And the real killer is still out there. And maybe after me. And it's not random—it has to be somebody I know. And it's not my imagination. And you have to call Campbell and see what's going on. He's railroading an innocent person. Somebody needs to solve this crime. Preferably somebody with a badge."

My brother didn't respond.

"Lance, it's not my imagination."

"It probably is, but I can't do anything anyway. I'm not supposed to have any contact with you—"

"But you never told me why."

"—or anyone on this case. I'm on desk duty. Chief got a call making…allegations about me…"

"What kind of allegations?"

"I'm not supposed to say."

"Tell me. You know I'm not letting this drop. It sounds serious. Is it serious?"

"Yes," he said quietly.

"Tell me. I won't breathe a word. You know I won't."

"Three anonymous calls this week. Maybe from the same person, maybe not. Said I bought booze one night on shift and drove away drinking it. Said I offered to get someone out of a ticket in exchange for a—"

"Don't say it!"

"—sexual favor. And," he took a deep breath, "that I'm covering up for you in the murder of your agent by tainting evidence."

"What evidence? What are they talking about? You haven't done any of that!"

"I know. And I hope Chief knows. But until it's all straightened out, I'm pushing papers and getting coffee." Pause. "Charlee, you can't say anything about this and you can't help me. I'll do what I can to find out about Detective Campbell, but I'm warning you, it won't be much. And you shouldn't get too deep into this either."

"I have to do what I have to do. And you do too. You be careful, Lance. This is your career. Everything you've always worked for."

"You be careful too, Space Case. Everything will be fine, but still. And call Mom. She's worried. But she doesn't know anything about this. Keep it that way."

"Okay."

My mind whirled with questions, finally landing on one: maybe whoever was trying to frame me was also trying to ruin Lance's career. Who did we know who hated us both that much?

I hung up and dialed Mom, almost relieved when she didn't answer. Otherwise I knew I'd start crying or blabbing. "Hi, Mom. Sorry I haven't returned your calls," I said to the voicemail, "but it's been a bit crazy with all this. I'm fine, though. I've got ... Lance and AmyJo and Ozzi. There's nothing you can do from Santa Fe but I'll call you when I have any news. Lance is fine too." I squinched my face, wishing I could grab those words back. She'd see right through that and know he wasn't fine. Mom Radar worked in person, over the phone, and probably in the vacuum of deep space. "Okay, talk to you later."

I fiddled with the phone in my hand. If Lance couldn't help me with Detective Campbell, there was only one other person who could.

Detective Ming-like-the-vase. I hadn't spoken to him since that first day, and I tried to put my finger on why I didn't trust him. That smarmy slicked-back hair, for one thing. But I couldn't come up with anything else.

I called and was put on hold for a long time. It gave me time to rehearse what I wanted to say, for a change. When he finally answered, I said, "Detective Ming? It's Charlee Russo. Can I ask you something?"

"Sure."

"It's about Detective Campbell. When he came over a little while ago—"

"Today?"

"Yes. He brought me coffee this morning and wanted to ask me some more questions."

"I see. Go on."

"It's just ... well, it seems like he's already decided that my neighbor Suzanne Medina is guilty of Melinda's murder, but he hadn't talked to some of the people I've talked to, so it seems like maybe he's jumping the gun a little?"

"You've been talking to people?"

"Um ... yes?"

"Who?"

"Everyone who read my manuscript. Melinda's mechanic. Sheelah's dentist. The photographer for Pleasure Center for Armadillos."

"I see."

*I see* was not a helpful phrase right now. I wasn't even sure he did see. "Detective Ming, I don't want to tell either of you how to do your job, but in my opinion, based on what I've seen and what he's told me, Detective Campbell is not being thorough in his investigation, and I'm worried that he's zeroed in on an innocent person and that the real killer may go free."

"Are you making a complaint against Detective Campbell?"

"No, of course not." Was I? Allegations like this could jam him up just like the ones against Lance. I didn't want that hanging on my conscience. "No, no official complaint. But can you just check into things and make sure he's going by the book?"

"Miss Russo, Detective Campbell has been on the job for a very long time. He has solved many a murder and sent lots of bad guys to prison. He knows what he's doing."

"Of course he does. But he's also really close to retirement and he told me about his last case that the DA threw out. He said he worked hard on it but they declined to pursue it. Isn't it possible that left a bad taste in his mouth? And since this will probably be his last case, isn't it possible he's cutting corners so he won't feel so invested if they decline to pursue this one too?"

"Those are some pretty heavy-duty allegations, and I certainly hope you haven't voiced them anywhere else. I suggest you let Detective Campbell do his job—"

"That's the point! I don't think he is."

"If you're not going to make an official complaint, I think this conversation is over. Good day, Miss Russo."

My mind wandered back through my conversation with Campbell that morning. Was Ming right? Was Campbell doing a good job? A doubt-spiral slowly pulled me down, like a slo-mo undersea whirlpool. Before it lugged me all the way down, though, I kicked and fought my way back to the surface.

Campbell wasn't doing his job. Suzanne didn't kill Melinda. My determination to figure it out strengthened.

Ming didn't see at all.

# Twenty

More weird dreams and continued poor sleep plagued me all night. This time, I dreamed a gigantic *Denver Post* knocked on my door and swallowed me whole, cackling and rattling its pages like a hurricane. I woke up sweating, shaking, and longing for Ozzi.

When I heard the huge Sunday paper thump against my front door, almost four hours after it was due, I retrieved it. The storm had blown in with a vengeance and covered everything with at least a foot of heavy, wet snow. In places, the wind had drifted it to mid-thigh. The summer-like blue sky belied the arctic air. No wonder the paper was late.

There hadn't been any articles the past few days with my name mentioned, and I hoped the same held true today.

I tore the paper from its orange plastic sleeve, pulling out the front section and flattening it on my kitchen table. Hope was a fickle thing, and it didn't take long to find a new article about me. Front page. Below the fold. This time it was illustrated with a graphic my publisher had put together for my last book tour—my photo centered above my newest release, *Pursued to Death*, with the dates and locations of my official signings in each corner. I'd hated that poster then, and I especially hated it now. They say all publicity is good publicity, but that can't be true. I thought about the phone call with Penn & Powell's attorney and my stomach lurched. My career was probably over anyway.

I read the article.

*Embezzlement Investigation Continues*. Most of it was my bio and career information, pulled verbatim from my website. Then a recap of Melinda's murder—still no mention of the mercury—and a reiteration of the royalty dispute already reported. Then a wildly inflated income bracket for me. I wish. And then, just like Jonathan Crier had promised, a lot of vague non-news, all attributed to anonymous sources.

I folded the paper and shoved away from the table to have a nice, self-indulgent cry in the shower.

My phone was dead—again—so I plugged it into the charger and texted AmyJo. She jumped at the chance to meet me at Espresso Yourself. I didn't feel guilty asking her to drive on a day like this; she loved challenging her enormous pickup in deep snow. I guess that's what happens when your brothers teach you to drive around the farm when you're eleven.

Personally, driving in weather like this scared me more than whatever bogeyman might be out to kill me. I had no control when driving on snow or ice, but at least when walking around, I could keep my guard up and have a modicum of control even on a snowy day like this. Plus, there was a bottomless cup of coffee and scrumptious non-walnut-y pastry waiting for me. Maybe two.

Forty minutes later, hair dried, wearing clean jeans, a funky sweater, and tall boots over my jeans, I felt presentable enough to leave my apartment. I'd also pep-talked myself that walking to the coffee shop wasn't likely to get me murdered. I wasn't convinced, but again, I hoped luck was with me.

I slid my phone and the newspaper into my messenger bag, bundled up, and set out for Espresso Yourself. Maybe I could find out if they'd had any recent break-ins.

It would have been faster to cut through the apartment's parking lot and move between the cars, but I'd seen enough movies to know that was a bad idea, pep talk or not. In fact, in one of my novels—*Fragments of Fear*—there was a chloroform abduction in a crowded parking lot. So I opted to tromp along the wide, curving sidewalk all the way around, wishing the maintenance crew had begun their snow removal on this side of the complex.

The pedestrian gate on the south side of the complex stood open. I remembered the shadows yesterday when Detective Campbell left. I glanced around and saw nobody, yet there were footprints in the snow. There were only two sets: mine and another that disappeared just past the gate and over the snowy grass. Glancing into my bag, I pretended to search for something, but behind my sunglasses, I cut my eyes toward the disappearing tracks. There were no apartments over there, just some carports and storage units. Easily capable of hiding someone.

I hurried through the gate, fighting with the drifted snow to close it behind me, but it wouldn't latch. I fiddled with it, trying to make it look like the gate was locked even though I knew the next person through probably wouldn't go to such trouble. I called the management office while I trudged through the snow. They weren't open, so I left a message. "Hi. This is Charlee Russo. The pedestrian gate on the south side is broken. Can you get somebody out here to fix it today? I know it's Sunday, but I pay for a secure building, and this doesn't seem very secure. Thanks." Even though it was a twenty-four-hour number, I wondered if they'd actually get the message today.

The sign for Espresso Yourself beckoned, relaxing me a bit. As I crossed the street, I heard whimpering and froze in the center of the street. No cars. No people. I strained, listening, but heard nothing. Must have been my imagination. I got to the opposite curb and heard it again. A little louder. Coming from the buildings on my right.

Every instinct told me it was a trap and to run into the warmth of the coffee shop for help, but I didn't. It sounded too much like Peter O'Drool. I moved slowly, picking my way across the snowy sidewalk. When the noise stopped, I stopped.

At the edge of a building, I crouched and peeked around the corner. Only the usual alley-way decorations: dumpsters, trash, a broken chair. I crouched there until my thighs burned, about twenty-two seconds. Shaking my head at my overactive imagination, I placed a palm against the wall for balance as I stood.

BAM! Something came at me and knocked me clear to Thursday.

I closed my eyes and flailed. Swung my bag. Kicked. Screeched. I scrambled backward into a snowbank on my already sore butt, bucking and twisting. No hands touched me. No voices spoke. When I felt like I'd settled, I braced myself and opened my eyes to my fate.

Three inches from my face was the mangiest, filthiest, most pathetic looking dog I'd ever seen. Medium-sized, but for all I knew half of that was mud. Staring at me with intense brown eyes. I slowly scooted backward in the snow. The dog took two steps toward me. Silently stalking.

"Shit," I whispered to myself.

The dog sat.

We stared at each other. It repeated the whimpering sound I'd heard earlier.

"What's the matter..." I bent to have a look-see. "Girl?" I held out my gloved hand for her to sniff. She placed her paw in it instead. I held out my other hand. She shook it too.

"C'mere."

She came closer.

Often during big snowstorms, dogs use drifted snow to climb over backyard fences and escape into the world. I felt around her neck for any collar or tags. Nothing. "What's your name?"

She cocked her head.

"Are you hungry?"

She cocked it again.

I rubbed the sides of her face with some snow and revealed a caramel-colored coat. "Where do you live? Why are you out here?"

She cocked her head twice more.

I suddenly felt ridiculous trying to have a conversation with a dog. Using the wall and the dog's head for support, I stood and brushed the snow off my butt. If I had to fall again, I was thankful to do it in a fluffy snow bank this time. Nothing felt any worse than it had when I woke up this morning, so I flung the strap of the messenger bag across my chest. The dog startled, ears back, and raced behind the dumpster.

"I'm sorry! Come back. It's okay." I crouched and she peeked out, taking tentative steps toward me. I held out my hand and she barrelled toward me, again stopping three inches from my face.

I straightened up and looked around. Behind us was the sandwich-board sign on the sidewalk in front of Espresso Yourself. Handwritten in green marker was the invitation, *Come on in! It's warm in here. The coffee is hot and the customers are cool.* I'd seen other dogs inside. Probably very much against health codes, but as long as the dogs behaved, nobody seemed to care.

I looked down at the dog and she looked up at me. Her tail flicked side to side, brushing the snow, but just a little at the tip, as if she didn't want to hope for too much.

"Come on. Your prayers are answered. I'll introduce you to Lavar and Tuttle." I hoped their generous spirit extended to filthy dogs and midlist mystery authors skewered in the press for a murder they didn't commit.

As I pulled open the door to swoon-worthy aromas of coffee, cinnamon, and sweet frosted delights, the dog hurried to a far corner. She turned three times and then settled in atop the heat register, nose buried in her tail, making herself right at home.

Waiting my turn behind two other customers, I drifted away on the hum of conversation and the delectable aromas until I heard Tuttle holler from the back, "Sweet baby Jesus! They doubled our blueberry butter braid order. Maybe now we won't run out."

"Charlee? The usual?"

Fingers snapped in my face.

"Girl, where you at?"

"Sorry, Lavar."

"That's okay. You got a lot on your mind. Nasty business, that." He poured my coffee. "Still prayin' for you. Even signed you up for a prayer bomb at church this morning."

"A prayer bomb?"

"Yes'm. E'rebody prays for you at the same time. Whole congregation." He pronounced it con-GREEEE-gation. "So if you feel the Spirit of the Lord at 4:15 this afternoon, you'll know why."

"That's sweet. Thanks, but wouldn't that be more of a prayer balloon, if it's going—" I jerked my head upward.

Lavar followed my eyes and crossed himself. "I guess it's both. Prayers go up and blessings come down." He plucked a plastic-wrapped muffin from the display and held it up.

"Can I have one of those blueberry butter braids? And a bacon mini quiche." I dug for my wallet but he waved me away.

"You got enough troubles."

"You read today's paper, I take it."

He pressed a lid on the coffee and handed it to me, leaning close. "Had to. Told that reporter I'd only talk if he mentioned Espresso Yourself. Sumbitch never said a word." He forced an extra quiche into my hand, tipping his chin toward the dog. "Nasty business," he repeated. "Seems like somebody's out to crucify you."

I sighed and thanked him, making way for the next customer. Suddenly the coffee shop seemed less friendly. If my pals would sell me out for a shout-out in the newspaper, what would my enemies do?

I pulled out a chair at a table near the dog. She opened one eye as if to say, *We okay here?* I unwrapped one of the quiches and broke off a piece. I held it down and she delicately plucked it from my fingers. I unfolded a paper napkin and placed it near her, plopping the rest of the quiche onto it. She cocked her head. If she were a person she would have placed a hand over her powdered bosom and exclaimed in a Southern drawl, "I do declare! Is this for little ol' me?"

She nibbled at the quiche, clearly hungry but remembering her manners even so.

I was less polite, inhaling my butter braid in three bites.

I opened up the *Denver Post* again, avoiding the article about me on the front page. I just wanted some quality time to commune with my coffee and my newspaper. It's not too much to ask. I leafed through the pages, getting caught up with the mundane and the horrific. So many times when I was reading an article I couldn't help but think about the people involved. When they woke up they'd thought it was a regular day, like most of the other days in their life. But then a car slammed into them. Or they won the lottery. Or their business burned to the ground. Or they received a Nobel Prize.

Or they were murdered.

Or they were accused of murder.

I shook my head, trying to get back to my quality time with my coffee and paper. Just a regular Sunday, like all the others in my life. Even last Sunday. A lifetime ago. I sipped and turned pages, reading articles I normally wouldn't just to keep my mind off my own troubles.

I gave the dog the second quiche, then stood to get her some water. Lavar used a damp cloth to wipe the counter.

"Can I get her a cup with some water?" I asked.

"Sure. When'd you get her?" Lavar filled a cup.

"About three minutes before we walked in here."

He raised an eyebrow and handed me the cup.

"Yeah, she was around the corner whimpering. No collar." I looked back at the dog, watching while she licked the floor around the napkin and then settled back in, nose to tail.

"Aren't you in those apartments?" Lavar asked.

"Yep."

"Do they allow pets?"

"Nope. Not anymore."

"Hmm."

"Indeed." I had no idea what I was going to do about the dog, but while there were no customers around I wanted to ask Lavar about any break-ins. I wasn't sure how to bring it up, though. *I know this is none of my business, and I've been in the paper recently for criminal acts, but how secure is your business?* Probably not like that. *So, I have this friend who likes to steal books…* Not like that either. Maybe I'll have to rethink it.

"Thanks for the water." I picked up the cup from the counter and moved toward my table.

Lavar said, "You know, maybe we could use a dog around here."

I turned back.

He walked to the café doors that separated the kitchen and office area from the customer area. "Hey, King Tut! Double-time it out here."

Tuttle came in wiping his hands on a towel. He smiled at me, then immediately pursed his lips. "Hey, Charlee."

"Hey, Tut."

Lavar draped one arm around his beefy shoulders and leaned his head close. "Look at the customer on the floor over there."

Tuttle snapped up his head. "On the—?"

Lavar pointed at the dog. "Can I keep her?"

"Did she follow you home from school?"

"No. But Charlee rescued her from a sad and lonely life on the mean streets and can't keep her in her apartment."

Tuttle looked between me, Lavar, and the dog about four thousand times before saying, "Sure. We could use a ... dog around the place."

I caught Lavar shooting Tuttle a look. Had he almost said "guard dog"?

I laid a trap. "I'm not sure how good a guard dog she'll be. She came right up to me even though she was scared and cold."

"Anything's better than nothing," Tuttle said. "We've had ... some trouble."

"Tut! Shh." Lavar peered around the coffee shop.

"What?" *Tell me all about the break-in, boys, so I can corroborate Suzanne's alibi.*

"It's nothing." Lavar waved at Tuttle. "He be jumping at shadows."

Tuttle leaned close and whispered, "I think we have a ghost."

"Do tell."

"Nothing specific, but stuff seems to be moved around some mornings when I come in. Books shelved wrong, chairs moved, stuff missing. That kind of thing."

Lavar rolled his eyes. "It's jus' his imagination."

"Don't you track inventory? Can't you tell if something's been stolen?" I asked.

Lavar shrugged. "We don't have what you'd call a *system*." He used air quotes.

"So, if someone broke in and stole your books, you'd never know it?"

"If they stole all of them, I bet we'd figure it out."

Tuttle nodded. "Probably."

Oy vey. No slam-dunk corroboration of Suzanne's alibi, but definitely tipping the scale closer. I leaned toward them and whispered, "You need more than a dog, boys," before delivering the water to their new dog.

I held it low enough so she could drink. "Found you a home but didn't lock down the alibi," I muttered. In baseball when you bat .500, it's considered off-the-charts successful, but here it felt an awful lot like failure. When she finished drinking, I rubbed her velvety ears. "But I'll get to see you whenever I want, so that's something." The dog closed her eyes and leaned into the ear rub. I wondered how she'd found herself out in the world. Clearly she'd been trained and loved by someone.

"Lavar? Tut?" I waited while they turned toward me. "You should take her to the shelter or a vet and have her checked for a microchip. Someone might be missing this one."

"We were just talking about that. She needs a bath, too," Tuttle said.

At the word "bath," the dog scrabbled on the linoleum, toenails looking for purchase as she tried to push herself further into the corner. I reached down to rub her ears again. "Not this minute, sweetie. Relax."

She did, but eyed Tuttle suspiciously.

I went back to my newspaper and coffee. I turned pages in the *Lifestyles* section until I came to a full-page spread with photos of well-dressed local philanthropists posing in front of, and sometimes with, zoo animals. There was one of the Channel Nine news anchors each holding a ferret. An elephant hugging the governor with its trunk. Balding John Elway flanked by two enormous football players struggling to hold the ends of a huge snake draped around his neck. Jake

Jabs with a tiger cub, perhaps one of his own. And last but not least, Kell, holding hands with a chimpanzee. I smiled. When did this fundraiser happen? Why hadn't Kell mentioned it?

I read the blurb at the top of the page. Last Sunday night. Oh, that was why. Because the next critique meeting was when all hell broke loose. I looked at more of the photos but didn't recognize anyone else. Until I got to the last one.

Melinda and her husband smiling at the camera, a colorful parrot perched on his shoulder.

She and Kell were at the same party, the night before she was murdered. And he didn't think to tell us that?

# Twenty-One

swirled the dregs of my coffee and stared at the photo of Melinda, all angles and sharp features visible in an elegant strapless gown. Henry, softer, with his rounder face, wore an impeccably tailored suit that showed off his perfect V-shaped torso. This had been her very last party and she didn't even know it. Weird to see her reincarnated like this, and looking so happy. I tried to think of when I'd really seen Melinda happy. Getting book deals made her happy. Rejecting bad authors made her happy. A perfectly cooked rib-eye steak made her happy. Her zippy little car made her happy. But then I was stumped. Was she happy? I didn't know.

Were any of us really happy? I tried to think what people would assume about my life after I was dead. They'd know coffee made me happy. And movies. And lasagne. And writing, at least up until recently.

I studied Melinda and Henry again. The closer I examined the photo, the less happy she seemed. She smiled straight ahead at the camera, even though her handsome husband was gazing at the huge red-yellow-and-blue parrot sitting on his shoulder. And they weren't even standing that close together. No touching, arms by their sides.

I studied the photos of the other women at the event. Each one wore the same perfect smile. Not too toothy, not big enough to create wrinkles. Their public smile.

The one Melinda flashed for the camera too.

Henry was clearly more captivated by the parrot than by his wife, but was that normal? They'd been married a long time and he probably didn't have a parrot on his shoulder for very much of it. The only thing I really knew about Henry was that women looked at him like he was a diamond necklace and they wanted to wear him. And that he was going to be my new agent, whether I liked it or not. He was holding me to the letter of my contract despite the circumstances. He was clearly a tough businessman, despite his love for tropical birds at the zoo.

With a jolt, I remembered that Kell had said he was on the red-eye returning from Chicago last Monday. How could he have been at a fancy fundraiser in Denver Sunday night, then fly home from Chicago early Monday morning?

My tremor intensified and I wrapped both hands around my coffee. I really needed to connect with his secretary to confirm he was on that flight. But even if she verified it, why would he have made such a quick a trip? It made no sense. I checked the article for the date of the fundraiser again. Yep, last Sunday.

The music in Espresso Yourself had changed from Irving Berlin to Cole Porter and I listened to a haunting arrangement of "Night and Day." AmyJo still hadn't arrived, and I considered calling her. Instead I called Kell.

I got right to the point. "You and Melinda were at the same fundraiser for the zoo the night before she died and you didn't tell me?"

"Were we? Half of Denver supports the zoo," Kell replied. "I don't know about Melinda, but I'm on a million nonprofit boards. I don't do anything, just throw money at them and show up to their parties. Presumably it's the same for her and her husband." Kell corrected himself. "Was the same."

"Do you know her husband?"

"I don't think so." Kell spoke to someone in the background. "Hey, Charlee, I've got to go. Is that all you wanted?"

Is that all I wanted? Hmm. No. I wanted a fully stocked refrigerator. I wanted my royalty payments higher. I wanted the police to arrest the murderer so I could get on with my life. I wanted Kell not to be a murderer. "Just one more thing. You went to Chicago after that party and came home barely a few hours later?"

It took him a moment longer than was reasonable to reply. When he did, his voice had a somber tone. "Yes, Charlee. I did. I had to." He cleared his throat. "I'll see you tomorrow."

I clicked away but toyed with the phone until it went dark. The first notes of "You're the Top" wafted through the coffee shop along with the image of my mom singing it to me as she brushed and braided my hair into pigtails. I drifted on the clouds of nostalgia until the song ended. I thought about calling my mom, but I knew it would be a bad idea to talk to her in public. Meltdown potential was too high.

I reached down to rub the dog's soft ears again. I straightened when AmyJo plunked herself at the table.

"Goalie spit, it's cold out there."

"It must be, if it makes you use such foul language."

She pulled off her gloves and unswaddled the 9,000-foot-long scarf around her neck, piling it in a heap on top of the newspaper. "Doing your crossword?"

"Nope." I turned the paper so she could see the photo of Melinda and Henry, but kept to myself the fact that the Sunday crosswords were simply too difficult for me.

She read the caption on the photo and her face fell. "That was her last party."

I nodded, then pointed at the photo of Kell. She studied it, then glanced up at me. "He was there, too?"

"Yeah, but he says he didn't even realize it."

"Do you believe him?" AmyJo struggled out of her knee-length puffy coat and draped it on the back of her chair, apologizing way too much to the man behind her.

"I don't know. Why would he lie?"

AmyJo leaned in conspiratorially. "Why wouldn't he?" My raised eyebrows and tilted head had apparently stirred up her conspiracy theories. She glanced around the coffee shop and whispered, "Maybe he and Melinda had a lovers' spat."

I wasn't sure why, but I leaned in too and whispered back, "They were lovers?"

"I don't know. But it makes sense."

"It makes no sense." I sat back in my chair. "Kell's so nice and she's so … not. Like a panda cub dating a razor blade. Can't picture it. But even so, you think he'd kill her? Could a kitten slay a dragon?"

"If the kitten was rich enough, he could hire someone to slay the dragon for him."

"But why?"

AmyJo played Connect the Dots with some coffee stains on the table. "To prove he's not a kitten? To get some real-life experience to change his milders into thrillers?"

I thought about our critique group conversations involving the early drafts of *Mercury Rising*. Kell had loved the murder scene, even

214

when it wasn't polished. But did he love it because of the writing or because it was just the information he needed?

"I don't know what to think, Ames."

"Me neither. But why would he keep it a secret that they were both there?"

"Maybe he really didn't know. Maybe these fancy events are huge and you don't get the chance to mingle. Maybe you just waltz in, drop off your enormous donation, eat a crab puff, then get your picture taken. Bing-bang-boom. He said he didn't know her husband, so maybe he really doesn't know her either."

"Maybe." AmyJo waved her fingers at Tuttle. "But wasn't he flying back from Chicago that night?"

As I relayed Kell's opaque explanation, Tuttle picked his way through the crowd with a coffeepot and an empty cup, which he set down in front of AmyJo.

"Hey, darlin'." He pecked her cheek, then filled our cups. "Can't chat. These folks need caffeine like a buzzard needs roadkill."

"Eww," she said as he moved away, glad-handing and refilling mugs. She took a sip and made happy noises.

I leaned on the table, chin in my palm. "I'll check into Kell's alibi of being on that red-eye. If he can lie about the fundraiser, he could certainly lie about that."

"Who else besides Kell is still on your list?"

"Einstein, Heinrich, Henry, Melinda—" When AmyJo looked at me askance, I added, "Melinda was on antidepressants. Far-fetched, but maybe she killed herself."

"Very far-fetched. And Henry?"

"Husbands are prime suspects. Didn't you tell me that? Maybe he was having an affair."

"Maybe." She blew across the top of her cup. "And Einstein and Heinrich?"

"I don't know. They're avoiding me. When I was on campus the other night, I swear Einstein looked me right in the eye, then raced away in the opposite direction. And, get this, Jenica told me Heinrich knows my brother because of some police problem at the high school a few years back." I stuck my face in my cup to avoid saying anything more about Lance.

"That's it!" AmyJo spoke loudly enough that people turned to stare. Quieter, she added, "Heinrich is framing you to get revenge on Lance."

"That doesn't make much sense." I hoped I sounded more confident than I felt. "I have the feeling that Lance already got in some kind of trouble over it. Jenica said there was a hearing Heinrich testified at."

"What does Lance say about it?"

I chose my words carefully so nothing could slip and hurt Lance. "Never asked him. The fact that he's never mentioned it must mean he doesn't want to talk about it. I'm sure it was nothing. They let him keep being a cop, after all."

"I guess."

AmyJo sipped her coffee while I played with the crumbs on my plate. Finally, she pushed her cup away and proclaimed, "Nobody in our critique group could have killed Melinda." She brushed her hands together as if that were the final dispensation of the case.

"There is one more suspect." I told her about what Suzanne had been up to, ending with, "I'm eighty-five percent sure she's innocent, but I need to be a hundred percent. What are you doing late tonight?"

AmyJo clapped her hands. "Going undercover?"

"Wanna come over now and make a surveillance plan?" I lowered my voice. "Theoretically, tonight's the night Suzanne breaks into this place. We can see if she goes all cat burglar in here. I can bribe you with cookies and banana bread." Nope, I'd given both of those to Suzanne. "Correction. I can bribe you with smushed brownies."

"You sure know how to sweet-talk guests. I'll pull the truck around front." It wasn't until she'd gathered her coat, scarf, and gloves in her arms that AmyJo saw the stray dog on the floor. "Friend of yours?"

"Nah, just met her earlier. Thought we'd share a snack."

AmyJo picked her way through the tables, holding her bundle of winter wear over her head. The end of the scarf came loose and brushed across the heads of everyone she passed.

I cleared our table but left the newspaper in a neat pile for someone else to peruse. On second thought, I dug through the pile to keep the sections with the articles about myself and the zoo fundraiser, then straightened the pile again.

Lavar and Tuttle were busy with customers, so I decided not to say goodbye. The place was packed now, all the tables full both on the café side and the bookstore side, plus people perched on the ledge in front of the window. I planned my route: try to slide by a table of six people clustered around a table for four, or backtrack past a couple with a toddler in a highchair?

I chose the highchair, but hadn't seen the enormous diaper bag on the floor. While the dad worked at shoving it under the table with his foot, I felt a hand on my shoulder.

A voice whispered in my ear, "I've got a gun."

Without thinking, I jammed the highchair forward toward the dad and scrambled behind it, pushing chairs, people, and tables out of my way until I reached the counter. I forced my way in front of the customer who was ordering.

"Charlee! What the hell?" Tuttle said.

"He's got a gun!" I whispered. I pointed at a man holding my newspaper.

Before Tuttle could react, the man called over the din. "Are you done? Can I have your newspaper?"

Relief and humiliation flooded my core. I nodded weakly and gave an apologetic smile to the couple trying to comfort their now-screaming toddler. Hanging my head so my hair covered my face, I slipped away from the counter and hurried toward the door before I misunderstood anyone else.

Glancing at the dog on my way out, I was a bit hurt she hadn't even woken up. Some watchdog.

# Twenty-Two

As I expected, AmyJo took advantage of the non-existent traffic and wild amount of snow, gunning her truck around the block back to my apartment. In the passenger seat, I gripped the strap with my right hand and braced myself with my other hand on the dashboard, hoping I wouldn't hurt my wrist again. AmyJo gleefully slid around corners and headed toward an area in the far corner of the complex parking lot without any cars, where she could perform a reckless series of doughnuts. I closed my eyes and hoped she'd take pity on me.

"Woohoo!" She did a little dance with her shoulders. "Isn't this a hoot?"

"No. Can we be done yet?" I opened one eye.

"Spoilsport." She slammed on the brakes, fishtailed, and slid into a perfectly executed finale, the nose of the truck pointing directly at my apartment building. It was a move that would make any stunt driver bow down in solidarity. Or so she said.

She coasted closer to the building and pulled into an empty spot between two compact cars. Without crampons, carabiners, or a Sherpa to guide me, I rappelled from the summit of Mount Chevrolet until I'd descended far enough to distinguish the tiny car next to me.

AmyJo regarded me with bemusement, as she did every time I tried to free-climb out of her truck.

"I have to go slow or I'll get the bends," I explained.

"I think that's only when you come up too fast. And in the ocean."

As we approached my building, I saw that the maintenance crew still hadn't made it this far with their plowing. There were several sets of footprints on the sidewalk and leading up to my door. I held out my arm to block AmyJo, trying to determine if the footprints all belonged to me. I moved my right foot as far away from my body as I could before tamping it into some virgin snow. I compared the print to the ones heading toward my door.

They weren't all mine.

AmyJo started to say something but I put my finger to my lips, then felt for my keys. When I had them, I mouthed the word "Run!" and we raced for my door. I jammed the key into the lock and slammed the door behind us, breathing hard.

We barely got our coats off before someone knocked. Again, I put my finger to my lips, then tiptoed to the peephole.

Ozzi. I released a hysterical giggle and so did AmyJo. I opened the door.

He flashed his dazzling smile, shaming every toothpaste commercial ever created. "Hey, beautiful. Can I come in?"

I stepped aside and waved him in, afraid to speak for fear I'd embarrass myself in my relief.

"Hi, AmyJo," he said.

AmyJo kept giggling. I rolled my eyes at her, forgetting that she hadn't been jumping at shadows all week.

Ozzi carried two big reusable grocery bags into the kitchen. We followed him. He set the bags down, then stepped forward to kiss me. I took a half-step back and he returned to the bags, not appearing to take offense.

"I noticed your car hasn't moved all week and I figured you were running low on supplies," he said.

He began opening cabinets and the refrigerator, expertly placing everything in its rightful place. I caught AmyJo's eye and she caught the hint to leave the kitchen.

"Actually, I've been out a lot," I said. "And I have an assigned space. Remember?"

"I know. But I needed something to say, right? Some piece of perfect dialogue?"

I watched him work while I tried to sort out my feelings for him and our relationship. Yes, he'd rebuffed my booty call and then pretty much accused me of killing Melinda, but I recalled accusing him of the same thing. And his sister. I'd accused lots of people of murder that week, at least in my thoughts. Was that such a bad thing? How else would I figure out what had happened? We'd both said some things we probably shouldn't have, and man-oh-man, was he trying hard to make up. Calls, texts, flowers, and now a full refrigerator?

"Thanks for this."

He leaned out from behind the refrigerator door. "You're welcome." He finished emptying one bag, folded it, and started on the other. "Now for the good stuff."

Apparently he knew I needed healthy stuff as well as comfort food because this second bag was brimming with all the things I loved. A half-gallon of ice cream, Fig Newtons, chocolate mini-donuts, a variety pack of crackers with an enormous block of cheese, cinnamon raisin bread, a pound of butter, the protein bars I liked, pancake mix, and real maple syrup.

And coffee. Glorious, marvelous coffee.

How could I stay mad after all that?

He folded the bag and leaned against the sink. "How are you? Getting any sleep?"

I leaned on the doorjamb, suddenly self-conscious and shy. "Not really." My thumbnail became fascinating to me and I studied it. "So, you hacked my computer ... "

"Did you like that? I worked really hard on it."

I looked up and saw him smiling at me.

"Oz ... how did you ... what did you—"

"If you're asking if I did anything illegal, I can assure you I did not. And you should be more careful with your passwords."

"I'm going to ask you something that might make you mad, but I have to know—"

"There's a red X up in the corner of the animation. Just click it away and your desktop comes back."

"Yeah, I already figured that out." I hoped AmyJo wasn't eaves-dropping. "It's not that. Did you hack into Melinda's computer? You didn't actually answer me before, when we were fighting."

"No!" He pushed away from the sink and stood straight, fists balled. "Why would I? What for?"

"To figure out my royalty problem, like I said."

He ran a hand through his perfectly tousled hair. "Charlee, I would never do anything like that. You've gotta know me better than that."

"You thought I killed my agent."

He slumped against the sink again and looked at the floor. "That was stupid of me. I was so stunned by the news, and then you didn't

222

call. I didn't know what to think." He raised his head and looked me in the eye. "I know you didn't do it."

Just as I was about to rush him for a sorely missed kiss and hug, there was a wild, insistent banging at my door. I jumped. Ozzi must have seen the fear in my eyes because he pushed past me and ran to the peephole. He turned toward me as he opened the door.

"It's just Sheelah."

She hurried in, taking her gloves off. "Well, thanks, Ozzi. Nice to see you, too."

"I just meant—"

"I know. I'm kidding. I'm here to whisk Charlee to a movie and away from her misery for a while." She clapped her hands at me. "Hurry up, chop-chop. We only have forty-five minutes if we want to make the next show."

I didn't move.

"C'mon, it's that one you've been wanting to see." When I still didn't move, she said in a sing-song voice, "Ryan Gosling."

When AmyJo came out of the bathroom and saw Sheelah standing in my living room, a grimace flashed across her face and then disappeared just as quickly, like it physically hurt her to see Sheelah there. Jealousy is a weird thing. Couldn't I have two friends? This was too much to deal with.

"Hi, AmyJo," Sheelah said. Her grin had morphed to a grimace too.

AmyJo mumbled a greeting.

"C'mon, Charlee. Today's the first day in a week my tooth doesn't hurt so I want to celebrate." Sheelah tipped her head toward Ozzi. "I guess you two made up?"

"We were about to," I said with exasperation. "AmyJo, why don't you and Sheelah go to the movies?"

AmyJo looked like I'd asked her to strip naked and recite the complete works of Shakespeare while performing a tarantella.

Sheelah said, "Um, well, I ... "

Ozzi walked over to me and planted a soft kiss on my mouth. Delicious. Then he gently pushed me away. "Go to the movies. Take your mind off things. Go out with your friends, get a good night's sleep. We'll have a real date tomorrow night. I'll make reservations someplace nice. Okay?"

I looked from him to AmyJo and Sheelah, both looking so hopeful. "Okay," I finally conceded with a sigh. "But you two need to take me to lunch first."

Sheelah flirted shamelessly with the teenage ticket seller and scored us Early Bird pricing, even though after eating lunch and driving to the theater it was almost 3:00, long past the cutoff. Then she waltzed over to the concession area and wrangled us three free popcorns and a box of Junior Mints, my first love. I laughed at her antics and willingly accepted the candy, but when I offered some to AmyJo, she shot me an annoyed smile and turned away.

I ate all the candy and most of my popcorn but couldn't concentrate on the film. I checked the time at 4:13 and remembered that Lavar and his con-greee-gation would be sending out their prayer bomb in two minutes. I braced myself against the Spirit of the Lord that would soon be cascading upon me, but only felt popcorn hitting the back of my head. I've heard God works in mysterious ways, but I doubted his medium was whole grains. I disentangled a kernel from my hair and glared backward. Another one hit me. Then another.

AmyJo went full Mama Grizzly and stormed up the aisle to confront three teenage boys sitting next to two girls. Clearly they were not as interested in Ryan Gosling as the rest of the audience. Sheelah and I watched wide-eyed as she slid into their row, facing them. The boys retreated as far as their seatbacks allowed. AmyJo bent at the waist. "If one more piece of popcorn goes anywhere near my friend's head, or anyone else's head, or anywhere that's not your mouth, I will personally come back here and shove every last kernel right up your ... noses. Do I make myself clear?"

In the dark theater, the whites of the boys' eyes shone so much brighter.

"Do I?"

They nodded.

She sidestepped back to the aisle, with a parting two-fingered *I'm keeping my eye on you* gesture.

When she sat down, Sheelah and I gaped at her.

AmyJo shrugged. "What?"

"Nothing," I said quickly. "Thanks."

Sheelah leaned forward and nodded her head. "Wow. Impressive."

Even though sitting on the barely upholstered seat was killing my tailbone, I turned my attention back to the screen, remembering too late about the group prayer. Nobody wanted to bless me, I figured. The movie had been a complete bust, too. While the rest of the audience sat transfixed by cinematic storytelling, I'd run through my list of remaining suspects in a continuous loop in my head, still coming up with no answers.

After the movie, Sheelah dropped us back at my apartment and AmyJo promised to be back later for our surveillance on Suzanne. I went inside, made some of the glorious coffee Ozzi brought, and opened the Fig Newtons. I texted him. *Come over?*

He replied immediately. *Made plans with my mom. Afterward?*

Probably for the best. I was sure to blurt out something I shouldn't about what was going on with Lance. Plus, I didn't want to explain my plans for Suzanne. I knew he wouldn't approve.

*That's okay. You were right. I should get some sleep tonight. See you to-morrow. oxox.*

I texted him again. *Quick question. Is it crazy hard to change time-stamps on the posts on a message board?*

*Almost impossible. Why?*

*Triple checking Q's alibi. Thanks. Say hi to your mom for me.*

*Will do. oxox*

I munched the soft, sticky cookies while reading my Yellow Tablet of Suspicion, even though I already knew exactly what it said. For one thing, complete blanks for both Einstein and Heinrich. I reached for my phone and dialed Heinrich. I must have tried calling him fifteen times over the last week. Maybe this time was the charm. I called his landline instead of his cell so he couldn't dodge my call unless he had Caller ID. While I waited for him to answer, I pictured him sitting in an easy chair chomping on a cigar.

Glancing over at the postcard of the two stylized couples I'd picked up at the art museum on Thursday, I realized that Heinrich was the reason why the two paintings on it felt so familiar. The man in each couple had a cigar parked between his lips.

"*Ja.*"

"Heinrich, it's Charlee."

"What's the matter?" His voice sounded worried.

"Nothing's the matter. I just wanted to ask you something, since you keep dodging my calls."

"*Ja.*"

*Ja*, he's been dodging my calls, or *Ja*, go ahead and ask? I chose the latter. "Why did you miss critique group the day Melinda Walter was killed?"

The silence stretched from here to Lichtenstein. "Heinrich? You still there?"

When he replied, I wished it had stretched farther. I could hear the anger in his voice, even though he fought to control it.

"You have no right to ask me this question. Shame on you." He also spoke a German paragraph, which might have only been one word. I guessed at the English translation from the way he spat it out, and I was glad it wasn't in English.

His stonewalling frustrated and angered me. "If you think you can punish my brother through me, you've got another thing coming," I snapped. "Lance made a rookie mistake, but you've got to let it go. I don't know everything that happened, but none of your kids were hurt. And I don't need this right now on top of everything else."

The longer the silence, the more I expected a stream of furious German expletives from him. Instead I heard laughter. "That *dummkopf* was your brother?"

"Still is."

"*Gott* save Denver. Thought he'd be fired by now."

"He's a good cop," I said angrily. "Why do you want to hurt him?"

"I don't." Heinrich sounded baffled. "I don't want to deal with him, but—"

Now I was baffled, too. "You're not trying to get revenge all these years later through me?" As I said it, I realized how truly ridiculous I sounded.

"You watch too much TV."

I wanted to tell him it was AmyJo's theory, so technically she might be the one who watched too much TV. But maybe now he'd be ready to give me an alibi. I'd made him laugh, after all. I didn't care any longer why he hadn't come to the critique group meeting, so I asked the more important question: "Do you have an alibi for when Melinda was murdered? Sunday night until Monday morning?"

"None of your business!"

"Is too!"

"Is not!"

Heinrich hung up before I could ask why he was being so secretive about his whereabouts. And why would it make him so angry at me? Surely he understood why I had to ask. Unless he had no alibi. But wouldn't he make one up if he was the killer and I came sniffing around?

No meaningful insights came to me, so I refocused on my list and tapped my pen on the pad of paper. Because I'd made up with Ozzi—even though we hadn't consummated our reconciliation—I decided to make nice with his sister, too, and perhaps get some answers. That old *get more flies with honey* thing, although why anyone wanted more flies had always puzzled me.

When Bubbles answered, I said, "I need to apologize to you for our last conversation. I didn't mean to accuse you of killing Melinda."

She must have heard from Ozzi that we'd reconciled, so she accepted my apology graciously.

We made a little small talk, and then I said, "Hey, I've been thinking. I'm not doing a whole lot of writing of my own these days, so I wanted to pay you back for reading and critiquing my manuscripts. I'd be happy to read something you've written and offer some feedback if you'd like."

"That's generous, Charlee, but I don't have anything. I don't actually write. I thought you knew that."

"You don't? Then why were you so insistent—er, excited when Oz introduced us?"

She laughed. "It's embarrassing, but I felt a bit like a fangirl. I'd never met a real author before."

"So you're not a wannabe writer?"

"Nope. I wanted to be one of your first readers because it seems so glamorous and exciting."

My turn to laugh. "Glamorous? Really?"

"Well, yeah. Until the cops came to question me."

# Twenty-Three

*W*hile waiting for AmyJo to come over, I finished the entire pot of coffee and twiddled my thumbs. She finally showed up a little before eleven, dressed all in black: sweatpants, sweatshirt, shoes, muffler around her neck. She also sported a black ski mask pushed up so it was just a hat, and she'd smudged her face with charcoal or something.

"Geez, Ames, we're not heading for the trenches on the Western Front," I whispered.

"So sue me," she whispered back. "I wanted to be prepared for my first stakeout. Why are we whispering?"

"Suzanne can hear every word we say over here."

"Everything? What about when you and Ozzi—"

"Yes. Everything."

We gave dual full-body shudders.

She eyeballed my outfit of jeans, boots, and Simpsons T-shirt. "Is that what you're wearing?"

I looked down. "Seems so."

"Not very"—she waved at her own clothes—"black." She dug in her purse. "At least rub this stuff on your face."

"Nope. But I will wear my black coat, if that'll make you happy."

"Hey, it's your surveillance. Speaking of which, I've been thinking. If she breaks into the bookstore tonight, how do you know she's not just doing it for show? You know, to prove her alibi to you."

I stared at AmyJo like Peter O'Drool might stare at an algebra book.

"Didn't cross your mind?"

I shook my head.

"No matter. We'll be able to tell by her body language and demeanor and stuff."

I doubted that was true, but I'd already polished off a pot of coffee so I wasn't sleeping anyway. We might as well blunder our way through this.

AmyJo turned off the lights and we waited at either end of the couch in my dark apartment.

It wasn't long before AmyJo was softly snoring and I'd felt my way to the bathroom to pee twice. The second time I decided to flush. I wasn't even sure Suzanne was home.

But as I settled back into my corner of the couch, I heard her front door open and close. I felt my way to the window and watched her walk across the parking lot. I craned my neck the opposite direction and saw her car parked in its regular spot, next to mine in the carport.

"AmyJo, this is it. Eagle has flown."

"Mfff?"

"I think Suzanne is headed for the coffee shop. Let's go."

We tiptoed to my car—as much as one can tiptoe through a foot of snow—and peeked over the hood until Suzanne reached the pedestrian gate. As soon as she went through it, we got in the car. I kept my distance, rolling up and down the lanes in the parking lot. As soon as

Suzanne had crossed the street, clearly heading to Espresso Yourself, I cut my lights, circled around to the other end of the alley, and watched her fiddle with the handle until the door opened.

"She's done this before," I whispered.

When Suzanne disappeared into the shop, AmyJo and I exited the Kia, being careful not to slam the doors. We scurried to the back of the coffee shop, but there were no windows.

AmyJo twisted the doorknob even though I shook my head so hard I hurt my neck.

"Locked," she whispered.

We made our way to the front, where I was suddenly overly aware of how we, meaning AmyJo, looked. A bit too conspicuous to be out for a midnight stroll in the frigid night air. I scurried to the front window with AmyJo right behind me. I pulled her arm until we were both squatting there, eyeballs even with the bottom of the window. I squinted into the dark but saw nothing unusual. The tables and chairs on the right side of the coffee shop were neatly stacked upside down, four to a table. Straight ahead there was no activity behind the counter, no lights on in the kitchen. In the book area on the left, everything was quiet as well. Overstuffed chairs sagged like bored employees lounging in a break room. Magazines and books piled on most of the end tables scattered around. A couple boxes with books peeking over the top waited for shelf space near the stacks.

AmyJo and I locked questioning eyes.

When I turned back to the window, though, two brown eyes and a hairy face peered out at me, head cocked. I hit the deck and pulled AmyJo to the sidewalk with me.

"The dog," I mouthed.

She responded by silently reenacting Edvard Munch's *The Scream*.

I placed my hand on the top of her head to keep her down while I raised myself up millimeter by millimeter. When my eyes reached the bottom of the window again, the dog's nose was pressed to the windowpane and her tail was wagging. She stared at me, beginning to get excited about this game, and then suddenly disappeared.

AmyJo struggled against the weight of my hand and I let go. She slowly raised herself to the level of the window and we both watched as Suzanne expertly managed the microwave in the dim light. The red light beeped and went out. She pulled something out and placed it on the floor, where the dog gobbled it up and then raised her head, expectations high. Suzanne gave her something else, which also disappeared, but this time, even though the pooch clearly wanted more, Suzanne instead patted her back and gave her some loving scritches before heading back behind the counter. She pulled a small loaf from cellophane, placed it on a baking sheet, and popped it in the toaster oven.

"Blueberry butter braid," I whispered.

"Your sense of smell is remarkable," AmyJo whispered back.

"No ... never mind."

We watched until Suzanne had pulled the pastry from the oven, sliced and placed it on a plate, and then headed to one of the small tables near the comfy chairs. She manhandled a big wingback chair so its back was to the window, then carried the table with the pastry on it so it was angled in front and to the right of the chair. She knew the correct angles to hide herself from view if anyone wandered down the sidewalk and peered inside, yet also remain in a pool of light cast by the street light so she would be able to read.

Ducking behind the bookshelves, she returned with three books. Two she dropped to the floor. She picked up the pastries and they disappeared, along with her, into the recesses of the wingback chair.

Yes, she'd done this before.

We watched for a while longer, but the only movement was the dog sprawling on the rug near Suzanne, clearly content with the snack and her company.

AmyJo ducked down and leaned her back against the wall. "How long do we have to do this? I'm freezing."

"Me too." I jerked my head toward the alley.

As soon as we climbed in the car and the relative warmth hit me, I had to pee again. "Dammit." I glanced around the dark alley. No good venues. "Let's talk this through and distract me from my bladder."

"Turn on the heater."

"She'll hear."

"Maybe, but she'll just think it's a car. And I doubt she'd hear it from all the way back here."

I turned the key. "But only until it gets warm."

"Fine."

"Now, talk."

"About what?"

"Suzanne. This." I fluttered both hands. "My investigation."

"Don't be cranky," AmyJo replied. "It's not my fault you have a bladder the size of a lentil. Let's see … Even if she is doing this for your benefit tonight, it's obvious she knows her way around in there."

"True. And I still can't come up with a motive for her. She has no connection to Melinda."

"That you know of." AmyJo yawned.

"That I know of." The car was warm enough, so I turned off the engine. Silence settled over us.

"Really? That's all we have to talk about?" I finally said.

AmyJo didn't answer. Her mouth hung open and she was fast asleep.

My full concentration was on my bladder now, and it was demanding some sort of action. I contemplated driving home and running inside to pee, but what if Suzanne left the coffee shop while we were gone? I had to pretend I was camping. Urban camping, since there were no trees nearby. I hated the idea, but I quietly shut the door of the Kia and picked my way through the snow toward the dumpster.

I held my breath, undid my jeans, and squatted. Relief was momentary because I heard a disembodied voice say, "You nasty, girl. Git yo'self outta here."

There is a physiological truth—at least for me—that once I begin peeing, I must finish the task completely. If I hold my breath, I must start breathing again soon. If I tense my muscles, I must start moving again soon. And now that I'd done all three, all systems had to, pardon the pun, go again.

So they did, even though the homeless person I'd disturbed began to stir. Something whacked at me, occasionally landing a soft blow on my arm or back. I was completely at his or her mercy, with my pants around my ankles at two in the morning in the snow in an alley behind a coffee shop.

I finished as quickly as possible, doing up my pants while on the move away from the voice and the dumpster.

"You white girls. Drink too much, then pee in somebody's house." A scraggly-bearded face wrapped tight in a blanket scowled at me in the faint moonlight. He waved a small hand-towel, which is what he must have been hitting me with.

My terror faded a bit, especially since I had my hand on the car door. "You're absolutely right, sir, that was terribly rude of me," I stage-whispered. I dove into the car and slammed the door shut behind me, locking it. I was gasping and panting, more scared now than when I was out there.

"My brain must have been so relieved, ugh, to pee that I didn't—" I turned to AmyJo. Sound asleep. I looked back toward the dumpster.

It was clear, I could see now, that it was makeshift housing: cardboard lean-to supported on one side by a full shopping cart, tarps and blankets cascading down to the asphalt. I was happy to see that I'd peed on a slight incline, directed away from his shelter.

I dug in my purse and pulled out a twenty and a protein bar. I tiptoed back to the man, whispering, "Hey, I want you to have this. I'm sorry for disturbing you."

He poked his head out and yelled, "Why do you keep bothering me? Leave me alone!"

I dropped the cash and weighed it down with the bar, then hurried back to my car again, hoping Suzanne wouldn't hear. It might not matter if she saw me, but if she was playing some game and using me as one of her pawns, then I should at least try to keep the upper hand.

But I'd rather both she and the homeless guy simply went back to what they were doing and ignore me.

I stared at the dumpster, finally seeing a hand reach out to snatch my apology from the snow.

AmyJo continued to snore while I tried to figure out exactly what I was doing out there. Suddenly I jolted and realized I'd fallen asleep, too. I had no idea if it had been a few minutes or an hour. Everything looked the same in the alley.

"Ames, wake up." I poked her in the upper arm until she stirred.

She straightened and groaned. "Ow. This is not a comfy car."

"I don't think they ever marketed it as a bed." I rearranged myself. "I fell asleep too. I'm going back around to see if she's still in there."

I snuck around the front of the building, again hoping nobody would see me. All this time and I still hadn't come up with a plausible reason for skulking around in the middle of the night. Not very good for a fiction writer.

I crawled the last few feet on my hands and knees until I was directly under the window again, glad that Lavar and Tuttle had cleared the sidewalk. I inched my way upward and peeked in. The furniture was still where Suzanne had moved it, but no dog sprawled on the rug. I raised myself higher. Still nothing. I stood mashed against the wall at the intersection where it met the window and craned my neck, sure I'd missed her.

I was about to give up and go home when the dog, tail wagging madly, raced over to the window. I ducked out of sight in case Suzanne was still inside. I peeked and saw the dog race across the bookstore side of the shop. She stopped in front of Suzanne, who held a medium-sized Amazon box. I watched her pluck titles off the shelves, read the backs, and replace most of them haphazardly until she'd dropped three books into the box. She slid the box onto the front counter and went around behind, returning with three cellophane-wrapped butter braids that she plopped into the top of the box. Squatting down, she rubbed and petted the dog, then picked up her box and headed toward the back of the shop.

I raced around the side of the building, slipping and sliding the whole way. When the Kia came into view, I frantically waved at AmyJo to move the car so Suzanne wouldn't see.

The car wasn't moving. When I got closer, I saw AmyJo wasn't either. Her mouth hung open and I knew she was snoring.

If Suzanne came out and looked to her left, she'd see my car at the other end of the alley. If she saw the car, she'd know I was there. If she knew I was there—oh my gosh! Did she lure me to the coffee shop for some reason? I dove back to the front of the building. I didn't know what to do. AmyJo was in the car. Was she in danger if Suzanne saw her? I peeked around the corner but didn't see Suzanne. I took some long strides toward the car.

I froze and let loose with a strangled cry when a pool of light spilled out the back door of the coffee shop. But it didn't quite reach me.

The homeless man stuck his head out of his tent. He stared at me, then the Kia, then Suzanne emerging from the shop, juggling her box. He scrambled out of his tarps and blankets. I stepped backward, ready to flee.

He shuffled toward Suzanne. "Hey," he said to her.

She jumped. "Oh, hey, Daryl. I didn't think you'd be out here tonight. You should be in the shelter."

"Hate the shelter. You know dat." He maneuvered around, taking the box from her and making sure her back was to me while she locked up Espresso Yourself. "That my blueberry?" He pulled out one of the butter braids. While they discussed the merits of blueberry over strawberry, he looked at me from over her shoulder and tipped his head toward the Kia. He turned back to Suzanne. "I ever tell you the story of when I was a professor?"

I took the opportunity to make a dash for the Kia after giving him a wave of gratitude. I slid into the car and before the engine had barely turned over, I reversed out of the alley.

AmyJo bolted upright, and I told her what had happened as I careened home. We raced for my regular parking spot and then for my front door. I kept the lights off and peeked out from behind the curtains. Less than ten minutes later, Suzanne trudged through the snow carrying the box.

A few minutes later we heard her front door open and close, and we collapsed on the couch.

My respite was short-lived, however, because about as soon as I finished peeing—again—I heard Suzanne's front door open. The clock on my microwave said 3:27. AmyJo was curled up on the couch with an afghan my mom had crocheted. I peeked out and saw Suzanne heading for her car wearing a parka and hospital green scrubs. She carried something in a plastic grocery bag.

I left AmyJo sleeping, and as soon as Suzanne was out of sight I hurried to the Kia and followed her. Since there were no cars on the road, I had to stay far back so she wouldn't see me. I was afraid I'd lose her.

She stayed on the main streets, not always performing precisely legal stops. It was clear she was going someplace she'd been before, hopefully the Senior Center so I could verify that part of her alibi. After about twenty minutes, I almost cheered as she pulled into the Senior Center parking lot and parked in a space close to the front door. She got out and took the bag with her.

I waited in my car for a bit, trying to decide what I should do. Now my surveillance had taken a turn into the unknown. I watched while she left the main building through a side door and entered another building. Lights flickered on, so it seemed she was staying there for a bit. Or at least I hoped so.

I parked on the other side of the lot and hurried into the main building. The door to the vestibule was open but the one into the rest of the building was locked. When I jiggled the door, a nurse looked up. She smiled and waved and then the buzzer sounded, allowing me in.

She took a few steps toward me, then frowned. "You're not the temp nurse."

I shook my head. "No, sorry."

She crossed her arms. "What can I do for you at four a.m., then?"

"I don't want to bother you, but I work weird hours and this was the only time I could stop in and inquire about this place for my, um, mother." My mom was barely AARP age, but nobody needed to know that. And if I told Mom about my inquiries, then it wasn't really a lie, right?

"Sure. You want a tour? I'm Sandy, by the way."

I sidestepped the introduction. "No, don't go to any trouble. I've just wondered what exactly this place is. A friend told me recently it was residential. And you have twenty-four-hour staff? I just saw someone come in who looked like she was going to work."

"Yeah, Suzanne. Oh, and she brought a butter braid. I just heated it up. You want some?"

"No, thanks. Is this a regular shift for her?"

"Yep, she's here four to noon every Monday." Sandy took a bite of pastry. "We have a large staff, mostly home health care workers trying to get some extra work. But we have some RNs on every shift too. You say your mom is looking to move to a facility?"

I nodded.

"I'm sorry I can't help you. We don't have any openings. I can put her on a waiting list, though."

"I'll talk to her about it. But I'm curious about that lady I saw come in just now. You say she comes in every Monday at this time?"

"Never misses."

"Never?"

"Not in the three years I've been here. She's as dependable as the day is long. Makes my job a dream. And the residents love her. She's always bringing us books and goodies. A real sweetheart." Sandy took another bite. "You sure you don't want a tour? It's no trouble. I can introduce you to Suzanne if you'd like."

"No, I won't bother you anymore. If there's no room, there's no room. Thanks anyway."

As I drove home, I knew Suzanne's alibi was not airtight, but it was tighter than many of the other suspects. Why was Detective Campbell so convinced of her guilt? My gut told me she wasn't Melinda's killer. Why didn't his?

# Twenty-Four

AmyJo flung open my door as soon as I reached it. She grabbed my sleeve and yanked me inside. When I regained my balance she pointed at the clock. "In four minutes I was going to call 911."

"I'm sorry. I didn't have time to leave you a note."

"Where were you?"

"Almost as soon as we got home, Suzanne left again so I followed her." I told AmyJo the rest of the story. I finished with, "I know she didn't do it. I'm crossing her off my list for good. I don't care what Detective Campbell says."

"But he's the one who gets to say."

"I know. So the only way I can keep Suzanne from going away for a very long time is to find the real killer."

"Who's left on the list? Go one by one and let's talk it through."

I crossed to the table and picked up the notepad. "Melinda."

"No way. Nobody kills themselves like that."

I nodded and sighed. "You're right. I've been avoiding crossing her off because if she killed herself, then nobody I know is a murderer." I put a line through Melinda's name as well as Suzanne's.

"Next."

"Melinda's husband, Henry."

AmyJo stared at a spot over my shoulder. "Don't you think if there was a whiff of guilt with Henry, the police would be all over him?"

"Yeah, but still, he has a pretty strong motive. I didn't think so until I went over there and he was all ready to step into Melinda's business. In less than two days he'd brought himself up to speed on all her clients."

"Maybe he'd always been involved in the agency."

"Maybe."

"And doesn't he run a successful business himself?"

"Seems like it. But maybe he ran up a ton of gambling debts or has a drug problem or spent a fortune on strippers."

"Don't you think the police would have found all that out by now?"

I nodded, glumly. "But if it can't be Melinda killing herself, I want it to be him. Everyone else is a friend of mine."

"I know." AmyJo was quiet a moment. "Plus, you said yourself that Detective Campbell was apparently taking the easiest path. Seems like the husband would be way easier than Suzanne. I've gotta believe they don't have anything on Henry." She gestured at the list. "Who's next?"

"Kell, of course." I checked the time. "In a couple hours I can try to catch his secretary and verify his alibi, before she gets busy." I looked at AmyJo and pursed my lips. "The only others are Heinrich and Einstein."

"I already told you what I think about Einstein. And Heinrich has that thing with your brother."

I rubbed my eyes. "I can't think straight. I've got to get some sleep. I'm going to sleep until dinnertime."

"You can't. It's Monday ... critique group day."

"I don't wanna."

"You have to. It'll give you an opportunity to cross off Heinrich, Kell, and Einstein. Maybe."

I knew she was right, but that didn't make me any more excited about going. How long had it been since I'd pulled all-nighters? A million years?

"Fine. But I'm taking a nap till it's time to go."

AmyJo grabbed my phone and set an alarm. "I turned the volume all the way up. No excuses."

"Yes, Mom." I ushered her out the door. "See you there."

Two and a half hours later the alarm blared, causing me to launch myself out of bed and flail around the room searching for it. I finally found it propped against my jewelry box where AmyJo left it.

I wasn't rested but I was standing, so I stepped into the shower, where I do my best thinking. I planned how I'd phrase my question about Kell's alibi. I preferred to cross him off before the meeting, if at all possible.

After making coffee and a piece of toast, I looked online for the flights Kell could have taken: one departing sometime after the fundraiser at the zoo Sunday night, the other returning early Monday morning, the day of Melinda's murder. Then I dialed his corporate phone number. I sat at my kitchen table and asked the receptionist to put me through to his office. Instead of using my name, I tried something different this time.

It worked, because instead of the receptionist taking my name and message again, Kell's private secretary answered. "Kell Mooney's office."

I crossed my fingers, hoping I'd remembered the right airline. "I'm calling on behalf of National Airlines. We found a Rolex watch on a recent flight and are checking with all of our first-class passengers to see if they've lost one."

"I'm sorry, but Mr. Mooney isn't in right now."

I gave her the flight information for the Monday morning flight. "Can you confirm he was on that particular flight? If not, then I don't need to bother him."

"Let me check."

While I listened to the hold music, I noticed my tremor was in perfect syncopation with the tune.

The secretary came back. "Yes, he was on that flight."

I took another wild stab. "That's good to hear, but I'm a bit confused, looking at this paperwork. I show that his flight from Denver to Chicago was just six hours earlier. Surely that's incorrect?"

She paused, then said, "No, that's right. He was escorting a minor child."

I loudly shuffled papers. "I don't see a second passenger on his itinerary."

"The child's mother bought the ticket."

"I don't understand."

"It was a spring break trip for the girl to visit her dad in Chicago." The secretary's voice took on a softness. "The mother couldn't take her there because at the last minute Mr. Mooney needed her in London for the company. He felt bad, so he escorted the daughter to Chicago, then flew right home. Never even left the airport. The things he does for his employees. Should I have him call you about the watch?"

"Only if he wants to claim it." I hung up without giving her any contact information. Let her think I was incompetent. But at least I'd been able to confirm Kell's alibi, cross him off my suspect list, and be reminded of what a nice guy he was.

It made it the teensiest bit easier to make the decision to attend my writing group. I bundled my coat around me.

The complex's parking lot was busy at this time on a Monday morning, with all the upwardly mobile young professionals on their way to their upwardly mobile careers. Cars moved in and out of parking spaces, half of them sweeping headlights across the lot, half of them dark. That's what overcast March mornings are like in Colorado. Never quite sure when daylight is.

My fellow residents and I cautiously picked our way over icy spots and snow drifts. With as much snow as we'd had Saturday night, no matter how fastidiously walks got shoveled and parking lots got plowed, no one could get it all. The unlucky commuters without covered spots had to scrape ice from windshields and push off flawless mounds of snow that added almost a foot of height to their cars. They also had to excavate the drifts packed against their tires. As was the habit of most people who lived in snowy climes, nobody thought to allow extra time to do this. There is nothing more karmic—or dangerous—than commuters in a rush who fail to clear the snow from the roof of their car, only to stop suddenly and have it all slide forward onto the windshield, blinding them.

Some of the complex's residents were heading toward Espresso Yourself for their daily grind before attempting their daily grind. At least I assumed they were residents. Some, perhaps, were in the midst of their walk of shame after an ill-advised one-night stand. I studied the bodies hunched against the morning chill, snow squeaking and crunching under their feet, to see if I could detect any of these unfortunate souls. But everyone looked the same—cold, cranky, and pressed for time.

The wind had kicked up and I clutched my celery-colored travel mug of coffee as I stepped from the sidewalk, head lowered against the blowing snow. I heard an engine rev to my left and raised my eyes. An SUV swerved around me at the last second. I stopped, hoping the driver saw my hands-up apology for not watching for traffic, expecting something similar in return. The car sped up, the driver never even glancing my way.

No acknowledgment at all? And he'd sped up. If this was one of my novels, I would make it clear the driver had purposely tried to run me down. But was this like fiction? Lately the line had kept blurring for me. Had someone just tried to run me down? Same as in Dave and Veta's neighborhood? I thought back to all my jumping at shadows and noises. There were explanations for all of them: Suzanne popping up unexpectedly, rabbits, that stray dog, maintenance men in the complex, jokers writing messages in the dirt on my car. All logical. My imagination was playing tricks on me and working overtime. But none of that eased the knot in my stomach. I hurried to my car, head on a swivel.

Even though I'd parked only a couple of hours earlier, my windows had iced over. I tramped around to the passenger side to ferret out the long-handled scraper I kept under the seat. I opened the door and saw the gigantic trash bag of Goodwill donations. Still there. I could drop it off on my way. I situated my coffee in the cupholder and then thrashed around, feeling with one arm for the scraper. I found it, dragged it out, and dropped my messenger bag on the floor in front of the Goodwill donation.

I worked up a sweat scraping, then slipped into the driver's seat. I took a sip of coffee and checked the clock on the dashboard. No time to swing by Goodwill after all, despite not having to stop at Espresso Yourself this morning thanks to Ozzi's gift of ground coffee from the grocery store.

I backed out of my parking space, bumping over the icy moguls I hoped would melt before July, and waited for a steady line of cars to pass. I took the opportunity to sip until a good Samaritan in a dark SUV finally took pity and waved me in. I hurriedly replaced my travel mug in the cupholder and swung into the lane, at the same time trying to bring up my hand in thanks. I hoped they saw, since I couldn't see through their tinted windows.

As I drove through the parking lot, I thought about the SUV that had almost hit me. The driver didn't really try to run me down, did he? We'd never made eye contact, so maybe he never actually saw me. Ozzi got that way sometimes when he was thinking about work. More than once I'd seen him let a perfectly chilled beer get warm while he stared into space, mulling some computer problem. When he returned to earth, he hadn't even realized he'd been gone. Maybe this snowy morning was like that for some other driver. I hoped they would snap out of it before something bad happened.

The streets became more and more major, yet not completely plowed, as I made my way through Aurora. I loved the diversity of the area. Colorado is very Caucasian, but my zip code had bodegas, Asian markets, authentic ethnic restaurants of every stripe, and was home to a huge Muslim population. Of course, it also had a notorious red-light district, plenty of meth houses, and an often large and unruly homeless population.

I wondered again about Daryl living behind Espresso Yourself. What was his story? How long had he been there? How long had he and Suzanne been friendly? What could I do for him?

I reached the freeway on-ramp and began to slow down sooner than I normally would because of the icy road. I crawled to a stop behind three cars at the ramp meter. I sipped my coffee. Still half-full, and I was halfway to Kell's. Perfect. More cars lined up behind me.

Was that the same SUV that almost hit me? I peered through my rear-view mirror but couldn't tell. Probably not. SUV is the new black, I decided. The new fashion vehicle. They were everywhere and probably all had those tinted windows.

The meter turned green for me and I gently stepped on the gas. My rear end fishtailed on the slick pavement. My coffee jostled in the cupholder while I got a rush of adrenaline. The freeway was crowded but flowed smoothly, since people were taking it easy with the road conditions. "Slow and steady wins the race," I reminded myself.

As I glanced back to check the freeway traffic, I saw the SUV behind me. I merged, took control of the lane like I was taught, and glanced behind to change lanes. The SUV was still right behind me. I changed lanes again. So did the SUV.

Almost as soon as I was traveling in my comfort zone—fast, but not overly so, in the fast lane—I came up on a Volkswagen driving well below the speed limit, even for the imperfect conditions. Texas plates. Figures. Scared of a little snow. I tapped my brakes but got a tad too close to their rear bumper, to make sure they knew I was there and not entirely happy with their choices this morning.

They didn't seem to care what I thought, so I passed them on the right and slipped back into the fast lane. So did the SUV. Weird. I flashed back to my book *Pursued to Death*, where the killer stalked my poor victim mercilessly until finally running her off the road. But that was set in a rural area, not a busy city freeway. But still. If somebody caused an accident and then sped off, I doubted any of these people would know what had happened. Everyone was in their own little bubble. The SUV was creeping me out, though, always behind me that way.

I increased my speed in the fast lane to pass a Honda traveling in the lane to my right, then eased in front of it, almost equidistant between it and a Subaru hatchback.

The SUV slid in behind the Honda even though the fast lane was clear. I watched to see if they were in the process of easing over toward the exit coming up. Nope. Knuckles white on my steering wheel, I decided to take the exit. I made a last-second dash for it, making other drivers hit their brakes as I stole the merge. I slid across two lanes to the off-ramp.

My coffee flew from the inadequate cupholder and bounced off the bag for Goodwill. The lid flew the opposite direction. "Dammit!" Warmth from the coffee spread over my right knee.

At the bottom of the exit, the light was green at the cross street. Knowing I couldn't stop to make a turn without sliding, I continued straight through, to the on ramp on the other side to get back on the freeway. Smart, I thought. I relaxed my grip on the steering wheel. I'd have to remember this for my next book. I merged back into freeway traffic, which was a bit lighter now, it seemed. I glanced back to change lanes.

The SUV was behind me again.

I peered through my mirror. Was it the same car? My imagination had been working overtime this past week. Was this another example? My eyes darted back and forth between it and the traffic in front of me. It seemed like the same one, but I was heading toward the Stepford suburbs where every soccer mom drove an SUV. I glanced to my left. Blue SUV. In front of it a green one. Two more black ones. Another blue one up ahead to my right.

But none of them with tinted windows like that. My imagination flared and my heart raced. That SUV was definitely following me. My tremor increased with my adrenaline and I gripped the wheel tighter. I made another last-minute, fishtailing dart across traffic to the next exit. It might have been the only time in my life I wished a cop would pull up behind me. I had to swerve to the right around the traffic slowing at Hampden Avenue.

The light was red, but I barely slowed as I turned right, glancing left to look for cars coming through the intersection. The visibility was bad, but I didn't see anyone and prayed it was true. I slid across two lanes and held my breath that any cars coming would see me. A blast of a horn told me they did and were none too happy about it.

If I kept going west, I'd hit University in a few miles. I could take it north, toward Lance's precinct. I was sure there was probably a closer police station, but I knew exactly where Lance's was. And if he was there, even better.

The roads were better plowed on the west side of the city, or perhaps they hadn't received as much snow, and I could see large patches of asphalt. I breathed a bit easier as I dodged through traffic, glad most people were at work or school already. It made it easier to travel. But also easier for a stalker to spot me.

The traffic light ahead changed and cars slowed in front of me. I stepped on the brake but it didn't depress. I wasn't sliding, but I was hurtling toward the cars at full speed. A sedan with a *Baby on Board* sign loomed in front of me. In desperation, I stomped my foot on the brake so hard I thought it would go through the floorboard. I yanked the wheel to the right to avoid a rear-end collision, and barely missed both the sedan and the honking Jeep in the right lane.

Everything was at a standstill at the red light, my car angled across two lanes. I released my white-knuckled grip on my steering wheel and felt around the brake pedal until I found shards of a smashed celery-colored travel mug. I refused to look at the driver of the Jeep, already knowing he was livid, and dropped the plastic pieces on the floor in front of the Goodwill bag.

The light changed and I pulled the rest of the way in front of the Jeep. I drove slowly, still shaky. Glancing around, I didn't see the SUV. I'd lost them.

As I traveled past the businesses on the opposite side of the intersection, a blush crept up my neck even though I was alone in the car. That SUV hadn't been following me. Just a coincidence. My overactive imagination. The stress of the last week. I exhaled slowly, sending up thanks that I hadn't hit anyone but furious at myself, and at that crazy SUV, for terrifying me.

Coming up on University forced a decision. To the right, to Lance's precinct? To the left, to Kell's and the critique group? I checked behind and still didn't see any sign of the SUV.

Left.

I bumped into Kell's driveway ten minutes late.

# Twenty-Five

*W*riting group was a bust. I suffered the acute humiliation of waltzing in with coffee soaked into my right pantleg from knee to ankle. We were all awkward around each other. AmyJo tried to cheerlead us through breakfast, but none of us knew what to say. The weight of the last week smothered us. We gulped down food, then raced through each perfunctory critique and response, no unnecessary words. Even worse, I didn't get to cross Einstein or Heinrich off my list because neither of them showed up.

I returned to my apartment just in time to see a police officer protect Suzanne's head as he guided her into the back of a squad car. The officer glared at me, and then he and his partner got in and drove away. Suzanne stared straight ahead.

I dialed my brother as I raced inside.

Voicemail.

"Lance, when you get this, call me right away. They just arrested Suzanne."

I paced around my apartment trying to figure out what to do or who to call. Suzanne needed me to find the real killer before this went any further. But how?

I grabbed my list of suspects. Einstein, Heinrich, and Henry.

I removed the business card tacked to my kitchen corkboard and dialed the phone. I asked for Detective Ming.

"Campbell."

"Detective Campbell? There's been a mistake. I asked for Detective Ming."

"Who is this?"

I debated hanging up. "It's Charlee Russo. Did you have Suzanne Medina arrested? She didn't kill Melinda Walter."

"Oh?"

"She didn't."

"Then who did?" I heard his chair squeak under his bulk as if he'd put his feet up on his desk.

"Melinda's husband, Henry." I said emphatically.

Campbell barked out an ugly guffaw. "Nope. Airtight alibi."

"Just like Suzanne."

"Oh, that's right," he laughed again. "At your storage unit with you."

"My investigation—"

"Your what?"

"Well, I'm not investigating, per se, but as you can imagine, this has hit me quite close to home, and . . . " If there were such a thing as irritated breathing, I was hearing it on the other end of the phone, so I rushed on. "Everyone who had access to my manuscript had means and opportunity. Some had motive, and I've been trying to ascertain"—*ascertain? I sound like Hercule Poirot*—"who had alibis and who did not."

I held my breath, half expecting him to tell me to sit tight because I was the one without an alibi and I might have lied to a detective and they'd be right over with the handcuffs and the dreaded perp walk.

Instead, Campbell said, "Well, aren't you just the cutest little Miss Marple."

That stung. I was much closer in age to Nancy Drew.

"Okay, I'll bite," he said. "What have you found out? Who have you exonerated? Give me your briefing."

Momentarily flustered that he wanted to hear my thoughts, I searched my notes. I flipped through the pages of the yellow legal pad and tried to read through all the scribblings. "I don't think Melinda killed herself. My boyfriend Ozzi was at work. His sister Bubbles, er, Beulah, spent the night with their mom. Dave and Veta Burr had people over and then went to bed, which I know isn't a good alibi, but really, they didn't have any motive to kill her and their garage door squeaks so loudly you probably could've heard it all the way to Kansas if they left that night, so I crossed them off." I realized I was talking too fast, which might sound like babbling, but if I had his attention even for a minute, I wanted to keep it. Maybe I could even convince him it wasn't Suzanne. "His boss told me Joaquin, that mechanic, had an alibi. And in my critique group, Kell was on a plane from Chicago, Sheelah was in the emergency room and then at her dentist's office, AmyJo was babysitting her nieces, and Jenica won tickets and backstage passes to the Fillmore Theater. Oh, and Cordelia's security system was on all night. And cameras. They show nobody came or went. And Queue Quaid has an alibi too, as you know." I kept quiet about Einstein and Heinrich.

"You've done good work, Miss Marple, but we knew all that within forty-eight hours of the murder."

I wanted to say *yes, but that's your job*, but I bit my tongue.

"There were other suspects and, as you know, actually an arrest this morning," he added.

It felt like he was playing with me. He was the quarterback and I was the football he was nonchalantly tossing in the air.

"Yes. But I'm trying to tell you, I know for a fact Suzanne Medina didn't kill anyone."

"You know this for a fact, eh?"

"I told you, we were together that night."

"So you did."

"That only leaves Melinda's husband." I wanted to ask about Heinrich and Einstein but couldn't bring myself to do so.

Campbell paused. "We've arrested someone. And it wasn't Henry Walter. Draw your own conclusion."

"But what about—"

"This has been loads of fun, Ms. Russo, but my coffee break is over, so I must—"

"Wait. On that website about Melinda and her rejections, the one Q is the webmaster for, there are a ton of deleted comments that probably describe really nasty things people want—wanted—to do to Melinda." I had a twinge of remorse. "Have you looked into them?"

"Ms. Russo, whether you want to believe it or not, we are good at our jobs over here. Been doing them a long time."

*Maybe so long you're jaded and burned out?*

"But did you?"

"Of course we did. Your manuscript was nowhere to be found on that server. Nobody on the forum read anything about mercury poisoning, at least not from your manuscript."

"Aha! So somebody could have—"

"A good detective doesn't grasp at straws. Miss Marple would know that." He let out a nasty chuckle.

"But—"

"One last time, Ms. Russo. We made an arrest. Goodbye."

*But the person you arrested didn't do it.*

# Twenty-Six

$\mathcal{I}$ stared into the distance for a long time after my conversation with Detective Campbell, finally drawing a line through Henry Walter's name on my suspect list. I fiddled with the pen, trying to picture Suzanne, his suspect, or Einstein or Heinrich, mine, killing Melinda. I couldn't do it.

My new art museum postcard was hanging crooked so I went over to straighten it, accidentally knocking it to the floor. I picked it up and studied it. When I'd brought it home and taped the art mat to it, I'd obscured some of the written description of the exhibit. So instead of reading about the *missing German art*, I simply saw *missing German* and thought of Heinrich.

When I'd first chosen the postcard, both of the reproductions on it seemed to convey jaunty characters from the flapper era. But now, the cigar-smoker in Wilhelm Lachnit's work stared straight at me with black, beady eyes, and his wife seemed indifferent to him, looking away even though they were side by side leaning out the window. In the other work, the one by Hans Christoph, the man was cutting his eyes to the side, decidedly shifty. His spouse's eyes could barely be seen. The man looked like Heinrich, with his round glasses and ever-present cigar.

Was the man in the painting mocking me? I moved the postcard sideways. His eyes didn't follow me like they would in a bad movie, but something still bugged me about it. He totally looked like Heinrich, but was Heinrich married? Had he ever been married? I racked my brain trying to remember if he'd ever said anything about a wife or ex-wife. Or, really, anything about his personal life. I knew he'd been an English teacher—more specifically, Jenica's English teacher, which seemed like it should be significant but I couldn't figure out why. I came up empty on any other facts, which led me again to wonder why Heinrich wouldn't tell me why he'd missed critique group that morning. He was hiding something, but what?

I knew I had to confront him in person, but I stopped and started to leave half a dozen times, each time with a new question, each time plopping onto my bed with a throaty groan. Was it wise for me to confront a potential murderer this way? Was this how I wanted to be dressed when they found my newly murdered body? How was it possible I knew a murderer? Could an English teacher really be a murderer? Should I drag someone with me? Should I call Lance or Detective Campbell or Ming and tell them what I was going to do?

It probably wasn't wise for me to confront Heinrich like this, but I didn't have a choice. Lance couldn't talk to me about it, and the detectives wouldn't talk to me, but I had to help Suzanne. I thought about dragging Ozzi, AmyJo, or Sheelah with me, but I knew they'd try to talk me out of it. And as much as I thought I needed to do this, I was afraid it would be too easy for someone to dissuade me.

I stood and stared at myself in the full-length mirror. "You have to do this, Charlee." I buttoned a red plaid flannel shirt over my comfy jeans and boots.

As a nod to good sense, I left a note addressed to Lance on my kitchen table. Then I used the GPS app on my phone to guide me to Heinrich's house.

I didn't know whether to hope he'd be there or not.

I saw him through the glass on his front door, talking on his kitchen phone. I debated whether to ring the doorbell or not, but my decision was made for me when he turned and saw me. His shoulders slumped and he lowered the phone to his thigh. He finally motioned me in. He was speaking in German but gestured he'd be finished soon, waving me into the living room to wait for him. I walked in and stood there, realizing I could be in the house of a murderer. What in the world was I thinking? I glanced around the room and only saw weapons, like I was in some kind of weird real-life game of Clue. Candlesticks on the mantle. An antique gun—that might not even be an antique—mounted above the mantle. Cords from the window blinds to strangle me. I noted fireplace tools I could lunge for if I needed a weapon. I sidled closer to them.

Through the other doorway, I could see into the kitchen. Knife-block filled with a dozen presumably sharp knives. Kitchen shears on the counter by the sink and, next to it, a tube of Glu-Pocalypse.

"What are you looking for?"

Heinrich came up behind me, making me jump.

"You have Glu-Pocalypse."

He adjusted his eyeglasses, then wiggled his butt. He pulled the unlit cigar from his mouth and sang, "If your force field comes unsealed, if your cup needs to be healed." He paused, trying to remember the jingle. "If your kitchen faucet drips, or upholst'ry got some rips, Glu-Pocalypse! Glu-Pocalypse! Glu-Poc-A-Lypse!" He punctuated the last four syllables by jabbing his cigar into the air. He returned the cigar to his mouth and said, "*Ja*, I have Glu-Pocalypse. Did you come all this way to borrow some?"

I shook my head and he stared, all the while chomping on his cigar.

"I think you know why I'm here, Heinrich." I tried to keep my voice steady and squeak-free.

He continued to stare and then abruptly turned his back on me and stomped out of the living room.

I leaped toward the fireplace, wondering which unseen weapon he was going after. Regardless, my best defense was the poker, which I grabbed in my right hand. I quickly shifted it to my left so I could dig the phone from the pocket of my jeans. I dialed the nine and the one, then switched hands again. The poker needed to be in my dominant hand. I wished I'd left *goodbye forever I love you* notes for my mom and Ozzi.

I also wished I'd never come here. Easily remedied. I was heading for the front door just as Heinrich came back in the living room. In his hand he held, not a weapon, but a photo album.

He saw me clutching the poker and my pre-dialed phone and shook his head. He spoke in German. When I didn't react, he translated. "You've got some balls."

He took a step toward me. I raised the fireplace poker, but he moved to the couch. If he was worried by my defensive pose, he didn't show it. He sat with the photo album on his lap.

"I'll tell you what I told the police."

"Was it the truth? Because that's all I'm in the mood for right now."

"*Ja*." He flipped pages of the album until he found a particular photo. He turned the book and motioned me to sit next to him.

I brought the poker with me and perched myself at the edge of the couch, poised to jump up if necessary.

He pointed to a teenage girl in a photo. She had long dark hair and matching dark eyes that I knew any man would lose himself in.

I cut my eyes at him, but he shook his head. "Nothing like that. I teach ESL, and Francesca here, one of my students, was in Mercy Hospital having a baby. I was there with her."

My bewildered brain rattled. Heinrich had never spoken of teaching English to foreigners and he sure as hell didn't seem like the nurturing Lamaze type. On the other hand, he would love telling a helpless pregnant girl what to do and when to do it. I didn't know what to think so I simply stared at him, mouth open, trying to keep my brain from rattling too loud.

Heinrich flipped through more pages of the album, smiling at the faces staring back at him.

I stood and waved my hand vaguely at the photo album. "So that's what you told the police?"

"Ja."

I returned the fireplace poker to the holder.

"Is it the truth?"

"Of course." Heinrich closed the album and placed it on an end table.

His landline in the kitchen rang. It startled me so much I almost pressed the final digit in my aborted 911 call. I erased the numbers as Heinrich headed to the kitchen. He called over his shoulder, "Close the door behind you."

I was thrilled to take his hint. I shoved my phone in my pocket and rooted around in my bag for my keys. As I searched my bag I heard Heinrich's voice, but the only word I recognized was "Thaddeus."

Had Einstein called him? It seemed Einstein was the only suspect left on my list.

I finally located my keys. When I got to the car, I locked the doors, drove half a block, parked, and then looked up the number for Mercy Hospital. I asked to be connected to the maternity ward. I knew Francesca would be long gone, but maybe one of the nurses had been on duty last Sunday night. The nurse who answered the phone was in fact on duty but didn't remember any German man with any of the patients. She asked two other nurses, but nobody remembered him.

Heinrich's alibi didn't hold up. Not even a little.

I whipped out of his neighborhood, finding a familiar arterial that I knew led to the interstate. I got off at University and drove all around, searching for a parking place on the DU campus.

I gave up and circled back to park illegally at a nearby Wendy's. If I was still alive after this, I'd buy something as rental on their parking place. I didn't really think Einstein would murder me with so many people around, so I set my taste buds for a single with cheese, small fries, and a chocolate Frosty. And a probable parking ticket.

I hurried toward campus, again asking everyone where the physics building was. Again, nobody knew for sure. Some pointed left, some pointed right, but I just kept barreling through until I finally found someone who seemed like they actually knew. They pointed to a familiar-looking building and I went up to the third floor—this time with much less pain. I hoped that would remain the case.

I flung open the door marked *Thaddeus Eichhorn* without knocking, quivering with adrenaline. I saw Einstein in his tiny office, sitting at a desk piled high with papers.

"Where were you the night before Melinda was killed?" I blurted.

"*Schtupping* Heinrich."

I yelped and felt the adrenaline drain from my body, leaving me to slump against the doorjamb. When I recovered a bit, I managed to squeak out, "Heinrich said he was at Mercy Hospital."

Einstein stood up, said "Excuse me," and walked to the opposite wall, which he faced. His back was to me, but he was only about five feet away. He pulled his cell from his pocket and started whispering into it.

I strained to hear, but I couldn't make out any of the conversation. I glanced around the office for any weapons he might use on me, or any I could use to defend myself. My only defense would seem to be hefting stacks of papers at him. And, of course, the enormous piles he'd have to step over to get to me would surely slow him down. I kept my hand on the door knob.

Suddenly he whirled around and was in front of me before I could even react. I gasped and my hand flew to my chest. Einstein jabbed the phone at me. I took it from him.

"Hello?" I asked tentatively.

"Yes, I teach ESL. Yes, one of my students had a baby. No, I wasn't at the hospital. Yes, I was *schtupping* Thaddeus." Click.

Heinrich and Einstein were lovers? Why was this such a big deal? Men in their sixties finding love was something to celebrate, not hide. Wasn't it? I opened and shut my mouth four thousand times. Handed Einstein's phone back without a word. He started to speak, then changed his mind. I started to speak, then changed my mind. He sat back down at his desk.

"You and Heinrich?"

A tiny smile cracked the edges of his mouth. Maybe he was glad I'd found out.

"Why the secrecy? What's the big deal?"

"No big deal. Just … personal."

"Are you worried about your job? Because there are laws—"

"No laws against parents."

"Aren't Heinrich's parents still in Germany?"

He nodded.

"Then why—" I remembered how angry Einstein had been when his publisher insisted his author name should be Thaddeus Eichhorn II. "Oh. Your father didn't like you flying your rainbow flag."

"He still doesn't." Einstein fiddled with a pair of eyeglasses on his desk.

"I thought your father was dead."

"To me he is."

I wanted to make him feel better, but this was out of my wheelhouse. "He's just one guy. Surely there are many others who would be happy for the two of you."

Einstein looked up and brightened. "I suppose that's true."

"So why was Heinrich so mad and evasive when I asked him about his alibi if he was with you? I'm no homophobe. Why lie about being at the hospital?"

"He's angry with me, not you. For wanting to keep this a secret."

I stared at him. "That's pretty insightful. You know, for you."

Einstein waved a dismissive hand. "Therapy. So much therapy."

"Well, if the therapy is helping so much, why did you run away from me the other night?"

He wrinkled his brow. "It seemed easier than talking to you."

"Easier for you, maybe."

"Of course for me." He genuinely looked puzzled.

"Of course." I pulled the door shut as I left, flashing him a grin and a wave.

Heinrich and Einstein. Einstein and Heinrich. Who knew?

I made my way back to the Wendy's where I'd ditched my car. I went inside and, suddenly famished, ordered a *double* with cheese, *large* fries, and a chocolate Frosty.

Staring at my plastic tray of food, my hunger vanished. I was glad neither Einstein nor Heinrich was a murderer, but they were the last two on my list. I'd crossed everyone off. I was back to zero. Technically below zero, since Suzanne was in custody and I knew she wasn't guilty. I'd failed. Suzanne would go to prison.

I dunked a couple of sturdy fries in my Frosty and scooped out some ice cream. There was something about combining the sweet with the salty that I liked. Peanut butter and honey. Chocolate-covered pretzels. French fries and ice cream. Not as comforting now, however.

I took two bites of my burger and shoved a few more Frosty-covered fries in my mouth, then dumped everything in the trash.

What I really wanted was a drink. Margarita, wine, beer, ethanol. Didn't care. The day had turned on a weird trajectory I never would have imagined. I was crazy to think I could investigate a murder. I couldn't investigate my way out of a paper bag. I needed to tell the cops about Suzanne's breaking and entering. She'd get in trouble for that, but it would be less trouble than murder. And on TV, at least, everybody gets some sort of plea deal if they help catch the real bad guy. But who was the real bad guy? I needed advice.

I called Ozzi. Voicemail. I texted him. *You busy?* No answer. Probably up to his elbows in computer code.

AmyJo never drank in the middle of the day, so I called Sheelah. "Are you busy? I need to stop by. I just found out something … intense." I didn't want to be so cryptic, but I really wanted to see her face when I told her about Einstein and Heinrich. And, despite their good news, I was afraid everything else I had to say would make me start sobbing right there at a Formica table in the middle of Wendy's.

When I got to Sheelah's, she opened the door and gave me a hug. "How are you?" She ushered me inside. "What's going on?"

"Well, for one thing," I said sarcastically, "I'm investigating the hell out of Melinda's murder."

"Are you?" She motioned me to sit on the couch next to her.

I nodded. "I'm checking everyone's alibi, but—"

Sheelah jumped up and held up one hand, traffic cop style. "Hold that thought. I left the iron on. Be right back."

While I waited, a text came in from Ozzi. He said the place he'd wanted to go for our dinner date was closed and asked me to choose a place. When I tried to tell him which restaurant I preferred, my phone died. I didn't want any kind of drama between us now that we were back on track, so I assessed my options. He wouldn't pick up a text from an unknown number, so I couldn't borrow Sheelah's phone. She was Android and I was iPhone, so I couldn't borrow her charger. But I saw Sheelah's computer and knew I could email him.

"Can I borrow your computer for a sec?" I called, plopping myself on her wheeled desk chair.

She didn't answer but I knew she wouldn't care. I jiggled the mouse and the dark screen lit up, showing the background image of a butterfly emerging from its cocoon behind her desktop files. It took me a minute to figure out which internet browser she used and where it was. As I searched for it, I saw a file marked "Melinda Walter."

"Sweet, she's trying to help me figure it out," I murmured. Curious, I opened the file. Mostly it contained the newspaper articles about Melinda's death, but there was also an image file. I clicked on it.

A mock-up of a prescription label for antibiotics filled the screen.

# *Twenty-Seven*

Sheelah stood in the doorway, holding something behind her back. "I just wanted to email Oz because my ... phone ... died." As I spoke, it dawned on me that the prescription image was one she must have created herself. To support her alibi. "But you had an alibi! I checked it myself," I blurted.

"Bleeding hearts will always rally to your defense if they think your ex-husband is violating his restraining order. That sap at the dentist was happy to lie for me to keep my imaginary ex from finding me."

A sudden chill hit my spine. "Sheelah, what have you done?"

"Something I've been waiting a long time to take care of." Her voice was like gravel.

"Killing Melinda?"

She shrugged indifferently. "Unfortunate by-product."

"Of what?"

"Of my real goal. Ruining your life."

I gasped. "My life? Why?"

"To see you suffer like I did at the hands of your father." She spat out the word like a bad taste.

"My father? What—?"

"God, you're stupid. So unaware." She sneered at me and my blood chilled. "You don't know what happened then, and you don't know what's happening now." She took a step toward me. I stood and rolled the chair between us, gripping the back tightly.

"Have you talked to your brother lately?" she asked.

I shook my head without thinking. Immediately regretted it. I thought about the note I'd left for Lance telling him I was on my way to Heinrich's. "But he'll be looking for me," I said. I backed away, slowly making my way toward the door, rolling the chair as I went.

"Not today he won't. You'll be long gone before anyone knows you're missing. Especially him. It's amazing what some well-worded anonymous calls can do to a police officer's career."

Goose bumps rose on my arms. "Sheelah, what are you doing? What's going on? What does Lance have to do with anything? Or my dad?" My whiny voice sounded unpleasant and humiliating.

"I told you. Your dad was the cause of all my pain. He got himself killed by his snitch that day, but worse, he got my Hal killed." Her face clouded as she walked toward me. "And my kids were taken from me."

My mind raced. She was talking about the shoot-out in that strip mall parking lot. What did she have to do with that? Was she there? "My dad would never kill a kid."

"I never said my kids were dead. But because of the shoddy way your dad handled the investigation, he may as well have."

I narrowed my eyes and lowered my voice, keeping the rolling chair between us. "You tell me what happened in that parking lot." If I was going to die, I was going to die knowing the truth. "Everything."

She laughed again. "Sure. You want to know? I'll tell you. My husband was Hal Hollingsway. Ring a bell?"

The name sounded familiar, but I couldn't place it. Until she started humming a tune that I recognized as an advertising jingle. "He was that car guy?"

"Owned dealerships, Executive Director of the Chamber of Commerce, on the school board—"

"I interviewed him for my school paper in middle school."

"So you did."

I frowned. "He wasn't married. Didn't have kids. I remember. I asked." I tried to conjure memories of how this might tie in to my dad back at that time.

Sheelah kept one hand behind her back and put a finger to her grinning lips. "Nobody knew. Nobody knew a lot of things. Like how we made a fortune from runaways."

"You were a pimp?"

She wrinkled her nose. "That's such a vulgar term. Like 'white slaver.' So ugly. I've always preferred 'human trafficker.'"

I couldn't believe what she was telling me. "You were a human trafficker?"

"I was *the* human trafficker." She straightened her posture and smiled. "I was the brains behind the business. Hal was the well-respected frontman. Together we built a huge empire." Her smile vanished. "Until your dad came along and turned that snitch on us. We flipped him back, but then everything went sideways when he grabbed your dad's gun. He even took himself out. My one consolation all these years was that nobody knew he'd been your dad's informant. With the two of them dead, all the suspicion was on your dad. He was in street clothes, dead next to a known criminal and a fine upstanding citizen, his own gun the weapon that killed them all. Everything pointed to him being a dirty cop. I couldn't have staged it any better."

Memories of the day my dad died flooded my sense. The smell of charred hot dogs. Cancelled Fourth of July plans as day turned to night, still no Dad. Melted peach ice cream. Another event ruined because Dad had put his job before his family. He loved his job, even when it meant he let us down. But he was a good cop, a conscientious one. "He wasn't dirty."

"Facts don't matter. Perception matters." Sheelah regarded me with pity, dripping in superiority. "You said yourself there were whispers and innuendo and his fellow officers were forced to attend his funeral while they covered it all up."

My head felt like it might burst. What did I really know about my dad or myself or that day or Sheelah? "So by framing me for killing Melinda, you, what, bring your kids and husband back to life?"

"My kids aren't dead," she snapped. "After Hal died—was murdered—we lost everything. I couldn't get at the money. I had to abandon the kids at a church, change my name, change my life. I'll never see them again."

"Ironic, since that's what you did to other people's children."

A guttural roar exploded from deep inside her. Sheelah hurtled forward, thrusting the pickle jar she held behind her back toward me.

I leaped back, keeping the rolling chair between us.

She unscrewed the lid. There were no pickles. My eyes darted between her face and the jar—I tried to see what was in it but needed to keep aware of her movements as we performed this tango. We were in the middle of her living room. The only thing between me and the front door was a leather recliner. The sun glinted off the contents of the jar.

My stomach turned to jelly and I quivered, releasing the rolling chair and drawing my arms around myself protectively. "Sheelah! Is that...mercury?"

I didn't want to lose what was left of my cool, but events were conspiring against me. I turned into a human windmill trying to get away from her. I shoved the wheeled chair toward her as hard as I could. She sidestepped it, lunging toward me. My elbow hit the jar. The open jar flew into the air and turned end over end, silvery blobs of mercury in a contrail behind it. The mercury landed on the carpet three feet from the recliner. The small beads oozed back together, forming a large blob.

"Don't step in that, Sheelah." I maneuvered around the recliner. "If that blob turns into tiny beads, it'll contaminate your carpet and make us both sick."

"Don't you think I already know that?" She scowled at me from the opposite side of the recliner.

I knew the room was big and well-ventilated, so if the blob stayed big, with less surface area than a bunch of small beads, everything should be okay. I tried to sidestep the mercury and keep Sheelah talking in order to divert her attention. I continued to edge toward the door.

"You really killed Melinda?" I knew in my head that it had to be true, but it wasn't really sinking in despite the circumstances.

"What do you think?" Sheelah screamed, face turning purple, shaking the pickle jar lid at me. She was done bragging and explaining. Now she was beyond reason, completely out of control. A different person than the one I knew. Thought I knew.

By now I'd backed all the way to the front door, Sheelah matching me step for step, less than a foot away. The mercury was still in a big blob about four feet behind her. I reached back and grappled for the knob.

Sheelah's eyes followed my hand. Trying distraction again, I said, "Why did we go to the movies yesterday? You seemed so … so normal."

"I had other plans for us until you invited that simp to join us."

"I thought you wanted to ruin me, not kill me."

She smiled like a jack-o'-lantern. "Death by a thousand cuts. Drive you crazy."

My hand froze against the door. "You made the footprints under my window. You drove those SUVs. You rammed me behind the movie theater."

"God, you're such an idiot. Why would I dirty my hands like that? I was powerful—am powerful. People still owe me favors." She cackled and wistfully closed her eyes, as if recalling an enchanting memory. "Ruining your brother's career was a—"

With her eyes closed, I took the opportunity to yank the door open. But she was still quicker. She slammed it shut again with an open palm. I ducked under her arm. She grabbed at me as I squeaked by her, dodging and weaving just out of her grasp. She let out another roar and dove after me. Her tackle landed me face first with a loud "Ooof!" as the wind was knocked out of me.

I struggled for breath, crawling and kicking away from her.

She held tight to my ankle, dragging me backward. I grabbed for a handhold on the recliner, finding the lever for the footrest. I held tight.

Sheelah's fury seemed to give her super-human strength. She dragged me and the recliner toward the mercury blob. I lost my grip on the chair and flew into the pile of mercury, scattering it in a shower of tiny, deadlier beads. My chest heaved. She scrambled on top of me, sitting on my low back, her knees restraining my arms. She pushed my face into the mercury.

The vapor was in my nose. I tasted metal in my mouth, felt it constricting my lungs. I was dizzy. Sheelah was screaming nonsense.

I summoned all my strength and rolled over, pinning her to the floor. I twisted her head to the side so she felt the effects of the mercury. She tried to shake me off, bucking her body from side to side. I needed to keep her near the mercury while keeping myself away from it. If she was weaker and quit fighting me, I could get us both outside to fresh air and safety. My dizziness was getting worse. I began to doubt I could drag myself across the room and out the door, let alone both of us.

Suddenly she quit bucking. Her mouth went slack.

"Sheelah!" I planted my feet on either side of her and yanked her arms. Dead weight. I squatted and lifted her under her arms. The room spun. My vision narrowed to a pinhole. I wasn't sure where the door was. But I kept dragging her backward, away from the mercury, until I ran into the wall.

My reduced vision swam through a prism of gray and black waves. I felt for the door, knowing that if it was more than arms distance, Sheelah and I would not make it out of this room alive. I couldn't hold her any longer and felt her thud at my feet.

I slapped and banged my hands blindly on the surfaces around me. The knob. I turned it and immediately felt the cool outside air clear my senses a bit. My vision slowly opened up and I saw Sheelah on the floor, ashen, lips blue. I grabbed her arms and pulled her down the two concrete steps leading to the snowy front yard. Right into the amazed face of a woman out walking her dog.

"Call 911," I gasped.

# Twenty-Eight

$\mathcal{L}$ance screamed up in his patrol car while I sat wrapped in a blanket in the back of an ambulance. I wanted to go back into Sheelah's house to get my bag, but the hazmat crew wouldn't let me.

Lance raced over, holding his phone to his ear, nodding. When he reached me, he said, "She's right here, Mom. She's fine."

He held the phone out to me. Tears transformed the scene in Sheelah's yard to a hazy blur when I heard my mother's voice. "Bug, are you really okay?"

"I'm fine, Mom." I swiped at my eyes, trying to remain calm and controlled so she would too. "Little shook up, but the EMTs checked me out and said I'm fine. And now Lance is here, too. I'm fine." I didn't want to lose my composure or scare her, so I said, "They want to talk to me some more. I'll call you later."

"I love you, Bug."

"Love you too, Mom." I handed the phone back to Lance. "Thanks for calling her."

"I called as soon as I heard. How are you?" He turned to the EMTs. "How is she?"

"She'll be fine. Not too much exposure, no prolonged direct contact, and the ventilation was pretty good."

Lance nodded, lips pursed. "And the perp?"

I preempted the EMT's diagnosis. "She'll be fine too. When they had her on the gurney she summoned the strength to say to me, 'I'd tell you to go to hell but I never want to see you again.' Pretty cogent, if you ask me. And a sentiment I share, by the way."

The EMT chuckled. "Yeah, she'll be a handful in jail."

"Campbell and Ming here?" Lance glanced around the scene in Sheelah's front yard, looking for the detectives. Neighbors, cops, medical personnel, hazmat guys, all standing around in clusters. But not Campbell and Ming.

"On their way, apparently. Can I borrow your phone? I need to call Ozzi."

Lance handed it over.

I punched in the number and burst into tears the minute I heard Ozzi's voice. Damn. And I'd been holding it together so well. I returned the phone to Lance and he filled Ozzi in while I tried to rein in my emotions. Then he pocketed the phone and said, "He'll be here in ten minutes."

"He works twenty minutes away."

"Speed limit's just a suggestion some days."

"Call him back and tell him to be careful," I sniffled.

Lance crossed his arms and smirked. "Riiight."

Detectives Campbell and Ming walked up behind Lance and he stepped aside, but he stayed close. Campbell whipped out his notepad. "Tell us everything."

"You mean starting with how I told you Suzanne didn't do it?"

Lance made a noise I couldn't decode. It was either a warning or a choked-back laugh. Probably both. But I was right, plus I was recovering in an ambulance, so I got special dispensation to say I told you so.

Ming winced and rubbed the back of his neck. "Point taken."

"So you know she was innocent."

"She's not stupid, Ms. Russo," Detective Campbell said. "Her attorney met us at the station and she confessed to the breaking and entering. She was off the hook for the murder as soon as we checked in with the owners of Espresso Yourself." He narrowed his eyes and lowered his head, leveling a glare at me. "You, on the other hand, lied to us about your whereabouts that night."

"Only to save Suzanne from being railroaded by you. You were —"

Ming interrupted. "Stand down, both of you. We follow leads no matter where they take us. Some take us further afield than we'd like. But under the circumstances"—he cut his eyes at Campbell—"no charges will be filed against you. And Ms. Medina will be fine. Espresso Yourself isn't pressing charges if she'll come work for them to organize inventory and help upgrade their security. Now tell us exactly what happened here."

Relieved for Suzanne, and myself, I recounted the day's events. They took notes, asked clarifying questions, and made lots of *mm-hmm* noises.

Behind them, I saw Ozzi's Prius pull up, blocking in Lance's police car. He jumped out and, without closing the car door, raced across Sheelah's lawn.

The detectives must have seen my face because they both turned to see what had captured my attention. They parted as I leaped out of the ambulance, throwing the blanket to the EMT inside. Ozzi caught me in his arms and held me while I sobbed. I cried for Melinda, I cried for Sheelah, I cried for my dad, I cried for all the hurt and anger and stress I'd caused and received over the past week.

"Shhh. It's over. It's all over," Ozzi whispered, nuzzling my neck. "Everything's fine."

I took a deep, shuddery breath and kissed him, soft at first, then hard and hungry. I turned toward the detectives and EMTs who were pretending not to stare at us. "Can I go?"

Campbell looked at Ming, who nodded. Then they both looked at the EMTs. "Yeah, she's fine," the medic said. "Take it easy, though, and call the hospital if anything changes."

I snorted. Everything had already changed.

# Twenty-Nine

The next Monday at critique group, I bumped into Kell's driveway five minutes late. I thought I'd allowed myself plenty of time to drink my coffee in the parking lot where my dad was killed and still get to the meeting on time. But I sat too long, staring at the blood stain that had long ago disappeared while considering my reputation, which he'd worried so much about even when I was just a teenager. He was right, of course—all you really had was your reputation.

Melinda Walter would always be remembered as a ruthless bitch. Unless she was remembered for her philanthropy.

Sheelah would always be remembered as a murderer. Unless she was remembered for her skills as a book doctor.

Dad will be remembered for single-handedly dismantling a human trafficking ring. Unless he's remembered for going rogue, not following protocol, and getting himself, his informant, and a local businessman killed.

*And me? What will I be remembered for, Dad?* I couldn't even imagine.

Kell's valet hurried toward me when I pulled up and helped me with the huge balloon bouquet in my backseat. I carried it into the library where my entire group, sans Sheelah, was gathered.

Near the buffet, Kell and Cordelia chatted and sipped from china cups. AmyJo, Jenica, and Einstein sat at the enormous table enjoying breakfast. Heinrich filled his plate at the buffet.

They all turned when I walked in and went to arrange the balloons in the center of the table. Puzzled looks crossed their faces.

Jenica gestured at the bouquet with her fork. "Who made a sale this week?"

"Nobody. These are apology balloons. I'm sorry for suspecting, um, all of you for killing Melinda."

Kell set down his cup and hugged me. "Don't be silly. We would have done the same thing in your place. I guess we all could have been a bit more forthcoming."

"You think?" I asked with a sarcastic smirk.

AmyJo nodded emphatically. "And we thought you might have killed her, too." Nobody spoke. "C'mon. It crossed your minds."

They all looked from one face to the other.

Cordelia broke the silence first. "Okay, fine. It crossed my mind."

"Me too." Jenica said.

"Me three."

"Same here."

"Ja."

I laughed. "Good to know. But in all seriousness, I'm not completely at peace with my thought process or behavior."

Cordelia placed one hand on my forearm. "But everything turned out for the best."

"Fill your plate, Charlee." Kell waved an arm over the buffet table.

I dropped my messenger bag and filled a plate with scrambled eggs, crisp bacon, and raspberry Danish. Heinrich placed a cup of coffee in front of me. As he set it down, he kissed me on the cheek.

"What was that for?" I asked, tilting my head.

He winked at me. "Just felt like it, *liebling.*"

I pointed a piece of bacon across the table. "I still have a question, though, Jenica. Why did you lie about volunteering at the hospital?"

She straightened her spiked collar. "Ruins my image. Plus, Dooley's parents hate me but I still want to visit his little sister whenever her asthma flares up and she gets admitted. So I just take off my Goth and hide in plain sight."

"That's exactly what Sheelah did," I said.

"Don't worry. I'll stay on the right side of the law, ma'am."

"See that you do. I don't want to investigate my friends for murder ever again." I folded the bacon into my mouth.

AmyJo asked, "So Sheelah was the one feeding info to the reporter?"

I nodded, my mouth full.

Einstein asked, "Why didn't the police check Sheelah's alibi and figure out she wasn't where she said she was?"

"According to Lance, they did check. She really did have an appointment for her fake emergency but she convinced the receptionist an ex-husband was stalking her and she had to cancel it. Told an epic story about the ex tracking her everywhere and using all kinds of impersonations—"

"Including cop?" Jenica guessed.

"Including cop. So in a fit of righteous female solidarity, the receptionist lied and said Sheelah was in the dentist's chair when she wasn't. Even got one of her friends to do the same at the ER the night before. She's lucky she didn't get thrown in jail too. But it just goes to show you what a master manipulator Sheelah is."

"How did Sheelah get into Melinda's car to fill it with the mercury?" Kell asked.

I laughed and a bit of egg shot across the table. "Sorry." I pinched it between my fingers and placed it on the side of my plate. "Seems she disguised herself pretty well and flirted with the guard at the gatehouse into Melinda's neighborhood. She told him her car broke down and she was waiting for a cab, then asked if she could warm up in the gatehouse. She must have laid it on pretty thick, too, because he left her there when he went to do his rounds. She slipped out, Melinda's car was unlocked, and the rest is history."

"Just like how she flirted at the movies the other day." AmyJo looked at the rest of the group. "Raise your hand if anyone has ever given you the early bird price two hours after it was over *and* free popcorn." When no one did, she said, "I know, right?"

AmyJo began passing out her submission for the meeting. "All this has taught me something. My life isn't as boring as I thought. And I've decided that *write what you know* isn't such bad advice after all. I know things this week that I didn't know last week. Like, Charlee's new BFF sucked as a BFF. The slightly overweight longtime friend is and always has been an excellent BFF. Heinrich and Einstein can have true love, even though they're so old." She scrunched her face. "Sorry. And Glu-Pocalypse might be the perfect metaphor. So this is the first chapter of a new thing I'm working on. It's a YA paranormal romance—again, no offense, guys. One mean girl"—AmyJo made it a point to eyeball me—"who might be a vampire, I'm not sure yet, and lives in a haunted house, ditches her old friend for a new bestie who is definitely a shapeshifter infected with something that makes her prey on humans to survive, but I don't want her to be a zombie or a cannibal so I'm not sure yet how that works. But anyway, two ill-fated lovers"—she shrugged and smiled at Heinrich and Einstein—"stick to each other like Glu-Pocalypse even while the two BFFs who *seem* closer actually fall apart as soon as the haunted house starts to come alive. My working title is *Glu-Pocalypse Can't Fix Everything*."

AmyJo finished passing out the pages and sat down to a stunned silence.

I jogged my papers into a neat pile and smiled at her. "Can't wait to read it."

We spent the meeting reading, dissecting, and brainstorming AmyJo's submission.

As we walked to our cars, which were arranged in a perfect line around Kell's circular driveway, I flung my arm around my old friend's shoulders. "I think you're right. Write what you know makes perfect sense."

AmyJo nodded. "And you know how to write mysteries. Don't forget that."

"I won't. Dinner tomorrow?"

"Can we go to Bonita Fajita?"

"No."

She pouted. "Fine. But then you have to pay."

"Fine."

In the garden next to my car, the snow had melted in a perfect circle around the early-blooming crocuses. I saw purple and lemon-colored blooms peeking from the earth, reminding me that some things just happen. There will always be flowers that bloom in the spring, just like there will always be unstable people in the world. I had no power over either phenomenon.

Sliding into my Kia, I flicked Dad's locker key hanging on the rearview mirror. "Miss you, Dad."

I held my hand in front of my face. No tremor.

## Acknowledgments

It has taken a village to raise me. I couldn't have written a paragraph, much less a book, without the many critique groups, writing and professional organizations, and very fine writers I'm lucky enough to know. A special shout-out goes to Sisters in Crime national and my stupendously awesome Colorado chapter. They're my fun, my friends, my absolute inspiration. I also owe my beta readers more than I can ever repay. Cynthia Kuhn, Karla Jay, MB Partlow, and Jessica Cornwell give me insightful constructive feedback, even when I don't want to hear it.

And you, dear reader. There's nothing more gratifying than hearing that I've entertained you for a bit. It's my distinct honor and privilege when you choose to read my books. On the flip side, there's nothing worse than hearing that I've made you cranky about something, so let me confess right here, right now, that I made up almost everything about the Denver Police Department to suit my fictional needs, so please don't storm the castle with torches aflare to tell me they don't use precincts and such. I already know. Please don't be cranky.

I'd be remiss if I didn't point out that my agent Jill Marsal and my publishing team over at Midnight Ink are really good sports about everything I've written in this book. I'm thrilled to say that none of them are remotely like anyone I've depicted.

## About the Author

A highly functioning chocoholic, Becky Clark is the seventh of eight kids, which explains both her insatiable need for attention and her atrocious table manners. She likes to read funny books so it felt natural to write them, too. She's a native of Colorado, which is where she lives with her indulgent husband and quirky dog.

Becky loves to present workshops to writing groups and is a founding member of the Colorado Chapter of Sisters in Crime. Visit her on Facebook and at BeckyClarkBooks.com for all sorts of shenanigans.